"I would give a year of my life for one night in your arms."

His voice was muffled against her skin as she lifted her hand to touch his hair.

Isobel gasped. It was all her fantasies about Giles, all her wicked longings, offered to her to take. All she needed was the courage to reach out.

Almost as soon as he said it, she felt him hear his own words. The enchanted bubble that surrounded them shattered like thin glass. Giles's body tensed under her hands, then he released her and stepped back.

"I am sorry. I should never have spoken, never touched you." His face was tight with a kind of pain that his physical injuries had not caused. "I did not mean— Isobel, forgive me. I would not hurt you for the world."

He turned on his heel and walked away without looking back.

* * *

Rumors
Harlequin® Historical #1153—September 2013

Author Note

To be asked to write about a place I know well and love is a rare privilege and I did not have to think twice when it was suggested that I set a novel among the real inhabitants of Wimpole Hall, a magnificent National Trust property in Cambridgeshire, England.

Everything I read about the Yorke family, who lived at Wimpole at the beginning of the nineteenth century, convinced me they must have been delightful people and I knew my hero and heroine would relish their company, too. I hope you enjoy exploring Wimpole Hall and its lovely park alongside Isobel and Giles as they fall in love. It is a love that seems doomed, but then, as now, Wimpole Hall has a certain magic and things may not be as black as they seem!

Rumors

—

Louise Allen

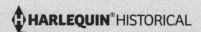
HARLEQUIN® HISTORICAL

Recycling programs
for this product may
not exist in your area.

ISBN-13: 978-0-373-29753-5

RUMORS

Copyright © 2013 by Melanie Hilton

Printed in U.S.A.

⊕ HARLEQUIN®
™ www.Harlequin.com

**Did you know that these novels are also
available as ebooks? Visit www.Harlequin.com.**

For the staff at Wimpole
who were a mine of information and
who were so patient with my endless questions.

LOUISE ALLEN

has been immersing herself in history, real and fictional, for as long as she can remember. She finds landscapes and places evoke powerful images of the past—Venice, Burgundy and the Greek islands are favorite atmospheric destinations. Louise lives on the North Norfolk coast where she shares the cottage they have renovated with her husband. She spends her spare time gardening, researching family history or traveling in the U.K. and abroad in search of inspiration. Please visit Louise's website, www.louiseallenregency.co.uk, for the latest news, or find her on Twitter, @LouiseRegency, and on Facebook.

Chapter One

February 2nd, 1801—the Old North Road,
Cambridgeshire

The chaise rattled and lurched. It was an almost welcome distraction from the stream of bright and cheerful chatter Isobel's maid had kept up ever since they left London. 'It isn't *exile* really, now is it, my lady? Your mama said you were going to rusticate in the country for your health.'

'Dorothy, I know you mean to raise my spirits, but *exile* is precisely the word for it.' Lady Isobel Jervis regarded the plump young woman with scarce-concealed exasperation. 'To call it *rustication* is to draw a polite veil over the truth. Gentlemen rusticate when they have to escape from London to avoid their creditors.

'I have been banished, in disgrace, and that is exile. If this was a sensation novel the fact that it is completely undeserved and unjust would cast a romantic glow over the situation. But this is not a novel.' She stared out through the drizzle at the gently undulating farmland rolling past the post-chaise window. In reality the injustice only increased her anger and misery.

She had taken refuge in the country once before, but that had been justified, essential and entirely her own doing. This, on the other hand, was none of those things.

'That was the sign to Cambridge we've just passed,' Dorothy observed brightly. She had been this infuriatingly jolly ever since the scandal broke. Isobel was convinced that she had not listened to a word she had said to her.

'In that case we cannot be far from Wimpole Hall.' Isobel removed her hands from under the fur-lined rug and took the carriage clock from its travelling case on the hook. 'It is almost two o'clock. We left Berkeley Street at just before eight, spent an hour over luncheon and changing horses, so we have made good time.'

'And the rain has eased,' Dorothy said, bent on finding yet another reason for joy.

'Indeed. We will arrive in daylight and in the dry.' The chaise slowed, then swung in through imposing gateposts. From her seat on the left-hand side Isobel glimpsed the bulk of a large brick inn and a swinging sign. 'The Hardwicke Arms—we are in the right place, at least.'

As they passed between the gateposts Isobel began to take more interest in the prospect from the window: it would be her home for the next two months.

The tree-dotted parkland rose gently on the left-hand side. She glimpsed a small stone building on the top of one low knoll, then, as the carriage swung round, the house came into view.

'Lawks,' Dorothy observed inelegantly.

'It *is* the largest house in the shire,' Isobel pointed out. 'I thought it might be a small palace from what Mama said, but it looks curiously welcoming, don't you think? Quite like home at Bythorn Hall.' It was no simple mansion, to be sure, but the red brick looked warm, despite the chill of the sodden February air.

The chaise drew up close to the double sweep of steps that led to the front door. *Too soon.* Isobel fought the sudden wave of panic. The Earl and Countess of Hardwicke had offered her shelter for the sake of their old friendship with her parents—Philip Yorke, the third earl, had met her father, the Earl of Bythorn, at Oxford—so they were hardly strangers, she told herself, even if she had not met them for several years.

'Be on your best behaviour, Dorothy,' she warned. 'The earl has been appointed the first Lord Lieutenant of Ireland, so he will soon be the king's representative.'

'Foreign, that's what Ireland is,' the maid said with a sniff. 'Don't hold with it.'

'It is part of the new United Kingdom,' Isobel said repressively. 'You enjoyed the celebrations at the beginning of the year, do not pretend that you did not! I must say I would like to see Dublin when the earl and countess move there in April, but they will have far more important things to worry about then than a house guest.'

In fact it was very kind of Lord Hardwicke and Elizabeth, his witty blue-stocking countess, to give sanctuary to their old friend's disgraced daughter at such a critical juncture in their lives. It might suit the Jervises to put it about that Isobel was helping the countess with her preparations, but she was sure she would be more of a distraction than a help.

She had wanted to flee to her friend Jane Needham's cheerful country manor in the depths of the Herefordshire countryside. It was remote, it was safe and it held warmth and love. But Mama had be‿‿‿‿‿ ‿‿ if scandal forced her daughter to retreat from Lond‿ then she would do so, very ostentatiously, under the wing of a leading aristocratic family.

The doors opened, footmen came down the steps, and Dorothy began to gather up their scattered shawls and reticules as Isobel tied her bonnet ribbons and strove for poise.

It was too late to back away now: the carriage door was opened, a footman offered his arm. Isobel put back her shoulders, told herself that the shivers running down her spine were due entirely to the February chill and walked up the steps with a smile on her lips.

'My dear Isobel! The cold has put roses in your cheeks—let me kiss you.' The entrance hall seemed full of people, but Lady Hardwicke's warm voice was an instant tonic, lifting spirits and nerve. 'What a perfectly ghastly day, yet you have made such good time!'

Caught before she could curtsy, Isobel returned the embrace wholeheartedly. 'Thank you, ma'am. It was an uneventful journey, but it is a great relief to be here, I must confess.'

'Now please do not *ma'am* me. Call me Cousin Elizabeth, for we are related, you know, although rather vaguely on your mother's side, it is true. Come and greet my lord. You are old friends, I think.'

'My lord.' This time she did manage her curtsy to the slender man with the big dark eyes and earnest, intelligent face. Philip Yorke was in his mid-forties, she recalled, but his eager expression made him look younger.

'Welcome to Wimpole, my dear Isobel.' He caught her hands and smiled at her. 'What a charming young woman you have grown into, to be sure. Is it really four years since I last saw you?'

'Yes, sir. After Lucas…after Lord Needham's funeral.' As soon as she said it Isobel could have bitten her tongue. Her host's face clouded with embarrassment at having reminded her of the death of her fiancé and she hurried into speech. 'It is delightful to meet you again in happy circumstances—may I congratulate you upon your appointment to the lieutenancy?'

He smiled in acknowledgement of her tact. 'Thank you, my dear. A great honour that I can only hope to be worthy of.' Behind him one of the two men standing beside the butler shifted slightly. 'You must allow me to introduce our other guests.' The earl turned to motion them forwards. 'Mr Soane, who is doing such fine work on the house for us, and Mr Harker, who is also an architect and who is assisting in some of Mr Soane's schemes for improvements in the grounds. Gentlemen, Lady Isobel Jervis, the daughter of my old friend the Earl of Bythorn.'

'My lady.' They bowed as one. Isobel was fairly certain that she had shut her mouth again by the time they had straightened up. Mr Soane was in his late forties, dark, long-faced and long-chinned, his looks distinctive rather than handsome. But Mr Harker was, without doubt, the most beautiful man she had ever set eyes upon.

Not that she had any time for handsome bucks these days, but even a woman who had vowed to spurn the male sex for ever would have had her resolution shaken by the appearance of this man. He was, quite simply, perfection, unless one would accept only blond hair as signifying true male beauty. His frame was tall, muscular and elegantly proportioned. His rich golden-brown hair was thick with a slight wave, a trifle overlong. His features were chiselled and classical and his eyes were green—somewhere, Isobel thought with a wild plunge into the poetic, between shadowed sea and a forest glade.

It was preposterous for any man to look like that, she decided while the three of them exchanged murmured greetings. It was superfluous to be quite so handsome in every feature. There must be *something* wrong with him. Perhaps he was unintelligent—but then, the earl would not employ him and Mr Soane, who had a considerable reputation to maintain and who had worked for the earl at Hammels Park before he succeeded to the title, would not associate with him. Perhaps he was socially inept, or effeminate or had a high squeaky voice or bad teeth or a wet handshake…

'Lady Isobel,' he said, in a voice that made her think of honey and with a smile that revealed perfect teeth. He took her hand in a brief, firm handshake.

Perfection there as well. Isobel swallowed hard, shocked by the sudden pulse of attraction she felt when she looked at him. A purely physical reflex, of course—

she was a woman and not made of stone. He would be a bore, that was it. He would talk for hours at meals about breeding spaniels or the importance of drainage or the lesser-known features of the night sky or toadstools.

But the perfect smile had not reached his eyes and the flexible, deep voice had held no warmth. Was he shy, perhaps?

The two architects drew back as the countess gave instructions to the butler and the earl asked for details of her journey. Isobel realised she could study Mr Harker's profile in a long mirror hanging on the wall as they chatted. What on earth must it be like to be so good looking? It was not a problem that she had, for while she knew herself to be tolerably attractive—*elegant* and *charming* were the usual words employed to describe her—she was no great beauty. She studied him critically, wondering where his faults and weaknesses were hidden.

Then she saw that the remarkable green eyes were fixed and followed the direction of his gaze, straight to her own reflection in the glazing of a picture. She had been staring at Mr Harker in the most forward manner and he had been observing her do it.

Slowly she made the slight turn that allowed her to face him. Their gazes locked again as she felt a wave of complex emotion sweep through her. Physical attraction, certainly, but curiosity and a strange sense of recognition also. His eyes, so hypnotically deep and green, held an awareness, a question and, mysteriously, a darkness that tugged at her heart. Loneliness? Sadness? The thought flickered through her mind in a fraction of a second before they both blinked and she dismissed the fancy and was back with the social faux pas of having been caught blatantly staring at a man. A man who had been staring at her.

The polished boards did not, of course, open up and swallow her. Isobel fought the blush that was rising to her cheeks with every ounce of willpower at her disposal and attempted a faint smile. They were both adult enough to pass this off with tolerable composure. She expected to see in return either masculine smugness coupled with flirtation or a rueful acknowledgement that they had both been caught out staring. What she did *not* expect was to see those complex and haunting emotions she had observed a moment earlier turn to unmistakable froideur.

The expression on Mr Harker's face was not simply haughty, it was cold and dismissive. There was the faintest trace of a sneer about that well-shaped mouth. She was no doubt intended to feel like a silly little chit making cow's eyes at a handsome man.

Well, she was no such thing. Isobel lifted her chin and returned his look with one of frigid disdain. *Insufferable arrogance!* She had hardly been in the house five minutes, they had exchanged a handful of words and already he had taken a dislike to her. She did not know him from Adam—who was he to look at her in that way? Did he think that good looks gave him godlike superiority and that she was beneath him? He no doubt produced an eyeglass and studied women who interested him without the slightest hesitation.

'Shall we go up?'

'Of course, ma'am…Cousin Elizabeth,' Isobel said with the warmest smile she could conjure up. 'Gentlemen.' She nodded to the earl and Mr Soane who were in conversation, ignored Mr Harker, and followed her hostess through into the inner hall and up the wide staircase.

That snub on top of everything else felt painfully unjust. What was wrong with her that men should treat her so? Isobel stumbled on the first step and took herself to task. *She* had done nothing to deserve it—they were simply unable to accept that a lady might not consider them utterly perfect in every way.

There was a faint odour of paint and fresh plaster in the air and she glanced around her as they climbed. 'Mr Soane has done a great deal of work for us, including changes to this staircase,' the countess remarked as they reached the first-floor landing. She did not appear to notice that her guest was distracted, or perhaps she thought her merely tired from the journey. 'There was a window on the half landing on to an inner court and that is now filled in and occupied with my husband's plunge bath, so Mr Soane created that wonderful skylight.' She gestured upwards past pillared balconies to a view of grey scudding clouds. They passed through double doors into a lobby and left again into a room with a handsome Venetian window giving a panoramic view across the park.

'This is your sitting room. The view is very fine when the sun shines—right down the great southern avenue.' Lady Hardwicke turned, regarding the room with a smile that was almost rueful. 'This was one end of a long gallery running from back to front until Mr

Soane put the Yellow Drawing Room into what was a courtyard and then, of course, the upstairs had to be remodelled. We seem to have lived with the builders for years.'

She sighed and looked around her. 'We had just got Hammels Park as we wanted it and then Philly's uncle died and he inherited the title and we had to start all over again here ten years ago.'

'But it is delightful.' Lured by sounds from next door, Isobel looked in and found that her pretty bedchamber had an identical prospect southwards.

Dorothy bobbed a curtsy as they entered and scurried through a door on the far side to carry on unpacking. Isobel saw her evening slippers already set by the fire to warm and her nightgown laid out at the foot of the bed.

'Catherine, Anne and Philip will have been sorry not to be here to greet you.' The countess moved about the room, shifting the little vase of evergreens on the mantelpiece so it reflected better in the overmantel mirror and checking the titles of the books laid out beside the bed. 'We did not expect you to make such good time in this weather so they went out after luncheon to call on their old governess in Royston.'

'Cousin Elizabeth.' On an impulse Isobel shut the connecting door to the dressing room and went to catch the older woman's hand so she could look into her face. 'I know you wrote that you believed my account of the affair—but was that simply out of your friendship for Mama? You must tell me honestly and not try to be kind. Mama insisted that you would never expose your daughters to a young woman who had participated in a veritable orgy, but I cannot help but wonder if you perhaps think that there was no smoke without some flicker of fire?

'Do you believe that I am completely innocent of this scandal? I feel so awkward, thinking you might have reservations about my contact with the girls.' She faltered to a halt, fearful that she had been gabbling. Guilt for sins past and hidden, no doubt. But this scandal was here and now and the countess, however kind, had a reputation for strict moral principles. It was said she did not even allow a beer house in the estate village.

'Of course I believe you would never do anything immoral, Isobel.' Her conscience gave an inward wince as the countess drew her to the chairs set either side of the fire. 'But your mother was so discreet I have no idea exactly what transpired. Perhaps it is as well if I know the details, the better to be prepared for any gossip.'

Isobel stared into the fire. 'When Lucas died I was twenty. I stayed in the country for almost a year with my old school friend Jane, who married Lucas's half-brother. You will recall that he drowned in the same accident. Jane was pregnant, and their home was so remote: it helped both of us to be together.

'I wanted to remain there, but Mama felt strongly that I should rejoin society last year because I had missed two Seasons. I hated it—I was older than the other girls, none of the men interested me in the slightest and I suppose I allowed it to show. I got a reputation for being cold and aloof and for snubbing gentlemen, but frankly, I did not care. I did not want to marry any of them, you see.

'Mama thought I should try again this year and, to ease me in, as she put it, I went to the Harringtons' house party at Long Ditton in January. I knew I was not popular. What I did not realise was that what might have been acceptable in a beauty with a vast fortune was merely regarded as insulting and irritating in a tolerable-looking, adequately dowered, second daughter of an earl.'

'Oh, dear,' Lady Hardwicke murmured.

'Quite,' Isobel said bitterly. 'It seems that instead of being discouraged by my snubs and lack of interest, some of the gentlemen took them as an insult and a challenge and resolved to teach me a lesson. I was sitting up reading in my nightgown late one night when the door opened and three of them pushed in. They had all been drinking, they had brought wine with them and they were bent, so they said, on "warming me up" and showing me what I had been missing.'

A log collapsed in a shower of sparks, just as one had in the moment before the door had burst open that night. 'I should have screamed, of course. Afterwards the fact that I did not seemed to convince everyone that I had invited the men there. Foolishly I tried to reason with them, send them away quietly before anyone discovered them. They all demanded a kiss, but I could see it might go further.

'I pushed Lord Halton and he collapsed backwards into a screen which smashed with the most terrific noise. When half-a-dozen people erupted into my room Halton was swigging wine from the bottle where he had fallen, Mr Wrenne was sprawled in my chair egging on

Lord Andrew White—and he had me against the bed-post and was kissing me, despite my struggles.

'One of the first through the door was Lady Penelope Albright, White's fiancée. No one believed me when I said I had done nothing to encourage the gentlemen, let alone invite them to my room. Lady Penelope had hysterics, broke off the engagement on the spot and has gone into such a decline that her parents say she will miss the entire Season. Lady Harrington packed me off home at dawn the next day.'

'Oh, my dear! I could box Maria Harrington's ears, the silly peahen. Had she no idea what the mood of the party was? I suppose not, she always had more hair than wit.' Lady Hardwicke got to her feet and paced angrily to the window. 'And what now? Do your parents think this will have died down by mid-April when we go to Ireland and you return home?'

'They hope so. And I cannot run away for ever. I suppose I must face them all some day.' Isobel put a bright, determined smile on her face. The thought of going into society again was daunting. But she could not live as a recluse in Herefordshire, she had come to accept that. She had parents and a brother and sister who loved her and who had been patient with her seemingly inexplicable desire to stay away for far too long.

She might wish to be removed from the Marriage Mart, but not under these humiliating circumstances. And London, which she enjoyed for the theatres and galleries, the libraries, the shops, would become a social minefield of embarrassment and rejections.

'That is very brave,' the countess said. 'I could call

out all those wretched young bucks myself—such a pity your brother is too young to knock their heads together.'

'I would certainly not want Frederick duelling at sixteen! It is not as though I feel any pressing desire to wed. If I had found a man who was the equal of Lucas and this had caused a rift with him, then I would have something to grieve over, but as it is…' *As it is I am not faced with the awful dilemma of how much of my past life to reveal to a potential husband.*

Chapter Two

Isobel stared into the fire and finally said the things she had been bottling up inside. She had tried to explain at home, but it seemed her mother would never understand how she felt. 'I suppose I should be fired up with righteous indignation over the injustice of it all. I was so hurt and angry, but now I feel no spirit for the fight any more. What does it matter if society spurns me? I have not felt any burning desire to be part of it for four years.'

She bit her lip. 'The men believe I am putting on airs and think myself above them, or some such foolishness. But the truth is, even if I did wish to marry, they all fail to match up to my memories of Lucas. I still remember his kindness and his intelligence and his laugh. People say that memory fades, but I can see his face and hear his voice.'

'But you are no longer mourning him, only regretting,' the countess suggested. 'You have accepted he is gone.'

'Oh, yes. I know it, and I have accepted it. There was

this great hole full of loss and pain and now it is simply an empty ache.' And the constant nagging doubt—had she done the right thing in those months after Lucas's death? The decisions had seemed so simple and yet so very, very hard.

'I do not want to go through that again. Or to settle for something less than I felt for him.' Isobel turned, reached out to the older woman. 'Do you understand? Mama does not, she says I am fanciful and not facing up to reality. She says it is my duty to marry.'

'Yes, I understand.' Lady Hardwicke gave her hand a squeeze. 'But I should not give up on men *quite* yet,' she added with a shake of her head. 'Do you mind if I tell Anne in confidence what happened at the house party? She is almost eighteen now and will be making her come-out in Dublin. She might pick up something from gossip in friends' letters and I would have her know the truth of matters. It will serve as a warning to her.'

'To fawn on young gentlemen in case they turn on her?' Isobel enquired.

'To lock her bedroom door at night and to scream the moment she feels any alarm,' the countess said with a smile.

'No, I do not mind.' Isobel returned the smile. The older woman was right to reprove her for that note of bitterness. If she became a sour old maid as a result of this, then those rakes would have made her exactly what they jeered at her for being.

'I will have tea sent up and hot water. Relax and rest until dinner time, then you will feel strong enough to face at least some of my brood. Charles and Caroline must have nursery tea and wait until the morning to meet you, but I will allow Lizzie and Catherine to have dinner with us, and Anne and Philip will be there, of course.'

'And the architects?' Isobel asked with studied nonchalance.

'Yes, they will join us. Mr Soane will travel back to London tomorrow. It is never easy to persuade him to stay away from his wife and his precious collection of art and antiquities in Lincoln's Inn Fields, but Mr Harker is staying. I confess, I wish he were not *quite* so good looking, for the girls are all eyes and attitudes whenever they see him, but to do him credit, he gives them not the slightest encouragement, which is just as well, considering who he is.'

She swept out, adding, 'Do not hesitate to ring if you need anything, my dear, I am so pleased to have you here.'

Isobel sank back into the chair, puzzled. *Who Mr Harker is? He* was an architect, but so was Mr Soane. Architects of good breeding—or even the sons of bricklayers like Mr Soane, if they were cultivated and successful—were perfectly acceptable socially, even at the dining table of an earl. Mr Harker's accent had been impeccable, his manners—if one left aside his hostile gaze—without reproach, his dress immaculate. He was a gentleman, obviously, and as eligible as a houseguest as Mr Soane. But who *was* he? Isobel shrugged. 'Why should I care?' she asked the crackling fire. 'He is insufferable whoever he is.'

* * *

The clock in the inner hall struck seven as Isobel reached the foot of the stairs. Where was everyone? There were no footmen to be seen and the doors ahead and to the right were closed, giving her no clues.

'If you say so...' A low masculine rumble. At least two of the party were down already, she realised with relief. It was always so awkward, standing around in a house one did not know.

Isobel followed the voices into the front hall and realised they came from the rooms to the left of the entrance. The cues lying on the billiard table in the first hinted that perhaps some of the gentlemen had only recently left. The conversation was clearer now, coming from the room beyond. The door stood ajar.

'...pleasant young lady, she will be companionship for Lady Anne, no doubt.' That was Mr Soane. Isobel stopped in her tracks. Was he talking about her?

'She is a good six years older than Lady Anne,' Mr Harker replied with disastrous clarity. 'One wonders what she is doing unwed, although I imagine I can hazard a guess. She has too bold an eye—no doubt it attracts the wrong sort of attention, not honourable proposals.'

'*You...*' Isobel bit back the words and applied her eye to the crack between door and hinges.

'You think she might prove to be an embarrassment?' the older man asked. He sounded concerned. 'I have seen the lengths you have to go to to prevent young ladies from becoming...um, attached.'

'I have no intention of allowing her to so much as

flirt with me. She was staring in the most brazen manner in the hall—presumably she thinks it sophisticated. That, or she is on the shelf and signalling that she is open to advances.'

Harker was strolling around the room, looking at the pictures that hung on the panelling. For a moment the exquisite profile came into view, then he vanished with a flick of dark blue coat tails.

You arrogant, vain swine! Isobel's fingers uncurled, itching to slap that beautiful face.

'I do hope not.' A slice of Soane's long, dark countenance appeared in the slit, furrowed by a frown. 'Lady Hardwicke would be most upset if there was any untoward flirtation. You know her reputation for high standards.'

'And it would rebound on you by association, Soane, as I am your protégé. I have no intention of risking it, have no fear. It is hardly as if she offers irresistible temptation in any case.' Both men laughed, covering Isobel's gasp of outrage.

'A pity gentlemen cannot have chaperons in the same way as the ladies,' Soane remarked. 'Being a plain man myself, I never had any trouble of that kind. Find yourself a wife, preferably a rich one, and settle down as I have, that is my advice, but I have no doubt you enjoy your freedom and your dashing widows too much, eh, Harker?'

'Far too much, sir. Besides, finding the right wife, in my circumstances, will take more application than I am prepared to expend upon it just now.'

As if anyone would have you! The words almost left

Isobel's mouth as the sound of their voices faded away. Her vision was strangely blurred and it took a moment to realise it was because her eyes had filled with tears of anger and hurt. It was so unjust to be stigmatised as a flirt, or worse, simply for staring at a man. And then to be labelled as *on the shelf* and too ordinary to offer any temptation to a connoisseur, such as Mr Harker obviously considered himself to be, was the crowning insult.

It took a few moments to compose herself. Isobel turned back the way she had come, unwilling to risk walking into them again. Was that cowardice or simply the wisdom to keep well away from Mr Harker while her palm still itched to slap him?

There was a footman in the hall when she emerged. 'May I help you, my lady? The family is in the saloon, just through here, ma'am.'

Ushered back through the inner hall, Isobel found herself in a pleasant room with a large bay window. It was curtained now against the February darkness, but she assumed it would look out onto the gardens and park stretching off to the north.

The earl was poring over what looked like architectural drawings with Mr Soane and a fresh-faced youth was teasing a giggling girl of perhaps twelve years— Lord Royston and Lady Lizzie, she guessed.

The countess sat on a wide sofa with Lady Anne and her fifteen-year-old sister, Catherine, who were making a show of working on their embroidery.

Mr Soane must have come through a connecting door, but there was no sign of the viper-tongued Mr Harker. Where was he? Isobel scanned the room, conscious of butterflies in her stomach. The evidence of nerves gave her another grudge against Mr Perfection.

The children saw her first. 'Ma'am.' Philip bowed. 'Welcome to Wimpole Hall.'

'Are you our Cousin Isobel?' Lizzie was wide-eyed with excitement at being allowed to a grown-up party. Isobel felt her stiff shoulders relax. *He* was not here and the children were charming.

Giles Harker straightened up from his contemplation of the collection of Roman *intaglio* seals in a small display table set against the wall. Lady Isobel had entered without seeing him and he frowned at her straight back and intricate pleats of brown hair as she spoke to Philip and Lizzie. She was a confounded nuisance, especially in a household presided over by a lady of known high standards. Lady Hardwicke's disapproval would blight his chances of commissions from any of her wide social circle. She might be a blue-stocking and a playwright, but she was the daughter of the Earl of Balcarres and a lady of principle.

The Yorke daughters were charming, modest and well behaved, if inclined to giggle if spoken to. But this distant cousin was another matter altogether. At his first sight of her a tingle of recognition had gone down his spine. She was dangerous, although quite why, Giles would have been hard pressed to define. There was something in those wide grey eyes, her best feature. Some mystery that drew his unwilling interest.

Her frank and unabashed scrutiny had been an unwelcome surprise in an unmarried lady. He was used to the giggles and batted eyelashes of the young women making their come-outs and made a point of avoiding them. His birth was impossibly ineligible, of course, even if his education, style and income gave him the entrée to most of society. But he was unmarriageable and dangerous and that, he was well aware, was dinned into the young ladies he came into contact with.

Yet those very warnings were enough to make some of them think it irresistibly romantic that the illegitimate son of the Scarlet Widow was so handsome and so unobtainable.

For certain married ladies Giles Harker was not at all unobtainable—provided his notoriously capricious choice fell on them. Something the son of the most scandalous woman in society learned early on was that one's value increased with one's exclusivity and he was as coolly discriminating in his sins as his mother was warmly generous in hers. Even in her fifties—not that she would ever admit to such an age despite the incontrovertible evidence of an adult son—her heart was broken with delicious drama at least twice a year. His remained quite intact. Love, he knew from observation, was at best a fallacy, at worst, a danger.

Lord Hardwicke and Soane straightened up from their litter of plans, young Lord Royston blushed and the countess smiled. 'Come in, my dear. Philip, bring that chair over to the sofa for Cousin Isobel.'

Giles watched as she walked farther into the room with an assurance that confirmed him in his estimate of her age. 'Thank you, Lord Royston,' she said as he brought her chair. 'And you are Lady Lizzie?'

'Lady Isobel.' He proffered the glass, keeping hold of it so that she had to respond to him.

'Thank you.' She glanced up fleetingly, but did not turn her body towards him. 'Would you be so good as to put it on that side table, Mr Harker?' He might, from her tone, have been a clumsy footman.

Giles put the glass down, then spun a chair round and sat by her side, quite deliberately rather too close, to see if he could provoke her into some reaction. He was going to get to the bottom of this curiosity about her, then he could safely ignore her. As good breeding demanded, Lady Isobel shifted slightly on the tightly stuffed blue satin until he was presented with her profile.

Now she was rested from her journey she was much improved, he thought, hiding a connoisseur's assessment behind a bland social smile. Her straight nose was no longer pink at the tip from cold; her hair, freed from its bonnet, proved to be a glossy brown with a rebellious wave that was already threatening her hairpins, and her figure in the fashionable gown was well proportioned, if somewhat on the slender side for his taste.

On the other hand her chin was decided, her dark brows strongly marked and there was a tension about her face that suggested that she was braced for something unpleasant. Her mouth looked as though it could set into a firm line of disapproval; it was full and pink, but by no stretch of the imagination did the words *rosebud* or *bow* come to mind. And she was quite definitely in at least her fifth Season.

Lady Isobel took up the glass, sipped and finally

turned to him with a lift of her lashes to reveal her intelligent dark grey eyes. 'Well?' she murmured with a sweetness that did not deceive him for a second. 'Have you studied me sufficiently to place me in your catalogue of females, Mr Harker? One well-bred spinster with brunette plumage, perhaps? Or do I not quite fit into a category, so you must bring yourself to converse with me while you decide?'

'What makes you think I have such a catalogue, Lady Isobel?' Giles accepted a glass of claret from the earl with a word of thanks and turned back to her. Interesting that she described herself as a spinster. She was perhaps twenty-four, he guessed, five years younger than he was. The shelf might be in sight, but she was not at her last prayers yet and it was an unusual young woman who would admit any danger that she might be.

'You are studying me with scientific thoroughness, sir. I half expect you to produce a net and a pin to affix me amongst your moth collection.'

Moth, he noted. *Not butterfly. Modesty? Or is she seeing if I can be provoked into meaningless compliments?*

'You have a forensic stare yourself, ma'am.'

Her lips firmed, just as he suspected they might. *Schoolmarm disapproval*, he thought. Or embarrassment, although he was beginning to doubt she could be embarrassed. Lady Isobel seemed more like a young matron than an unmarried girl. She showed no other sign of emotion and yet he could feel the tension radiating from her. It was strangely unsettling, although he should be grateful that his unwise curiosity had not led her to relax in his company.

'You refer to our meeting of eyes in the hall? You must be tolerant of my interest, sir—one rarely sees Greek statuary walking about. I note that you do not relish being assessed in the same way as you study others, although you must be used to it by now. I am certain that you do not harbour false modesty amongst your faults.'

The composure with which she attacked began to nettle him. After that exchange she should be blushing, fiddling with her fan perhaps, retreating from their conversation to sip her drink, but she seemed quite calm and prepared to continue the duel. It confirmed his belief that she had been sounding him out with an intention to flirt—or more.

'I have a mirror and I would be a fool to become swollen-headed over something that is due to no effort or merit of my own. Certainly I am used to stares,' he replied. 'And do not welcome them.'

'So modest and so persecuted. My heart bleeds for you, Mr Harker,' Lady Isobel said with a sweet smile and every appearance of sympathy. Her eyes were chill with dislike. 'And no doubt you find it necessary to lock your bedchamber door at night with tiresome regularity.'

'That, too,' he replied between gritted teeth, then caught himself. Somehow he had been lured into an utterly shocking exchange. A well-bred unmarried lady should have fainted dead away before making such an observation. And he should have bitten his tongue before responding to it, whatever the provocation. Certainly in public.

'How trying it must be, Mr Harker, to be so troubled by importunate members of my sex. We should wait meekly to be noticed, should we not? And be grateful for any attention we receive. We must not inconvenience, or ignore, the lords of creation who, in their turn, may ogle as much as they please while they make their lordly choices.'

Lady Isobel's voice was low and pleasant—no one else in the room would have noticed anything amiss in their conversation. But Giles realised what the emotion was that had puzzled him: she was furiously angry. With him. Simply because he had reacted coldly to her unladylike stare? Damn it, she had been assessing him like a housewife looking at a side of beef in the butchers. Or did she know who he was and think him presumptuous to even address her?

'That is certainly what is expected of ladies, yes,' he said, his own temper rising. He'd be damned if he was going to flirt and cajole her into a sweet mood, even if Lady Hardwicke noticed their spat. 'Certainly unmarried ones—whatever their age.'

Her chin came up at that. 'A hit, sir. Congratulations. But then a connoisseur such as yourself would notice only ladies who offer *irresistible temptation*. Not those who are *on the shelf and open to advances*.'

She turned her shoulder on him and immediately joined in the laughter over some jest of Philip's before he had time to react to the emphasis she had put on some of her phrases. It took a second, then he realised that she was quoting him and his conversation with Soane a few minutes earlier.

Hell and damnation. Lady Isobel must have been outside the door. Now he felt a veritable coxcomb. He could have sworn he had seen the glitter of unshed tears in her eyes. Now what did he do? His conscience stirred uneasily. Giles trampled on the impulse to apologise. It could only make things worse by acknowledging the offending words and explaining them would simply mire him further and hurt her more. Best to say nothing. Lady Isobel would avoid him now and that was better for both of them.

Chapter Three

'Dinner is served, my lady.' There was a general stir as the butler made his announcement from the doorway and the party rose. Giles made a hasty calculation about seating plans and realised that ignoring Lady Isobel might be harder than he had thought.

'We are a most unbalanced table, I am afraid,' the countess observed. 'Mr Soane—shall we?' He went to take her arm and the earl offered his to Lady Isobel. Giles partnered Lady Anne, Philip, grinning, offered his arm to fifteen-year-old Catherine and Lizzie was left to bring up the rear. When they were all seated Giles found himself between Lady Isobel and Lizzie, facing the remaining Yorke siblings and Mr Soane. Conversation was inevitable if they were not to draw attention to themselves.

Lizzie, under her mother's eagle eye, was on her best behaviour all through the first remove, almost unable to speak to him with the effort of remembering all the things that she must and must not do. Giles concluded it would be kinder not to confuse her with conversation, which left him with no choice but to turn and proffer a ragout to Lady Isobel.

'Thank you.' After a moment she said, 'Do you work with Mr Soane often?' Her tone suggested an utter lack of interest. The question, it was obvious, was the merest dinner-table conversation that good breeding required her to make. After his disastrous overheard comments she would like to tip the dish over his head, that was quite clear, but she was going to go through the motions of civility if it killed her.

'Yes.' Damn it, now he was sounding sulky. Or guilty. Giles pulled himself together. 'I worked in his drawing office when I first began to study architecture after leaving university. It was a quite incredible experience—the office is in his house, you may know— like finding oneself in the midst of Aladdin's cave and never knowing whether one is going to bump into an Old Master painting, trip over an Egyptian sarcophagus or wander into a Gothic monk's parlour!

'I am now building my own practice, but I collaborate with Soane if I can be of assistance. He is a busy man and I owe him a great deal.'

Lady Isobel made a sound that might be interpreted, by the wildly optimistic, as encouragement to expand on that statement.

'He employed me when I had no experience and, for all he knew, might prove to be useless.'

'And you are not useless?' She sounded sceptical.

'No.' *Hell, sulky again.* 'I am not.' Deciding what to do with his future during that last year at Oxford had not been easy. It would have been very simple to hang on his mother's purse strings—even her notorious extravagances had not compromised the wealth she had inherited from her father, nor her widow's portion.

Somehow the Dowager Marchioness of Faversham kept the *bon ton*'s acceptance despite breaking every rule in the book, including producing an illegitimate child by her head gardener's irresistibly handsome soldier son, ten months after the death of her indulgent and elderly husband. She was so scandalous, so charming, that Giles believed she was regarded almost as an exotic, not quite human creature, one that could be indulged and permitted its antics.

'I work for my living, Lady Isobel, and do it well. And I do not relish indolence,' he added to his curt rejoinder. He would have little trouble maintaining a very full, and equally scandalous, social life at the Widow's side, but he was not prepared to follow in her footsteps as a social butterfly. Society would have to accept him as himself, and on his own terms, or go hang if they found him too confusing to pigeonhole.

'You had an education that fitted you for this work, then?' Lady Isobel asked, her tone still inquisitorial, as though she was interviewing him for a post as a secretary. Her hands were white, her fingers long and slender. She ran one fingertip along the back of the knife lying by her plate and Giles felt a jolt of heat cut through his rising annoyance with her, and with himself for allowing her to bait him.

Stop it, there is nothing special about her. Just far more sensuality than any respectable virgin ought to exude. 'Yes. Harrow. Oxford. And a good drawing master.'

Lady Isobel sent him a flickering look that encompassed, and was probably valuing, his evening attire—from his coat, to his linen, to the stick-pin in his cravat and the antique ruby cabochon ring on his finger. Her own gown and jewellery spoke of good taste and the resources to buy the best.

'What decided you on architecture?' she asked. 'Is it a family tradition?'

No, she quite certainly did not know who he was or she would never have asked that. 'Not so far as I am aware. My father was a soldier,' Giles explained. 'I did not realise at first where my talents, if I had any, might lie. Then it occurred to me that many of the drawings in my sketchbooks were buildings, interiors or landscapes. I found I was interested in design, in how spaces are used.' His enthusiasm was showing, he realised and concluded, before he could betray anything more of his inner self, 'I wrote to Mr Soane and he took me on as an assistant.' He lowered his voice with a glance down the table. 'He is generous to young men in the profession—I think his own sons disappoint him with their lack of interest.'

And now, of course, many of his commissions came from men he met socially, who appreciated his work, liked the fact that he was 'one of them' and yet was sufficiently different for it not to be an embarrassment to pay his account. Giles was very well aware that his bills were met with considerably more speed than if he had been, in their eyes, a mere tradesman. And in return, he stayed well clear of their wives and daughters, whatever the provocation.

'So, have you built your own house, Mr Harker?'

'I have. Were you thinking of viewing it, Lady Isobel?'

'Now you are being deliberately provocative, Mr Harker.' Her dark brows drew together and the tight social smile vanished. 'I am thinking no such thing, as you know perfectly well. This is called *making polite conversation*, in case you are unfamiliar with the activity. You are supposed to inform me where your house is and tell me of some interesting or amusing feature, not make suggestive remarks.'

'Are you always this outspoken, Lady Isobel?' He found, unexpectedly, that his ill temper had vanished, although not all his guilt. He was enjoying her prickles—it was a novelty to be fenced with over dinner.

'I am practising,' she said as she sat back to allow the servants to clear for the second remove. 'My rather belated New Year resolution is to say what I mean. Scream it, if necessary,' she added in a murmur. 'I believe I should say what I think to people to their faces, not behind their backs.'

Ouch. There was nothing for it. 'I am sorry that you may have overheard some ill-judged remarks I made to Mr Soane earlier, Lady Isobel. That is a matter for regret.'

'I am sure it is,' she said with a smile that banished any trace of ease that he was beginning to feel in her presence. If she could cut with a smile, he hated to think what she might do with a frown.

'However, I do not feel that any good will be served by rehearsing the reason you hold such...*ill-judged* opinions.' Giles took a firm grip on his knife and resisted the urge to retaliate. He had been in the wrong—not to feel what he did, but to risk saying it where he might be overheard. Now he must give his head for a washing. He braced himself for her next barb. 'You were telling me about your house.'

Excellent tactics, he thought grimly. *Get me off balance while you work out how to knife me again.* 'My house is situated on a small estate in Norfolk. My paternal grandfather lives there and manages it for me in my absence.' It was also close enough for him to keep an eye on his mother on those occasions she descended on the Dower House of Westley Hall for one of her outrageous parties, causing acute annoyance and embarrassment to the current marquess and his wife and scandalised interest in the village. When she was in one of her wild moods he was the only person who could manage her.

'Your father—'

'He died before I was born.' It had taken some persuasion to extract his grandfather from the head gardener's cottage at Westley and persuade him that he would not be a laughing stock if he took up residence in his grandson's new country house. 'My grandfather lives with me. His health is not as robust as it once was.' Stubborn old Joe had resisted every inch of the way, despite being racked with rheumatism and pains in his back from years of manual labour. But now he had turned himself into a country squire of the old-fashioned kind, despite grumbling about rattling around in a house with ten bedchambers. Thinking about the old man relaxed him a little.

'How pleasant for you,' Lady Isobel said, accepting a slice of salmon tart. 'I wish I had known my grandfathers. And does your mama reside with you?'

'She lives independently. Very independently.' Things were relatively stable at the moment: his mother had a lover who was a year older than Giles. Friends thought he should be embarrassed by this liaison, but Giles was merely grateful that Jack had the knack of keeping her happy even if he had not a hope of restraining her wilder starts. To give the man his due, he did try.

'She is a trifle eccentric, perhaps?'

'Yes, I think you could say that,' Giles agreed. How quickly Lady Isobel picked up the undertones in what he said— No wonder she was able to slip under his guard with such ease when she chose.

'My goodness, you look almost human when you grin, Mr Harker.' She produced a sweet smile and turned to join in the discussion about the Irish language the earl was having with his eldest daughter.

You little cat! Giles almost said it out loud.

He had succeeded—far more brutally than he had intended—in ensuring he was not going to be fending off a hand on his thigh under the dinner table, or finding an unwelcome guest in his bedchamber, but at the expense of making an enemy of a close friend of the family. Now he had to maintain an appearance of civility so the Yorkes did not notice anything amiss. He could do without this—the tasks he had accepted to help

Soane were going to be as nothing compared with the challenge of keeping his hands from Lady Isobel's slender throat if she continued to be quite so provocative.

She was idly sliding her fingers up and down the stem of her wine glass as she talked. The provocation was not simply to his temper, he feared.

Giles took a reviving sip of wine and listened to young Lizzie lecturing John Soane on the embellishments she considered would make the castle folly on the distant hill even more romantic than it already was.

That was one possibility, of course: wall up Lady Isobel in the tower and leave her for some knight in shining armour to rescue. Which was a very amusing thought, if it were not for the fact that he had a sneaking suspicion that through sheer perversity she would never wait around for some man to come to her aid. She would fashion the furniture into a ladder, climb out of the window and then come after him with a battleaxe.

She laughed and he turned to look at her, the wine glass halfway to his lips. That laugh seemed to belong to another woman altogether: a carefree, charming, innocent creature. As if feeling his regard, she turned and caught his eye and for a long moment their glances interlocked. Giles saw her lips part, her eyes darken as though something of significance had been exchanged.

A stab of arousal made him shift in his chair and the moment was lost. Lady Isobel turned away, her expression more puzzled than annoyed, as though she did not understand what had just happened.

Giles drank his wine. He knew exactly what had occurred; two virtual strangers had discovered that they were physically attracted to each other, even if one of them might not realise it and both of them would go to any lengths to deny it.

There were people in her bedroom. Voices, too low to make out, a tug on the covers as someone bumped into the foot of the bed. Isobel opened her eyes to dim daylight and a view of lace-trimmed pillow. With every muscle tensed, she rolled over and sat up, ready to scream, her heart contracting with alarm.

There was no sign of the party of rowdy bucks who had haunted her dreams. Instead, three pairs of wide eyes observed her from the foot of the bed, one pair so low that they seemed on a level with the covers. *Children.* Isobel let out a long breath and found a smile, restraining the impulse to scoot down the bed and gather up the barely visible smallest child and inhale the warm powdered scent of sleepy infant. 'Good morning. Would one of you be kind enough to draw the curtains?'

'Good morning, Cousin Isobel,' Lizzie said. 'I knew it would be all right to wake you up. Mama said you should sleep in and eat your breakfast in your room, but I thought you would like to have it with us in the nursery.'

The contrast between her own dreams of drunken, frightening bucks invading her bedroom, of the presence of Giles Harker somewhere in the mists of the nightmare, and the wide, innocent gaze of the children made her feel as though she was still not properly awake.

'That would be delightful. Thank you for the invitation.' Isobel rubbed the sleep out of her eyes and regarded the other two children as they came round the side of the bed. 'You must be Caroline and Charles. I am very pleased to meet you.'

Charles, who was four, if she remembered correctly, regarded her solemnly over the top of his fist. His thumb was firmly in his mouth. He shuffled shyly round the bed to observe her more closely. Isobel put out one hand and touched the rosy cheek and he chuckled. She fisted her hands in the bed sheets. He was so sweet and she wanted…

Caroline beamed and dragged the wrapper off the end of the bed. 'You'll need to put this on because the passageways are draughty. But there is a fire in the nursery.'

The children waited while she slid out of bed, put on the robe, ran a brush through her hair and retied it into a tail with the ribbon before donning her slippers. 'I'm ready now.'

'We can go this way, then we will not disturb Mama.' Lady Caroline led her out of the door on the far side of the bedchamber, through the small dressing room and out of another door on to what seemed to be the back stairs. 'We just go through there and up the stairs to the attic—'

There was the sound of whistling and the soft slap of backless leather slippers on carpet. Across the landing a shadow slid over the head of the short flight of stairs that must lead to the suites at the back of the house. Someone was coming. A male someone. Trapped in the doorway, with a chattering seven-year-old in front of her, a small boy hanging on to her skirts and Lizzie bringing up the rear, Isobel just had time to clutch the neck of her wrapper together as Mr Harker appeared.

He stopped dead at the sight of them, his long brocade robe swinging around his bare ankles. His face was shadowed with his unshaven morning beard, his hair was tousled and an indecent amount of chest was showing in the vee of the loosely tied garment. He must be naked beneath it. 'Good morning, Lady Isobel, Lady Lizzie, Lady Caroline, Master Charles. I hope you do not represent a bathing party.'

Cousin Elizabeth had said something about a plunge bath in this area, so that was presumably where he was going. He might have had the decency to have turned on his heel the moment he saw them, Isobel thought, resentment mingling with sensations she tried hard not to acknowledge. Now she was in the position of having to exchange words with a scarcely clad man while she was in her nightwear. The fact that her wrapper was both practical and all-enveloping was neither here nor there.

'We are going to the nursery for breakfast,' she said, her gaze, after one glimpse of hair-roughened chest, fixed a foot over his head. 'Lead the way, please, Caroline.'

'Good morning, Mr Harker,' the children chorused. Isobel scooped up little Charles as a shield and they trooped across the landing, past the architect and through into the sanctuary of the door to the attic stairs. She was furiously aware that she was peony-pink and acting like a flustered governess. All her anger-fuelled defiance of him over dinner was lost in embarrassment.

They climbed the stairs and Caroline took them around the corner and on to a landing with a skylight overhead and a void, edged with rails and panelled boards, in the centre. As she tried to orientate herself Isobel realised it must be above the inner hallway her room opened on to, with the snob-boards to prevent the servants looking down on their employers.

'Papa had Mr Soane make him a plunge bath in the old courtyard that used to be behind the main stairs.' Lizzie waved a hand in the general direction. 'I think it would be great fun to learn to swim in it, but Mama says it is for Papa to relax in, not for us to splash about.'

Now I have the mental picture of Mr Harker floating naked in the warm water... Thank you so much, Lizzie.

'Here we are. This is where Caroline and I sleep, and here is Charles's room and here is the nursery. Nora, we have brought Lady Isobel, I told you she would like to have breakfast with us.'

A skinny maid bobbed a curtsy. 'Oh, Lady Lizzie! I do hope it is all right, my lady, I said you'd be wanting to rest, but off they went...'

'That is quite all right. I would love to have breakfast here.' The children and their staff appeared to occupy this entire range of south-facing rooms with wonderful views over the long avenue and the park towards Royston. A pair of footmen carried in trays. Charles twisted in her arms and she made herself put him down.

'I told them to bring lots of food because we had a special guest. Those are my designs for the tower—Mr Soane says I show a flair for the dramatic,' Lizzie pronounced, pointing at a series of paintings pinned on the wall. 'I expect I get that from Mama. She writes plays, you know and sometimes when we have a house party they are acted in the Gallery. Papa says she is a veritable blue-stocking. We will go for a walk this morning and I will show you the tower.' Lizzie finally ran out of breath, or perhaps it was the smell of bacon that distracted her.

'That would be very pleasant, provided your mama does not need me.' Isobel sat down at the table. 'It would be wonderful to get out in the fresh air and it looks as though the morning will be sunny, which is such a relief after yesterday's drizzle.' And there was the added advantage that if she was out of the house she would be at a safe distance from Mr Harker's disturbing presence.

While she ate she contemplated just how maddening he was. He was arrogant, self-opinionated, far too aware of his own good looks, shockingly outspoken and did not do his robe up properly. He was, in fact, just like the drunken bucks at the house party, only sober, which was no excuse, for that meant he should know better. He also made her feel strangely unsettled in a way she had almost forgotten she could feel. There was no doubting that his relaxed, elegant body would strip to perfection, that his skin would feel—

Isobel bit savagely into a slice of toast and blackcurrant conserve. What was the use of men except to make women's lives miserable? She contemplated Master Charles, chubby-cheeked, slightly sticky already, full of blue-eyed innocence. Little boys were lovely. She felt a pang at the thought of what she was missing.

Kind fathers and husbands like her own papa, or

Lord Hardwicke, were obviously good men. Lucas had been almost perfect. But how on earth was one to tell what a candidate for one's hand would turn out to be like? Most males, by the time they turned eighteen, appeared to be rakehells, seducers, drinkers, gamblers...

Perhaps she could become an Anglican nun. They did have them, she was sure, and it sounded safe and peaceful. A mental image of Mr Harker, laughing himself sick at the sight of her in a wimple, intruded. She would look ridiculous and she would be quite unsuited to the life. Besides, she would not be free to travel, to visit Jane and the children. An eccentric spinster then. She had enough money.

Only she did not *want* to be a spinster. She would rather like to fall in love again with a good man and marry. Her daydream stuttered to a halt: he would doubtless want children. But where did she find one she could trust with her heart and all that was most precious to her? And even if she did find this paragon, was he going to want her when he knew the truth about her?

Chapter Four

'More coffee, Cousin Isobel?'

'Thank you, Lizzie.' Her mind was going round in circles. Isobel forced herself into the present. 'At what time shall we go for our walk?'

'Shall I meet you in the garden at ten o'clock?' the girl suggested. 'I must explain to Miss Henderson, my governess, that I am going on an educational nature expedition with you.'

'You are?'

'There are the lakes—we will see all kinds of wild birds,' Lizzie said with irrefutable logic. Isobel found herself experiencing a pang of sympathy for the unfortunate Miss Henderson.

A visit to Lady Hardwicke's unusual semi-circular sitting room, almost next to her own, reassured Isobel that her hostess did not require her assistance, and that Lizzie was permitted to escape from French conversation for one morning.

Isobel snuggled her pelisse warmly around herself as she stepped out into the garden that lay between the north front and the parkland. It wanted at least fifteen minutes until ten o'clock and there was no sign of Lizzie yet. The bleak, wintry formal beds held little attraction, but the shrubbery that lay to one side behind the service wing looked mysterious and worthy of exploration.

A glimpse of a small domed roof intrigued her enough to brave the dense foliage, still dripping on to the narrow paths after yesterday's drizzle. The building, when she reached it down the twisting paths, was small, low and angular with an odd dome and no windows that she could see. It looked vaguely classical, but what its function might be, she had no idea. The gloomy shrubbery seemed an odd place for a summer house. Perhaps it was an ice house.

Isobel circled the building. Under her boots the leaf mould yielded damply, muffling her footsteps as she picked her way with caution, wary of slipping.

The sight of a pair of long legs protruding from the thick clump of laurel bush that masked the base of the structure brought her up short. The legs were visible from midthigh, clad in brown buckskin breeches. The polished boots, smeared with mud, were toes down—their owner must be lying on his stomach. As she stared there was a grunt from the depths of the bush—someone was in pain.

A keeper attacked by poachers? A gardener who had fainted? Isobel bent and pushed aside the branches with her hands. Even as she crouched down she realised that gamekeepers and gardeners did not wear boots of such quality. She slipped, landed with an ungainly thump, threw out a hand and found she was gripping one hard-muscled, leather-clad thigh.

'Oh! Are you all right?' The man was warm at least—perhaps he had not lain there very long. There did not seem to be any room to move away now she was crouched under the thick evergreen foliage.

The prone figure rolled over and she went with him in a tangle of thin branches to find herself flat on her back, her body pinned under the solid length of a man who was quite obviously neither fainting nor wounded, but very much in possession of his senses. All of them.

'My dear Lady Isobel, have you come to assist me with the plumbing?' Harker drawled as he looked down at her through the green-shadowed gloom. After a fraught moment he raised his weight off her and on to his elbows.

'Plumbing?' Isobel stared at him. 'What on earth are you talking about? Let me go this—ouch!'

'You are lying on a hammer,' he explained. 'If you will just move your shoulder a trifle... There. Is that more comfortable?'

'No, it is not. Will you let me up this instant, Mr Harker!'

'The ground is quite dry under these evergreens and you are lying on sacking.' There was the hint of a smile tugging at one corner of those sculpted lips. 'You are being very demanding—I really do not feel you can expect anything better if you will insist on an alfresco rendezvous with me in early February.'

Isobel tried to sit up and succeeded merely in pressing her bosom against his chest. Harker's eyes darkened and the twitch of his lips became an appreciative smile. She fell back, opened her mouth to scream and then remembered Lizzie—the last thing she wanted was to frighten the child by bringing her to this scene.

Furious at her own powerlessness, she put up her hands and pushed against his shoulders. He did not shift. Isobel felt her breath become shorter. *Oh, the humiliation*—she was positively panting now and he doubtless thought it was with excitement. Even more mortifying was the realisation that he would be right— her instincts were responding and she *was* finding this exciting. This was her punishment for daydreaming about his body. The reality was just as deliciously hard and lean and—

'Get off!' She felt aroused, flustered and indignant, but she did not feel afraid, she realised as the green eyes studied her. 'I have not the slightest intention nor desire of making a rendezvous with you, Mr Harker, inside or outside.'

'Then whose thigh did you think you were fondling?' he asked with every appearance of interest.

'*Fondling?* How dare you! I lost my balance.' The feel of those taut muscles under the leather was imprinted on her memory. 'I thought a gardener had fainted, or hit his head, or a gamekeeper had been attacked by poachers or something.' His body was warm and hard and seriously disturbing to a lady's equilibrium, pressed against her just there…and the wretch knew it. He shifted slightly and smiled as she swallowed. Oh, yes, he was finding this *very* interesting. No doubt she should be flattered.

'And there I was, thinking that the sight of me in my dressing gown was enough to lure young ladies into a damp shrubbery,' Harker said. 'I was, of course, about to decline what I assumed was your most flattering offer.'

'Decline?' She stared at him. That he could imagine for one moment that she had actually followed him there in order to…to…canoodle… Indignation became fury. 'Why—?'

'Why? Because well-bred virgins are far more trouble than they are worth.'

'Oh!' The insufferable arrogance of the man!

'This is probably madness, but as we are here, it seems a pity to waste the moment.' She realised too late that her hands were still on his shoulders and tried to pull herself away, but there was nowhere to go. He bent his head and took her mouth, all with one smooth, well-practised movement.

The last man to kiss her had been both drunk and clumsy. Harker was neither. His mouth was hot and demanding and sent messages straight to her belly, straight to her breasts, as though wires connected every nerve and he was playing with them. Panic at her own response threatened for a fleeting moment and then she got one hand free, twisting as she did so. The smack of her palm against the side of his face was intensely satisfying.

'You…you *bastard*,' she spat, the moment he lifted his head. The word seemed to rock him off balance. The green eyes darkened, widened and he pushed himself up and away from her. The wave of anger brought her to her feet, shoving against him for balance as she crashed out of the shrubs onto the path. 'Is this revenge because I took you to task for your insulting words to Mr Soane last night? You arrogant, lustful, smug *bastard*!' It was a word she never used, a word she loathed, but now she threw it at him like a weapon.

'Cousin Isobel? Are you in the shrubbery?' Lizzie's voice sounded as though she was coming towards them.

'Stay there,' Isobel said fiercely, jabbing a finger at him. 'Just you stay there.' Harker straightened up, one hand rubbing his reddening cheek, his mouth twisted into a rueful smile. The mouth whose heat still seemed to burn her own.

Isobel turned on her heel and almost ran along the twisting path to meet the child. The tug of the ribbons at her throat stopped her in time to rescue her bonnet. She brushed leaf mould from her skirts, took a deep breath and stepped out onto the lawn.

'Here I am. I went exploring.' Somehow her voice sounded normal, if a little over-bright.

'Oh, I expect you found the Water Castle. *Castello d'Aqua*, Mr Soane calls it. He had it built to supply the boiler when the plunge bath was put in, but it hasn't been working very well.' Lizzie chattered on as she led the way across the garden and out of the gate into the park. 'Papa said the pressure was too low and the steward should call a plumber, but Mr Harker said he'd see if he could free up the valve, or something. I expect having a bath this morning reminded him.'

That must have been what he was doing in the bushes, not lying in wait for passing females to insult.

Apparently he could manage to do that with no prior warning whatsoever.

They let themselves out of the iron garden gates and Lizzie led the way across the park that lay between the house and the hill surmounted by the folly tower. A small group of deer lifted their heads and watched them warily.

'What a delightful park.' Isobel kept her side of the conversation going while she forced her somewhat-shaky legs to keep up with Lizzie's exuberant pace.

Harker had leapt to the most indecent conclusion about her motives—her desires, even. He had not let her get more than a word out, he had taken advantage of her in the most appalling way.

She had stood up to him last night—was this then to be her punishment? To be taken for a lightskirt? Or was this insult simply retaliation for her refusal to meekly treat him as wonderful? That made him no better than those wretched bucks who had invaded her bedroom and she realised that that was disappointing. Somehow, infuriating though he was, she had expected more of him.

She had responded to him, she thought, incurably honest, as she trudged in Lizzie's exuberant wake through a gate and across a narrow brick bridge crossing a deep stock ditch. Had he realised? Of course he had—he was experienced, skilful and had slept with more women than she had owned pairs of silk stockings. So now she could add humiliation to the sensations that would course through her when she next saw

Mr Harker and he, no doubt, would use it to torment her mercilessly for as long as the game amused him.

She toyed with the idea of telling Cousin Elizabeth, then realised that she did not come out of the incident well herself, not unless she was prepared to colour the encounter so she appeared a shrinking violet and he a ravisher.

'See—is it not splendid?' Lizzie gestured to the tower and ragged length of curtain wall that crowned the far hill. 'But I think Papa should have Mr Soane build an entire castle. Or Mr Harker could do it. He is younger so perhaps he is more romantic. It would not be an extravagance, for all the gamekeepers and under-keepers could live in it, which would be a saving in cottages.'

'Do you not think the keepers might find it uncomfortable?' Isobel enquired as they took the winding sheep path down towards the sheet of water. She resisted the temptation to remark that, in her opinion, Mr Harker was as romantic as a ravaging Viking horde.

'That had not occurred to me. You are very practical, Cousin Isobel.' Practicality did not seem to appeal much to Lizzie. She frowned, but her brow cleared as the lake opened out in a shallow valley before them. A long narrow ribbon of water ran away to their right. Ahead and to the left was a smaller, wider lake.

'When Mr Repton was here to do the landscaping he said we should have a ship's mast on the bank of the lower lake.'

'A rowing boat or a skiff, you mean?'

'No, a proper big ship's mast so the tops of the sails

would be seen from the house and it would look as though there was an ocean here.' Lizzie skipped down the somewhat muddy path. 'Papa said it was an extravagant folly. But I think it would be magnificent! I liked Mr Repton, but Papa says he has expensive ideas, so Mr Sloan and Mr Harker have come instead. You see, there is a bridge here.'

As they got closer Isobel could see that the valley had been dammed and that the smaller lake was perhaps fifteen feet above the lower one, with a bridge spanning the point where the overflow ran from one to the other.

Lizzie gestured expansively. 'Mr Repton said we need a new bridge in the Chinese style.' She ran ahead and leaned over the rail to look into the depths below.

Isobel dragged her mind away from trying to decide whether she ought to tell Cousin Elizabeth about Mr Harker's kiss, however badly it made her appear. 'That does look a trifle rickety. Do be careful. Lizzie!'

As she spoke the rail gave a crack, splintered and gave way. Lizzie clung for a moment, then, with a piercing shriek, tumbled into the water and vanished under the surface.

'Lizzie!' Isobel cast off her bonnet and pelisse as she ran. 'Help! Help!' But even as she shouted she knew they had seen no one at all in the broad sweep of park, let alone anyone close enough to help.

Could the child swim? But even if she could, the water was cold and muddy and goodness knew how deep. There were bubbles rising, but no sign of Lizzie. Isobel ran to the edge, waded in and forced her legs, hampered by her sodden skirts, through the icy water.

She couldn't swim, but perhaps if she held on to the bridge supports she could reach out a hand to Lizzie and pull her up.

Without warning the bottom vanished beneath her feet. Isobel plunged down, opened her mouth to shriek and swallowed water. Splinters pierced her palm and she lost her hold on the wooden supports. The light was blotted out as the lake closed over her head.

Giles cursed under his breath and held the grey gelding to an easy canter up the sweeping slope. Had he completely misread her? Had Lady Isobel simply chanced to come upon him in the shrubbery and lost her balance as she maintained? He had thought it a trick to provoke him into kissing her and that her protests had been merely a matter of form. But now his smarting cheek told him her protests had been real enough. So had her anger last night. He had let his desires override his instincts and he had completely mishandled the situation.

Bastard. He had learned to accept and ignore that word, to treat it with amusement. But for some reason it had stung more from her lips than the flat of her hand on his cheek had done

He should seek her out and apologise. *Hell.* If he did, then she would either slap his face again or she would be all too forgiving and…and might kiss him again with that delicious mixture of innocent sensuality and fire.

No. Too dangerous. Concentrate on work and forget one provoking and unaccountably intriguing woman who, it was becoming painfully clear, he did not understand. She was no schoolroom miss—she would soon forget it, or at least pretend to.

He reined in as the grey reached the earthworks that marked the base of the old windmill. From here there was a fine view north over the lakes to the Gothic folly and, stretching south along the edge of the woodland, an avenue of trees leading to his destination, the Hill House.

The avenue stretched wide and smooth, perfect for a gallop. Giles gathered up the reins, then stopped at the sound of a faint shriek. A bird of prey? A vixen? He stood in his stirrups and scanned the parkland. There was nothing to be seen.

'Help!' It was faint, but it was clear and repeated, coming from the direction of the lakes. A woman's voice. Giles dragged the gelding's head round and spurred down the slope, heedless of wet grass, mud and thorn bushes. The deep stock ditch opened up before them and the grey gathered his hocks under him and leapt, then they were thundering down towards the lake.

As Giles reined in on the flat before the dam he could see no signs of life—only a bonnet and pelisse lying discarded at the water's edge.

There were footprints in the mud, small woman's prints, and a disturbance, bubbles, below the centre of the bridge where the rail was broken. Giles flung himself out of the saddle, wrenched off his coat and boots and strode into the lake. The muddy water churned and two figures broke the surface for a few moments, the larger flailing desperately towards the bridge supports, the smaller limp in her grasp before they sank again. Lady Isobel and Lizzie.

It took a dozen strokes to reach them. Giles put his head down and dived under, groped through the muddy water and touched a hand, so cold that for a moment he thought it was a fish. He kicked and broke the surface hauling the dead weight of both woman and child after him.

'Take her,' Isobel gasped as they broke the surface and she thrust the child's body into his reaching arms. When he tried to take hold of her too, she resisted. 'No, there's weed tangled round her. I couldn't... You'll need both hands to pull her free.'

Treading water, Giles wrenched and tugged and the slight body was suddenly floating in his arms. 'Hang on!' he ordered Isobel as though he could keep her afloat by sheer force of will. He towed Lizzie back to the shore, dumped her without ceremony and turned back to Isobel. She had vanished.

Chapter Five

Numb, shaking with cold and fear for Isobel, Giles launched himself back into the water in a shallow dive. She was beyond struggling now as he caught one slender wrist and pulled her, gasping and choking, back to the surface again.

As soon as they reached the shallows she managed to raise herself on hands and knees and shake off his hold. 'Go and see if she's breathing. Help her—I can manage.'

Giles stumbled to the shore and dragged Lizzie farther up onto the grass, turned her over his knee and slapped her hard between the shoulder blades. 'Come on, breathe!' She coughed, retched up quantities of muddy water, then began to cry.

'Lizzie, it is all right, Mr Harker rescued us,' a hoarse voice croaked beside him. 'Come here now, don't cry.' Somehow Isobel had crawled up the bank to gather the child in her arms, petting and soothing. 'There, there. We'll get you home safe to your mama, don't worry.'

Giles found his coat and wrapped it round them. Lady Isobel's hair hung in filthy sodden curtains around her face, her walking dress clung like a wet blanket to her limbs and she was shuddering with cold, but her voice was steady as she looked up at him. 'Please, go for help, Mr Harker.' She dragged the coat off her own shoulders and around the child.

He stared at her for a moment, a bedraggled, exhausted Madonna, somehow the image of desperate motherhood and feminine courage. 'Felix will take all of us at a walk, it will be faster.' He dragged on his boots and unsaddled the gelding to make room for the three of them. 'Let me get you up first, then I'll hand Lizzie to you. Can you manage?'

Lady Isobel let him drag her to her feet, then boost her onto the horse. She ignored the display of bare flesh as her skirts rode up her legs and held out her hands to steady Lizzie as the child was put in front of her. Giles vaulted up behind.

Felix, well trained and willing, plodded up the slope with his burden while Giles tried to hold Isobel and Lizzie steady as their shivering increased. Through his own wet shirt he could feel how cold Lady Isobel was growing, but she did not complain. He could hear her murmuring reassurance to Lizzie, the words blurred as she tried to control her chattering teeth.

'Thank God you can swim,' he said as the house came in sight. He steered Felix towards the service wing where there would be plenty of strong hands to help.

'I c-can't.'

'Then why the hell did you go in?' Giles demanded, his voice roughened with shock.

'I th-thought I might be able to reach her if I held

on to the bridge supports. She did not c-come up, you see. By the time I had got to the house and brought help she would have drowned. But the bottom shelved and I was out of my depth—as I went down I found her.' She broke off, coughed, and he did his best to support her until the racking spasms ceased. 'I untangled enough of the weed to push us up to the surface, but then I could not keep us there.'

Every other female of his acquaintance would have stood on the lakeside and screamed helplessly while the child drowned. 'Isobel, that was very brave.'

She did not react to the way he addressed her—she was probably beyond noticing such things. 'There didn't seem to be any other option—she was my responsibility.' The retort held a ghost of her tart rejoinders of the night before and Giles smiled with numb lips even as a pang of shame reminded him how easily he had judged this woman.

She seemed to slump and Giles tightened his arms around them. 'Steady now.' Isobel let her head fall back on his shoulder and she leaned against him as though seeking for the slight heat he could give her. He wanted to rip off their clothes, hold her against his bare flesh to force his remaining warmth into her. 'Almost there now, my brave girl.'

As they rode into the yard the boot boy gawped, a scullery maid dropped an armload of kindling, but one of the footmen ran forwards shouting, 'Here! Every-one—quick—and bring blankets! Hurry!'

Hands reached for Lizzie and Isobel and he let them

be taken before he threw a leg over Felix's withers, dropped to the ground and ran to find the countess.

Isobel rather thought she had fainted. One minute she was held against Mr Harker's comfortingly broad chest, and he was calling her his brave girl, the next hands were lifting her down and then she found herself in the countess's sitting room with Cousin Elizabeth ordering hot baths and towels and more coals for the fire and no recollection of how she had got there.

'I'm sorry,' she managed to say when the hubbub subsided enough to make herself heard. Her voice sounded raspy and her throat was sore. 'The rail on the bridge broke and Lizzie tumbled in. Mr Harker…'

Mr Harker had saved her and the child. She looked at Lizzie, white-faced, her vulnerable, naked body and thin little arms making her look much younger than her years. She wanted to hold her, convince herself the child was safe, but that was not her right. Lizzie had her mother to hold and comfort her. Her mother was with her, every day, saw every change in her growing child, felt every emotion…

'Mr Harker said you went in after Lizzie even though you cannot swim,' Cousin Elizabeth said. She looked up from the tub where she was on her knees helping the nursery nurse rub her daughter's pale limbs amidst clouds of steam. Isobel blinked back the tears that had blurred her vision and with them the pang of jealousy towards the older woman with her happy brood of children all around her. 'She owes her life to you both.' The shock was evident on the countess's strained face, even though she managed to keep her voice steady.

'Let me help you into the bath.' Lady Anne, who had been peeling off Isobel's sodden, disgusting clothes, pulled her to her feet and urged her towards the other tub set before the fire. 'Papa insisted on sending his valet to look after Mr Harker. Tompkins went past just now muttering about the "State of Sir's Breeches" in capital letters. One gathers that Mr Harker's unmentionables may never be the same again.'

As Anne must have intended, the women all laughed and Isobel felt herself relax a little as she slid into the hot water. To her relief Lizzie began to talk, her terrifying brush with death already turning into an exciting adventure. 'And Mr Harker galloped up like a knight in shining armour and dived into the lake...'

He must have done—and acted without hesitation—or neither of them would be here now. He might be a rake, and an arrogant one at that, but he had been brave and effective. And kind in just the right way: brisk and bracing enough to keep them both focused.

Isobel bit her lip as Anne helped her out of the tub and into the embrace of a vast warm towel. She was going to have to thank Mr Harker, however hard that would be. 'Sit by the fire and let me rub your hair dry,' Anne said as she and the maid enveloped Isobel in a thick robe.

Finally Lizzie was bundled off to bed. Her mother stopped by Isobel's chair and stooped to kiss her cheek. 'Thank you, my dear, from the bottom of my heart. Will you go to bed now?'

'No. No, I want to move around, I think.' She was filled with panic at the thought of falling asleep and dreaming of that black, choking water, the weed like the tentacles of a sea monster, her fear for the child. As Lizzie had slid through her hands she had thought she had lost her. She shuddered. To lose a child was too cruel and yet they were so vulnerable. *No, stop thinking like that.*

'If you are sure.' The countess regarded her with concern. 'You are so pale, Isobel. But very well, if you insist. Perhaps you could do something for me—I know my husband will have said all that is proper, but will you ask Tompkins to tell Mr Harker that I will thank him myself tomorrow? For now I must stay with Lizzie.'

'Yes, of course. As soon as I am dressed,' Isobel promised. Anne pressed a cup of tea into her hands and stood behind her to comb out her hair.

'Mr Harker is very handsome, don't you think?' the younger girl remarked as soon as they were alone.

'Oh, extraordinarily so,' Isobel agreed. To deny it would be positively suspicious. 'Although I find such perfection not particularly attractive—quite the opposite, in fact. Do you not find his appearance almost chilly? I cannot help but wonder what lies behind the mask.' What was he hiding behind that handsome face? Puzzling over his motives kept drawing her eyes, her thoughts, to him. He had courage and decision, he was beautiful, like a predatory animal, but he was also rude, immoral...

'How exciting to have your come-out in Dublin,' she said, veering off the dangerous subject of rakish architects. 'And with your papa representing his Majesty, you will be invited to all the very best functions.'

The diversion worked. Anne chatted happily about her plans and hopes while Isobel let the strength and courage seep slowly back into her as the warmth gradually banished the shivers.

Mr Harker's rooms would be on the north side of the house, judging by his appearance en route to the plunge bath. There were three suites on the northern side and the westernmost one of those belonged to the earl. So by deduction Harker must be in either the centre or the eastern one. Isobel hesitated at her sitting-room door and was caught by Dorothy as her maid bustled past with an armful of dry towels.

'Lady Isobel! How did you get yourself dressed again? You should be in your own bed and wrapped up warm. Come along, now, I'll tuck you up and fetch some nice hot milk.'

'I would prefer to warm myself by exploring the house a little and for you to see what can be done with my walking dress. I fear it must be ruined, but I suppose it might be salvageable.'

There was a moment when Isobel thought Dorothy was going to argue, then she bobbed a curtsy and retreated to the dressing room with pursed lips, emanating disapproval.

Isobel's footsteps were muffled as she crossed the landing. Somehow that made the nerves knotting her stomach worse, as though she was creeping about on some clandestine mission. But she had to thank Mr

Harker for saving her life and she had to do that face-to-face or she would be uncomfortable around him for her entire stay at Wimpole. It did not mean that she forgave him for that kiss, or for his assumptions about her.

It occurred to Isobel as she lifted her hand to knock on the door of the central suite that this visit might reinforce those assumptions, but she was not turning back now.

She rapped briskly. A voice within, somewhat smothered, called 'Come!' Isobel rapped again. The door opened with a impatient jerk and Mr Harker stood on the threshold, a towel in his hand, his damp-darkened hair standing on end. He was in his shirt sleeves, without his neckcloth. Like this he seemed inches bigger in both height and breadth.

'Isobel?'

'Do not call me—' She took a breath, inhaled the scent of sandalwood and soap and moderated her tone. She was here to make peace, she reminded herself, not to lash out to prove to herself just how indifferent she was to him. 'I have a message from the countess and something I wish to say on my own account. Lady Hardwicke wants very much to thank you herself, but she feels she must be with Lizzie today and she hopes you will understand if she does not speak with you until tomorrow. I think you may imagine her emotions and will therefore forgive her sending a message.'

He tossed the towel away towards the corner of the room without taking his eyes from her face. 'I do not need thanking and certainly do not expect her to leave the child in order to do so. How is Lady Lizzie?'

'Much better than one might expect, after that experience. She will be perfectly all right, I believe.' She could turn tail and go now. Isobel took a deep breath instead. 'And I, too, must thank you, Mr Harker, on my own account. I owe you my life.'

'I was in the right place to hear you, that is all. Anyone would have done the same.' He frowned at her. 'You should not be here.'

For him to be preaching the proprieties was intolerable! 'Please, do not be afraid I have come with any improper purpose, Mr Harker. Surely even your elevated sense of self-esteem would not delude you into thinking that after this morning's experiences I have either the desire or the energy to attempt to seduce you.'

The acid in her tone made him blink and the sweep of those thick dark lashes did nothing to moderate her irritation with him. 'Rest assured,' she added rather desperately, 'I have no intention of crossing the threshold. Your...virtue is perfectly safe.'

He studied her in silence for a moment. Isobel pressed her lips together to control the other things she would very much like to say on the subject of men who made assumptions about ladies with no evidence and then discussed them with their friends and then ravished them in wet shrubberies and made them feel... made them...

'What a relief,' he said finally. 'I was about to scream for help.' She glared at him. 'However, I believe I have an apology to make.'

'Oh? So you are sorry for that outrage in the shrubbery, are you?' It was very hard to hang on to a sense of gratitude when the wretch stood there, the gleam in his eyes giving the lie to any hint of penitence in his voice.

'I am sorry for coming to an incorrect conclusion about your intentions. I cannot be sorry for the kiss, for I enjoyed it too much.'

'If that is intended to flatter, Mr Harker, it failed. I imagine you enjoy virtually any kisses you can snatch.' She should turn on her heel and walk away, but it was impossible to leave him before she had made her indifference to him clear beyond any possible doubt. It was very strange—the last time she had felt this stubborn and light-headed had been after an incautious second glass of champagne on an empty stomach.

'I do not find you in the slightest bit attractive and, even if I did, my upbringing and my personal standards would prevent me acting in any way that might hint at such foolishness,' she stated, crossing her fingers tightly in the folds of her skirt. 'If your delusions about your personal charms have suffered a correction, I can only be glad of it for the sake of other females you may encounter.' It must be the effect of expressing her irritation so freely, but she was feeling positively feverish. Isobel shivered.

Instead of taking offence at her lecture, or even laughing at her, Harker took a step closer, his face serious. 'Why are you not in your bed, Isobel?'

'Because I do not need to mollycoddle myself. And grateful as I am to you for rescuing me, I did not give you the use of my name.'

'If you desire to thank me for getting wet on your behalf, I wish you will let me use it. My name is Giles and I make you free of that,' he said as he lifted one hand and laid the back of it against her cheek. 'You are barely warm enough, Isobel. I am sorry for this morning, and last night. I have become…defensive about single ladies. I was wrong to include you with the flirts and, worse, upon no more evidence than a very frank stare and a willingness to stand up to me.'

Somehow his hand was still against her cheek, warm and strangely comforting, for all the quiver of awareness it sent through her. If her limbs felt so leaden that she could not move, or brush away his hand, then at least she could speak up for herself. 'Surely you are not so vain as to believe that good looks make you somehow superior and irresistible to women? That every lady who studies your profile or the width of your shoulders desires you?' Oh, why had she mentioned his shoulders? Now he knew she had been looking.

He did not take her up on that revealing slip. 'Unfortunately there are many who confuse the outer form, over which I have no control, and for which I can claim no credit, for the inner character. And, it seems, there are many ladies who would welcome a certain amount of…adventure in their lives.' He shrugged. 'Men are just as foolish over a pretty face, uncaring whether it hides a vacuous mind or fine intelligence. You must have observed it. But the pretty young ladies are chaperoned,' he added with a rueful smile.

'And no one protects the handsome men?' Isobel enquired. She had managed to lift her hand to his, but it stayed there instead of obeying her and pushing his fingers away. She felt very strange now, not quite in her own body. There was a singing in her ears. She forced herself to focus. 'You are telling me that you are the victim here?'

'We men have to look after ourselves. I am vulnerable, certainly. If I acquire a reputation for flirting, or worse, with the unmarried daughters of the houses where I work, I will not secure good commissions at profitable country estates.' His mouth twisted wryly. 'Repelling single young ladies has become second nature and a certain cynicism about the motives of those who show an interest is, under the circumstances, inevitable.'

'What circumstances?'

Giles had caught her left hand in his, his fingers long and strong as they enveloped it. 'You do not know? Never mind.' Isobel thought about persisting, then restrained herself—probably this was something that would reveal her as painfully naive. Giles drew her closer and slid his hand round to tip up her chin. 'You are exhausted and probably in a state of shock. Why will you not rest?'

'I do not want to dream,' Isobel confessed. 'I have night...' The man must be a mesmerist, drawing confessions out of her as she stood there, handfast with him. She should go at once, stop talking to him about such personal matters. If only her body would obey her, because she wanted to go. She really wanted...

'You suffer from nightmares?'

'When I have a lot on my mind.' Her voice sounded as though it was coming from a long way away. She stared at Giles Harker, who was moving. Or perhaps the room behind him was. It began to dawn on her that she was going to faint.

'You are in no fit state—' Harker caught her as her knees gave way and gathered her against his chest. He ought to put her down because this was improper. She should tell him… But he was warm and strong and felt safe. Her muddled brain questioned that—Giles Harker was not safe, was he?

There was the sound of footsteps on the great staircase below them, muted voices carrying upwards. Giles stepped back into his room, pulling her with him, and closed the door. 'Damn it, I do not want us found by a brace of footmen with you draped around my neck and me half dressed.' His voice was very distant now.

'Put me down, then,' Isobel managed as she was lifted and carried into another room, deposited on something. A bed?

'Stay there.'

'I do not think I could do anything else…' It was an effort to speak, so she lay still until he came back and spread something warm and soft over her.

'Go to sleep, Isobel. If any nightmares come, I will chase them away.'

He will, promised the voice in her head. It was telling her to just let go, so she did, and slid into a darkness as profound as the blackness of the lake water.

Chapter Six

Giles locked the door from his dressing room on to the landing and studied the sleeping woman stretched out on the chaise. Isobel must be utterly drained to have fainted like that. He supposed he should have done something, anything, rather than carry her into his room, but it was a trifle late to worry about that now and they were probably safe enough. The family would be too concerned about Lizzie to wonder where their guest had got to and his borrowed valet believed him to be resting and would not disturb him.

He sat down in a chair, put his elbows on his knees and raked his fingers through his damp hair. Nothing had changed, so why the devil was he ignoring the self-imposed rules that had served him so well all his adult life? Isobel was a single young lady of good family and one, it would appear, that he had misjudged. The wild sensuality he had sensed in her must have either been his own imagination or she was unaware of it in her innocence.

He shot a glance through the door into the dressing

room, but she seemed deeply asleep. He was discovering that he liked her, despite her sharp tongue and unflattering view of him. He admired her courage and her spirit, enjoyed the sensation of her in his arms. But all of that meant nothing. She should be, literally, untouchable and they both knew it.

Why, then, did she make him feel so restless? He wanted something, something more than the physical release that his body was nagging about. There was a quality, a mood, about Isobel that he simply could not put his finger on. Giles closed his eyes, sat back, while he chased the elusive emotions.

'Mr Harker. Giles! Wake up, you are having a nightmare.'

Giles clawed his way up out of a welter of naked limbs, buttocks, breasts, reaching hands and avid mouths. 'Where the hell am I?'

'In your bedchamber at Wimpole Hall.' He blinked his eyes into focus and found Isobel Jervis kneeling in front of him, her hands on the arms of the chair. His body reacted with a wave of desire that had him dropping his hands down to shield the evidence of it from her as she asked, 'What on earth were you dreaming about? It sounded very…strange.'

'I have no idea,' he lied. 'How long have we been asleep?' Long enough for her to have lost the pallor of shock and chill. Her body, bracketed by his thighs, was warm. *Hell.* 'You should not be here.' And certainly not kneeling between his legs, as though in wanton invitation to him to pull her forwards and do the outrageous things his imagination was conjuring up.

'I am well aware of that, Mr Harker! It is four o'clock. I heard the clocks strike about five minutes ago when I woke. Are you all right? You were arguing about something in your sleep.'

'I am fine,' Giles assured her. Already his head was clearing. It was the familiar frustrating dream about trying to break up a party at the Dower House, the one that had got completely out of hand. It was after that fiasco that he began to lay down the law to his mother—and to his surprise, she had listened and wept and things had become marginally better. But that night, when he had to cope with a fire in the library, a goat in the salon—part of a drunken attempt at a satanic mass—and the resignation of every one of his mother's long-suffering staff, had burned itself into his memory.

'I was supposed to be making sure you did not dream,' he apologised. 'And you had to rescue me instead.'

'I had no nightmares,' she assured him. 'But it was a good thing that your voice woke me.' Her hair had dried completely and the loose arrangement was beginning to come down in natural waves that made him want to stroke it as he might a cat's soft coat. Isobel shook it back from her shoulders and a faint scent of rosemary touched his nostrils, sweet and astringent at one and the same time, like the woman before him.

'You must go before anyone starts looking for you.' He kept his hands lightly clasped, away from temptation.

Isobel nodded and sat back on her heels and the simple gown shifted and flowed over breast and thighs. Giles closed his eyes for a moment and bit back a groan.

'I will go out of your dressing room and across the inner landing to my sitting room. Provided no one sees me leaving your chamber, there are any number of ways I could have reached my own door.'

'You have an aptitude for this kind of intrigue,' Giles said in jest. Isobel got to her feet in one jerky movement and turned towards the door in a swirl of skirts. He saw the blush on her cheek and sprang up to catch her arm. 'I am sorry, I did not mean that as it sounded. You think clearly through a problem, that is all.'

'Yes, of course.' She kept her head averted, but the tension in her body, the colour in her cheek, betrayed acute mortification. 'I have a very clear head for problems.' The unconcern with which she had knelt before him had gone—now she was uncomfortably aware of him as a man.

'Isobel.'

She turned, her eyes dark and her mouth tight. He no longer thought it made her look like a disapproving governess. This close, he could read shame behind the censorious expression.

'I am sorry.' How she came to be in his arms, he was not certain. Had she moved? Had he drawn her close— or was it both? But with her there, warm and slender, those wide, hurt grey eyes fixed questioningly on his face, it seemed the most natural thing in the world to kiss her.

Isobel must have sensed his intent, although once his arms had encircled her she did not move for a long moment. Then, 'No!' She jerked back against his hold, as fiercely as if he had been manhandling her with brutal intent. 'Let me *go*.'

Giles opened his hands, stepped back. 'Of course.' There had been real fear in her eyes, just for a moment. Surely she did not think he would try to force her? Perhaps she had recovered enough to realise just how compromising it was to be in a man's bedchamber.

Or was this all a tease, a way of punishing him for his kiss that morning? But then she would have to be a consummate actress. Puzzled, uneasy, he knew this was not the time to explore the mystery that was Isobel Jervis. In fact, now was the time to stop this completely before his curiosity about her got the better of him.

He opened the door and looked out. 'It is safe to leave.'

'Thank you,' Isobel murmured and brushed past him without meeting his eyes.

That was, of course, the best possible outcome. All he had to do now was to maintain a civil distance. He could only hope he was imagining the expression in her eyes and that he could ignore the nagging instinct that he should be protecting her from whatever it was that caused it.

'You're not having anything to do with that man, are you, my lady?' Dorothy set the breakfast tray across Isobel's lap with unnecessary firmness. 'You go vanishing goodness knows where yesterday when you should have been resting and I worry you were with him. He's too good looking for any woman to be around—it shouldn't be allowed. You can't trust any of them—men—he knows you're grateful for him saving you and the next thing you know he'll be—'

'I told you, I had a nap in one of the other rooms, Dorothy.' Isobel made rather a business of wriggling up against the pillows and setting the tray straight on her knees. 'Will you please stop nagging about it?'

'What your sainted mama would say if she knew, I do not know.'

'And how could you?' Isobel said between gritted teeth. 'There is nothing to know.'

'He's no good, that one. He's not a gentleman, despite all those fine clothes and that voice,' Dorothy pronounced as she bustled about, tidying the dressing table. 'They don't say much in front of me in the servants' hall, me being from outside, but I can tell that there's something fishy about him.'

'Dorothy, if Lady Hardwicke trusts Mr Harker sufficiently to entertain him in her own home, with her daughters here, I really do not feel it is your place to question her judgement.'

'No, my lady.'

'And one more sniff of disapproval out of you and you can go straight back to London.'

Silenced, the maid flounced out, then stopped to bob a curtsy in the doorway.

'May I come in?' Cousin Elizabeth looked round the door and smiled when she saw Isobel was eating. 'It seems everyone is much recovered this morning, although I have forbidden Lizzie to leave her room today.'

'How is she?' Isobel's sleep had been disturbed by

vivid dreams of loss, of empty arms and empty heart. She felt her arms move instinctively as though to cradle a child and fussed with the covers instead.

'She is fine, although a trifle overexcited. What would you like to do, my dear? Stay in bed? I can bring you some books and journals.'

The sun was pouring through the window with a clarity that promised little warmth, but exhilarating views. 'I thought I might take another walk, Cousin Elizabeth. If you do not require me to assist you with anything, that is. Perhaps Anne or Philip might join me?'

'Of course, you may go and enjoy this lovely weather, just as long as you do not overtire yourself.' She looked out of the window and nodded, as though she could understand Isobel's desire to be outside. 'Philip would join you, but his father has sent him to his studies—his tutor's report on his Latin was very unsatisfactory, poor boy. And Anne has fittings with the dressmaker all morning—I declare she has not a single thing fit to wear for her come-out.'

'Never mind. I do not mind exploring by myself,' Isobel said. 'It is such a sunny day and who knows how long the weather will hold at this time of year.'

'Do you want me to send one of the footmen to go with you?'

'Goodness, no, thank you. I will probably dawdle about looking at the view and drive the poor man to distraction.'

The countess smiled. 'As you wish. The park is quite safe—other than the lake! Mr Harker and my husband will be in a meeting this morning.' She delivered this apparent non sequitur with a vague smile. 'And now I fear I must go and have a long interview with the house-keeper about the state of the servants' bed linen. Do not tire yourself, Isobel.'

Isobel came down the front steps an hour later, then stopped to pull on her gloves and decide which way to go.

Over to her left she could glimpse the church with the stables in front of it. Time enough for viewing the family monuments on Sunday. A middle-aged groom with a face like well-tanned leather came out from the yard and touched his finger to his hat brim.

'Roberts, my lady,' he introduced himself. 'May I be of any assistance?'

'I was trying to decide which way to walk, Roberts.' Isobel surveyed the long avenue stretching south. It would make a marvellous gallop, but would not be very scenic for a walk. The park to the north, towards the lake, she did not feel she could face, not quite yet. To the east the ground was relatively flat and wooded, but to the west of the house it rose in a promising manner. 'That way, I think. Is there a good view from up there?'

'Excellent, my lady. There's very fine prospects in-deed. I'd go round the house that way if I was you.' He pointed. 'Don't be afeared of the cattle, they're shy beasts.'

Isobel nodded her thanks and made for the avenue of trees that ran uphill due west from the house. At the first rise she paused and looked back over the house and the formal gardens.

Why, she wondered, had Cousin Elizabeth made a point of mentioning where Giles Harker would be that morning? Surely she did not suspect that anything had transpired between them beyond his gallant rescue?

And what *had* happened? Gi…Mr Harker seemed to accept that she was not some airheaded flirt. She was, she supposed, prepared to believe that he suffered from an irritating persecution by women intent on some sort of relationship with a man of uncannily good looks. But that kiss in the shrubbery, the look in his eyes as they stood at the door of his room, those moments made her uneasily aware that she could not trust him and nor could she trust herself. He was a virile, attractive male and her body seemed to want to pay no attention whatsoever to her common sense.

There was something else, too, she pondered as she turned and strode on up the hill, her sturdy boots giving her confidence over the tussocky grass. There was another man behind both the social facade and the mocking rake, she was sure. He had a secret perhaps, a source of discomfort, if not pain.

Isobel shook her head and looked around as she reached the top of the avenue and the fringe of woodland. The less she thought about Giles Harker the better and she had no right to probe another's privacy. She knew what it was to hold a secret tight and to fear its discovery.

To her right was an avenue along the crest, leading to the lake and, beyond it, she could see the tower of the folly. To her left the view opened out beyond the park, south into Hertfordshire across the Cambridge road. A stone wall showed through a small copse. She began to walk towards it, then saw that it was the building she had noticed from the chaise when she had first arrived. As she came closer to the grove of trees it revealed itself as a miniature house with a projecting central section and a window on either side.

It was set perfectly to command the view, she realised, but as she got closer she saw it was crumbling into decay, although not quite into ruin. Slates had slipped, windows were broken, nettles and brambles threatened the small service buildings tucked in beside it.

Isobel walked round to the front and studied the structure. There was a pillared portico held up by wooden props, a broken-down fence and sagging shutters at the windows. The ground around it was trampled and muddy and mired with droppings and the prints of cloven hooves.

And through the mud there were the clear prints of a horse's hooves leading to where a rope dangled from a shutter hinge: a makeshift hitching post.

Giles Harker's horse? Why would he come to such a sad little building? Perhaps he was as intrigued by it as she was, for it had a lingering romance about it, a glamour, as though it was a beautiful, elegant woman fallen on hard times, perhaps because of age and indiscretion, but still retaining glimpses of the charms of her youth.

But he was not here now, so it was quite safe to explore. Isobel lifted her skirts and found her way from tussock to tussock through the mud until she reached the steps. Perhaps it was locked. But, no, the door creaked open on to a lobby. The marks of booted feet showed in the dust on the floor. Large masculine footprints. Giles.

With the delicious sensation of illicit exploration and a frisson of apprehension that she was about to discover Bluebeard's chamber, Isobel opened the door to her right and found the somewhat sordid wreckage of a small kitchen. The middle door opened on to a loggia with a view of the wood behind the building and the door to the left revealed a staircase. The footprints led upwards and she followed, her steps echoing on the stone treads. The door at the top was closed, but when she turned the handle it opened with a creak eerie enough to satisfy the most romantic of imaginings.

Half amused at her own fears, Isobel peeped round the door to find a large chamber lit patchily by whatever sunshine found its way through the cracked and half-open shutters.

It was empty except for a wooden chair and a table with a pile of papers and an ink stand. No mysterious chests, no murdered brides. Really, from the point of view of Gothic horrors it was a sad disappointment. Isobel cast the papers a curious glance, told herself off for wanting to pry and opened the door on the far wall.

'Oh!' The room was tiny and painted with frescoes that still adhered to the cobwebbed walls. A day-bed, its silken draperies in tatters, stood against the wall. 'A love nest.' She had never seen such a thing, but this intimate little chamber must surely be one. Isobel went in, let the door close behind her with a click and began to investigate the frescoes. 'Oh, my goodness.' Yes, the purpose of this room was most certainly clear from these faded images. She should leave at once, they were making her feel positively warm and flustered, but they were so pretty, so intriguing despite their indecent subject matter...

The unmistakable creak of the door in the next room jerked Isobel out of a bemused contemplation of two satyrs and a nymph engaged in quite outrageous behaviour in a woodland glade. She had heard nothing—no sound of hooves approaching the building, no footsteps on the stairs. The wind perhaps...but there had been no wind as she walked up the hill. The consciousness that she was not alone lifted the hairs on the nape of her neck.

Chapter Seven

'I know you are in there, Isobel.' Giles Harker's sardonically amused voice made her gasp with relief, even as she despised herself for her nerves and him for his impudence.

'How did you know?' she demanded as she flung the door wide.

He was standing hatless in the middle of the room in buckskins and breeches, his whip and gloves in one hand, looking for all the world like an artist's model for the picture of the perfect English country gentleman. He extended one hand and pointed at the trail of small footprints that led across the room to the doorway where she stood.

Isobel experienced a momentary flicker of relief that she had resisted the temptation to investigate what was on the table. 'Good morning, Mr Harker. I came up here for the view, but I will not disturb you.'

'I thought we were on first-name terms, Isobel. And I am happy to be disturbed.' Was there the slightest emphasis on *disturbed*? She eyed him warily. 'It is an interesting building, even in this sorry state. Whether I can save it, or even if I should, I do not yet know.'

So this was what he was about, the rescue of this poor wreck. 'It is charming. It is sad to see it like this.'

'It was built as a prospect house and somehow was never used very much for forty years. Soane had suggestions for it some time ago, Humphrey Repton countered with even more ambitious ones. His lordship points out that it cost fifteen-hundred pounds to build, so hopes that I, with no previous experience of the place, will tell him what can be done that will not cost a further fifteen-hundred pounds.' He smiled suddenly and she caught her breath. 'Now what is it that puts that quizzical expression on your face?'

'It is the first time I have heard you sound like an architect.'

'You thought me a mere dilettante?' The handsome face froze into pretended offence and Isobel felt the wariness that held her poised for flight ebb away as she laughed at his play-acting. Surely he was safe to be with? After all, he had let her sleep untouched when she was at her most vulnerable yesterday and the moment when they had stood so close and she had thought he was about to kiss her had been as much her own fault as his. But it had troubled her sleep more than a little, that moment of intimacy, the sensual expertise she knew lay behind the facade of control.

'I knew Mr Soane would not associate with you, nor the earl employ you, if that was so. But you are the perfect pattern of the society gentleman for all that. You should not object if that is all you are taken for.'

'Appearances are deceptive indeed. You should look out for the glint of copper beneath the plating when you think you are buying solid silver,' he said with an edge to his voice that belied the curve of his lips. He turned to the table before she could think of what to reply. 'You are that impossibility, it seems—a woman without curiosity.'

'Your papers? Of course I was curious, but curiosity does not have to be gratified if it would be wrong to do so.'

'Even if these are simply sketches and elevations?'

'For all I knew they might be the outpouring of your feelings in verse or love letters from your betrothed or even your personal accounts.'

'I fear I am no poet and there is no letter from a patient betrothed, nor even—do not think I cannot read that wicked twinkle in your eyes, Isobel—billets-doux from females of quite another kind.'

'I have no idea what you are talking about,' she said repressively. 'Tell me about this house. Or is it not a house?'

'A prospect house is a decoration for a view point, not for living in. As was fashionable when it was built, this room was designed as a banqueting chamber. It *is* rather splendid.' He swept a hand around the space which was perhaps twenty feet square. 'Repton's plans would make this open for picnics. He proposed moving the pillars up from the front portico to frame the opening and turning the ground floor into an estate worker's cottage.'

'Oh, no.' Isobel looked around her at the wide fireplace and the walls that had once been painted to resemble green marble. 'I love this as it is. Could it not be repaired?'

'I share your liking. But I fear the initial building was so poorly done that repair or alteration may be a positive money pit for the earl.'

'And there I was imagining it renovated and turned into a little house. I love looking at houses,' she confessed. 'I think I must be a natural nest-builder.' She could imagine herself, an almost-contented spinster, in a little house like this. But she would be alone with a cat, not with the sound of a child's feet running towards her—

'You found the painted room.' He strolled past her and into the little chamber she had been examining. Isobel shook off the momentary stab of sadness and followed. She would not be a prude, she would simply ignore the subject matter of the tiny, intricate scenes that covered the mildewed walls. 'The frescos are in the Etruscan style,' he explained. 'I think this room was intended for trysts, don't you?'

'Or as the ladies' retiring room,' Isobel suggested.

'So prosaic! I hoped you would share my vision. Or perhaps you have examined the designs and are shocked.'

It rankled that he should think her unsophisticated enough to be shocked. 'Your vision is of a history of illicit liaisons taking place here?' Isobel queried, avoiding answering his question.

'Do you not think it romantic?' Giles leaned his

shoulder against the mantel shelf and regarded her with one perfect eyebrow lifted.

'Thwarted young lovers might be romantic, possibly, but I imagine you are suggesting adulterous affairs.' She could easily imagine Giles Harker indulging in such a liaison. She could not believe that he was celibate, nor that he repulsed advances from fast widows or wives with complacent husbands, however much he might protest the need to keep young ladies at a safe distance.

'Not necessarily. How about happily married couples coming here to be alone, away from the servants and the children, to eat a candlelit supper and rediscover the flirtations of their courtship?'

'That is a charming thought indeed. You are a romantic after all, Mr Harker. Or a believer in marital bliss, perhaps.' She kept her distance, over by the window where the February air crept through the cracks to cool her cheeks.

'Giles. And why *after all*? An architect needs some romance in his soul, surely?'

'Yesterday your views on the relationships between men and women seemed more practical than romantic.' Isobel picked at a tendril of ivy that had insinuated itself between the window frame and the wall.

'Merely self-preservation.' Giles came to look out of the window beside her, pushing the shutter back on its one remaining hinge. 'How is it that you have avoided the snare of matrimony, Isobel?'

Surprised and wary, she turned to look at him. 'You regard matrimony as a snare for women as well as for men? The general view is that it must be our sole aim and ambition.'

'If it is duty and not, at the very least, affection that motivates the match, then I imagine it is a snare. Or a kindly prison, perhaps.'

A kindly prison. He understood, or could imagine, what it might mean for a woman. The surprise loosened her tongue. 'I was betrothed, for love, four years ago. He died.'

'And now you wear the willow for him?' There was no sympathy in the deep voice and his attention seemed to be fixed on a zigzagging crack in the wall. Oddly, that made it easier to confide.

'I mourned Lucas for two years. I find it is possible to keep the memory of love, but I cannot stay in love with someone who is no longer there.'

'So you would wed?' He reached out and prodded at the crack. A lump of plaster fell out, exposing rough stone beneath.

'If I found someone who could live up to Lucas, and he loved me, then yes, perhaps.' *He would have to love me very much indeed.* 'But I do not expect to be that fortunate twice in my life.'

'I imagine that all your relatives say bracingly that of course you will find someone else if only you apply yourself.'

'Exactly. You are beset with relatives also, by the sound of it.'

'Just my mother and my grandfather.'

Which of those produced the rueful expression? she

wondered. His mother, probably. He had described her as eccentric.

'If this paragon does not materialise, what will you do then?' Giles asked.

'He does not have to be a paragon. I am not such a ninny as to expect to find one of those. They do not exist. I simply insist that I like him and he is neither a rakehell nor a prig and he does not mind that I have… a past.'

'Paragons of manhood being fantastic beasts like wyverns and unicorns?' That careless reference to her past seemed to have slipped his notice.

Isobel chuckled. 'Exactly. I have decided that if no eligible gentleman makes me an offer I shall be an eccentric spinster or an Anglican nun. I incline towards the former option, for I enjoy my little luxuries.'

Giles laughed, a crow of laughter. 'I should think so! You? A nun?'

'I was speaking in jest.' How attractive he was when he laughed, his handsome head thrown back, emphasising the strong line of his throat, the way his eyes crinkled in amusement. Isobel found herself smiling. Slowly she was beginning to see beyond the perfect looks and the outrageous tongue and catch glimpses of what might be the real man hiding behind them.

There was that suspicion about secrets again. What would he be hiding? Or was it simply that his faultless face made him more difficult to read than a plainer man might be? 'I thought about a convent the other day when I was reflecting on just how unsatisfactory the male sex can be.'

'We are?' He was still amused, but, somehow he was not laughing at her, but sharing her whimsy.

'You must know perfectly well how infuriating men are from a female point of view,' Isobel said with severity, picking up the trailing skirts of her riding habit to keep them out of the thick dust as she went to examine one of the better-preserved panels more closely. Surely they could not all be so suggestive? It seemed they could. Was it possible that one could do that in a bath without drowning?

'You have all the power and most of the fun in life,' she said, dragging her attention back from the erotic scene. After a moment, when he did not deny it, she added, 'Why is the thought of my being a nun so amusing?'

Giles's mouth twitched, but he did not answer her, so she said the first thing that came into her head, flustered a little by the glint in his eyes. 'I am amazed that the countess allows this room to be unlocked. What if the girls came in here?'

'The whole building has been locked up for years. Lady Hardwicke told the children that they were not to disturb me here and I have no doubt that her word is law.'

'I think it must be, although she is a very gentle dictator. So—will you recommend that the place is restored?'

'I do not think so.' Giles shook his head. 'It was badly built in the first place and then neglected for too long. But I am working up the costing for the earl so he has a fair comparison to set against Repton's ambitious schemes.'

'But that would be such a pity—and you like the place, do you not?'

'It is not my money. My job is to give the earl a professional opinion. I am not an amateur, Isobel. I am a professional, called in like the doctor or the lawyer to deliver the hard truths.'

'But surely you are different? You are, after all, a gentleman—'

Giles turned on his heel and faced her, his expression mocking. 'Do you recall what you called me when I kissed you?'

'A…*bastard*,' she faltered, ashamed. She should never had said it. It was a word she had never used in cold blood. A word she loathed.

'And that is exactly, and precisely, what I am. Not a gentleman at all.'

'But you are,' Isobel protested. He was born out of wedlock? 'You speak like a gentleman, you dress like one, your manner in society, your education—'

'I was brought up as one, certainly,' Giles agreed. He did not appear at all embarrassed about discussing his parentage. Isobel had never heard illegitimacy mentioned in anything but hushed whispers as a deep shame. How could he be so open about it? 'But my father was a common soldier, my grandfather a head gardener.'

'Then how on earth…? Oh.' Light dawned. His *eccentric* mother. 'Your mother?' His mother had kept him. What courage that must have taken. What love. Isobel bit her lip.

'My mother is the Dowager Marchioness of Faversham.' Isobel felt her jaw drop and closed her mouth. An aristocratic lady openly keeping a love child? It was unheard of. 'She scorns convention and gossip and the opinion of the world. She has gone her own way and she took her son with her.' He strolled back into the large chamber and began to gather up the papers on the table.

'Until you left university,' Isobel stated, suddenly sure. A wealthy dowager would have the money and the power, perhaps, to insist on keeping her baby. Not everyone had that choice, she told herself. Sometimes there was none. 'She did not want you to study a profession, did she?' She made herself focus on the man in front of her and his situation. 'That was when you went your own way.'

'Perceptive of you. She expected me to enliven society, just as she does.' He shrugged. 'I am accepted widely—I know most of the men of my age from school and university, after all. I am not received at Court, of course, and not in the homes of the starchier matrons with marriageable girls on their hands.'

Isobel felt the colour mount in her cheeks. No wonder he was wary of female attention. If his mother was notorious, then he, with his looks, would be irresistible to the foolish girls who wanted adventure or a dangerous flirtation. Giles Harker was the most tempting kind of forbidden fruit.

'Of course,' she said steadily, determined not to be missish. 'You are not at all eligible. I can quite see that might make for some…awkwardness at times. It will be difficult for you to find a suitable bride, I imagine.'

'Again, you see very clearly. I cannot marry within society. If I wed the daughter of a Cit or some country squire, then she will not be accepted in the circles in which I am tolerated now. There is a careful balance to be struck in homes such as this—and I spend a lot of my time in aristocratic households. We all pretend I am a gentleman. A wife who is not from the same world will not fit in, will spoil the illusion.'

'It will be easier as your practice grows and your wealth with it.' Isobel bit her lip as she pondered the problem. 'You could wed the daughter of another successful professional man, one who has the education and upbringing to fit in as you do.'

Giles stopped in the act of rapping a handful of papers on the desk to align them. Isobel's reaction to his parentage was undeniably startling—it was almost as though she understood and sympathised. 'Do you plot all your friends' lives so carefully for them? Set them all to partners?'

'Of course not. It is just that you are a rather different case. Unusual.' She put her head on one side and contemplated him as though trying to decide where to place an exotic plant in a flower border or a new ornament on a shelf. 'I would never dream of actually matchmaking.'

'Why not? It seems to be a popular female preoccupation.'

Now, why that tight-lipped look again, this time accompanied by colour on her cheekbones? 'Marriage is enough of a lottery as it is, without one's acquaintances interfering in it for amusement or mischief,' she said with a tartness that seemed entirely genuine.

'You are the victim of that?' Giles stuffed his papers into the saddlebag he had brought up with him.

'Oh, yes, of course. I am single and dangerously close to dwindling into a spinster. It is the duty of every right-thinking lady of my acquaintance to find me a husband.'

There was something more than irritation over being the target of well-meaning matchmaking, although he could not put his finger on what it was. Anger, certainly, but beneath that he sensed a deep unhappiness that Isobel was too proud to show.

'Ah, well,' Giles said peaceably, 'we are both safe here, it seems. The Yorke girls are well behaved and well chaperoned and there are no eligible gentlemen for the countess to foist upon you.'

'Thank goodness,' Isobel said with real feeling. 'But I am disturbing you when you have work to do. I will go on with my walk now I have admired the view from up here.'

'I do not mind being disturbed.' He thought he had kept the double meaning out of his voice—he was finding her unaccountably disturbing on a number of levels—but she bit her lower lip as though she was controlling a sharp retort. Or just possibly a smile, although she turned abruptly before he could be quite certain. 'Where are you going to go now?'

'I do not know.' Isobel stood looking out of the window.

'The avenue running north from here is pleasant. It skirts the wood.'

'And leads to the lake.'

'That frightens you?'

'No. No, of course not.' The denial was a little too emphatic.

'Then you did not dream?' Giles buckled the saddlebag, threw it over his shoulder, picked up his hat and gloves and watched her.

'No…yes. Possibly. I do not recall.'

'I will come with you,' he said. 'I have been sitting too long.'

'But your horse—'

'I will lead him. Come and see the best view of the Gothic folly.'

Isobel followed him down the stairs and out into the sunshine, allowed him to take her hand as they negotiated the mud and then retrieved it as she fell in beside him. They walked beneath the bare branches of the avenue, Felix plodding along behind them, the reins knotted on his neck, the thin February sunlight filtering through the twigs.

Chapter Eight

Afterwards Giles found it difficult to recall just what they talked about on that walk. His memories seemed to consist only of the woman he was with. Isobel seemed to be interested in everything: the deer grazing in the park, the lichen on the tree trunks, the view of the roofs of the Hall, complex and interlocking, the reason why he had named his horse as he had and what an architect must learn. He made her laugh, he could recall that. She stretched his knowledge of botany with her questions and completed his verse when he quoted Shakespeare. But under it all there was still a distance, a wariness. She was no fool, she knew she was playing with fire being with him, but it seemed, just now, as if she was suspending judgement.

She held her bonnet against the breeze. 'A lazy wind—it does not trouble itself to go around,' she said. 'Oh.' The lakes spread out below them in the valley, chill and grey.

'And there is the folly.' Giles pointed to the tower on

the opposite hill to bring her eyes up and away from the source of her apprehension. 'Shall we go and look at it?'

If you fell off a horse, then the best thing was to get right back on, and the narrow bridge where the broken timbers showed pale, even at this distance, was her fall. 'Of course, if you are too tired…'

Isobel's chin went up. 'Why not?'

They followed the path down into the stock ditch and through the gate in the fence at the bottom. Felix's hoofprints from the previous day were clear in the turf. It had been a good jump, Giles thought as they climbed out at the other side.

Isobel was silent as they walked down the hillside towards the lake. Then, as the muddy patch where they had clawed their way out came in sight, she said, 'I thought she had drowned. I thought I was not going to be able to save her. What if you had not heard us?' The words tumbled out as though she could not control them and he saw her bite her lip to stem them. Her remembered fear seemed all for Lizzie, not for herself, and he recalled how she had cradled the child on the bank. For the first time it occurred to him that a single woman might mourn her lack of children as well as the absence of a husband.

'Don't,' Giles said. 'What-ifs are pointless. You did save her, you found her and hung on until I got there. Now run.'

She gasped as he caught her hand and sprinted down the last few yards of the slope, along the dam, on to the wooden bridge, its planks banging with the impact of their feet. Moorhens scattered, piping in alarm. A pair of ducks flew up and pigeons erupted from the trees above their heads in a flapping panic. Giles kept going, past the break in the rail and on to the grass on the other side.

He caught Isobel and steadied her as she stopped, gasping for breath. 'You see? It is quite safe.' Felix ambled in their wake.

'You—you—' Her bonnet was hanging down her back and she tugged at the strings and pulled it off. She was panting, torn between exasperation and laughter. 'You idiot. Look at my hair!'

'I am.' The shining curls had slipped from their pins and tumbled down her back, glossy brown and glorious. Her greatest beauty, or perhaps as equally lovely as her eyes. Isobel stood there in the pale February sunlight, her face flushed with exertion and indignation, her hair dishevelled as though she had just risen from her bed, her breasts rising and falling with her heaving breath.

Kiss her, his body urged. *Throw her over the saddle and gallop back to the Hill House and make love to her in the room made for passion.* 'You are unused to country walks, I can tell,' he teased instead, snatching at safety, decency, some sort of control. 'I will race you to the folly.' And he took to his heels, going just fast enough, he calculated, for her to think she might catch him, despite the slope.

There was no sound of running feet behind him. So much the better—he could gain the summit and give himself time to subdue the surge of lust that had swept through him. Just because Isobel was intelligent and poised and stood up to him he could not, *must not*, lose sight of the fact that she was a virgin and not the young matron she often seemed to be.

The thud of hooves behind him made him turn so abruptly that his heel caught in a tussock and he twisted off balance and fell flat on his back. Isobel, perched side-saddle on Felix's back, laughed down at him for a second as the gelding cantered past, taking the slope easily with the lighter weight in the saddle.

God, but she can ride, Giles thought, admiring the sight as she reached the top of the hill and reined in.

'Are you hurt?' Her look of triumph turned to concern when he stayed where he was, sprawled on the damp grass.

'No, simply stunned by the sight of an Amazon at full gallop.' He got to his feet and walked up to join her. 'How did you get up there?' She had her left foot in the stirrup and her right leg hooked over the pommel. Her hands were light on the reins and she showed no fear of the big horse. Her walking dress revealed a few inches of stockinged leg above the sturdy little boot and he kept his gaze firmly fixed on her face framed by the loose hair.

'There's a tree stump down by the fence. Felix obviously thought someone should be riding him, even if his master was capering about like a mad March hare.'

'Traitor,' Giles said to his horse, who butted him affectionately in the stomach. 'Would you care to explore the folly, Isobel?'

She sent an interested, curious glance at the building, then shook her head. 'We had better go back or we will be late for luncheon, will we not? Perhaps I can look at it tomorrow.'

Pleasure warred with temptation. They could be together safely, surely? He had self-control and familiarity would soon enough quench the stabs of desire that kept assailing him. It was too long since he had parted with his last mistress, that was all that ailed him. The challenge to make Isobel smile, make her trust him, was too great.

'I am not too busy to walk with you. Or we could ride if you prefer?'

'Oh, yes. If only it does not rain. I had better get down.' She lifted her leg from the pommel and simply slid, trusting him to catch her. Obviously his dangerous thoughts were not visible on his face. Her waist was slender between his hands. He felt the slide of woollen cloth over silk and cotton, the light boning of her stays, and set her down with care.

It took him a minute to find his voice again, or even think of something to say. 'What have you done with your bonnet, you hoyden?' Giles asked halfway down the hill as they walked back towards the lake. Isobel pointed to where the sensible brown-velvet hat hung on a branch beside the path. 'And what are you going to say to Lady Hardwicke about your hair if she sees you?'

'Why, the truth, of course.' Isobel sent him a frowning look. 'Why should I not? Nothing happened. We ran, my bonnet blew off, my hair came down. It is not as though we are in Hyde Park. Or do you think she will blame you in some way?'

'No, of course not. She trusts you, of course—she

would suspect no impropriety.' Now why did that make her prim up her lips and blush?

'Exactly,' Isobel said, her voice flat. But when they reached the garden gate and Giles turned to walk Felix back to the stables, she caught his sleeve. 'Thank you for chasing my nerves away at the bridge.'

'That is what friends do,' he said. That was it, of course: friendship. It was novel to be friends with an unmarried woman but that was surely what this ease he felt with Isobel meant.

She smiled at him, a little uncertain. He thought he glimpsed those shadows and ghosts in her eyes still, then she opened the garden gate and walked away between the low box hedges.

A friend. Isobel was warmed by the thought as she walked downstairs for breakfast the next morning. It had never occurred to her that she might be friends with a man, and certainly Mama would have the vapours if she realised that her daughter was thinking of an architect born on the wrong side of the blanket in those terms.

But it was good to see behind the supercilious mask Giles Harker wore to guard himself. After a few minutes as they walked and talked she had quite forgotten how handsome he was and saw only an intelligent man who was kind enough to sense her fears and help her overcome them. A man who could laugh at himself and trust a stranger with his secrets. She wished she could share hers—he of all men would understand, surely.

He was dangerous, of course, and infuriating and

she was not certain she could trust him. Or perhaps it was herself she could not trust.

Giles was at the table when she came in, sitting with the earl and countess, Anne and Philip. The men stood as she entered and she wished everyone a good morning as the footman held her chair for her.

'Good morning.' Giles's long look had a smile lurking in it that said, far more clearly than his conventional greeting, that he was happy to see her.

The morning was fine, although without yesterday's sunshine. They could ride. Isobel did not pretend to herself that she did not understand why the prospect of something she did almost every day at home should give her such keen pleasure. Perhaps she felt drawn to him because Giles was of her world but not quite in it, someone set a little apart, just as she was by her disgrace. She wanted to like him and to trust him. Could she trust her own judgement?

'Might I ride today, Cousin Elizabeth?'

'This morning? Of course. You may take my mare, she will be glad of the exercise. I have been so involved with the endless correspondence that this change in our life seems to be producing that I have sadly neglected her. And it is not as though my daughters enjoy riding, is it, my loves?'

A heartfelt chorus of 'No, Mama!' made the countess laugh. 'One of the grooms will accompany you, Isobel.'

Isobel caught Giles's eye. 'I…that is, Mr Harker is riding out this morning, ma'am, I believe. I thought perhaps…'

She feared the countess would still require a groom

as escort, but she nodded approval. 'I will have Firefly brought round at ten, if that suits Mr Harker?'

'Thank you, ma'am, it suits me very well. Shall I meet you on the steps at that hour, Lady Isobel?'

'Thank you,' she said demurely and was rewarded by a flickering glance of amusement. Was she usually so astringent that this meekness seemed unnatural? She must take care not to think of this as an assignation, for it was nothing of the kind. *Friendship*, she reminded herself. That was what was safe and that, she had to believe, was what Giles appeared to be offering her.

'Mama, I have been thinking,' Lady Anne said. 'With Cousin Isobel and Mr Harker here we might have enough actors to put on a play. We could ask the vicar's nephews to help if we are short of men. Do say *yes*, it is so long since we did one.'

'My dear, it is not fair to expect poor Mr Harker to add to his work by learning a part. He and Papa are quite busy enough.'

'You have a theatre here, Cousin Elizabeth?' Isobel asked, intrigued.

'No, but we have improvised by hanging curtains between the pillars in the Gallery.'

'That was where we had the premiere performance of Mama's play *The Court of Oberon*,' Lizzie interrupted eagerly. 'And then it was printed and has been acted upon the London stage! Is that not grand?'

'It is wonderful,' Isobel agreed. Many families indulged in amateur dramatic performances, especially during house parties. She caught Giles's eye and smiled:

he looked appalled at the possibility of treading the boards.

'Perhaps on another visit, Lizzie,' the countess said. 'I am writing another play, so perhaps we can act that one when it is finished.'

'The post, my lord.'

'And what a stack of it!' The earl broke off a discussion with his son to view the laden salver his butler was proffering. 'And I suppose you will say that all the business matters have already been dispatched to my office? Ah well, distribute it, if you please, Benson, and perhaps my pile will appear less forbidding.'

'Feel free to read your correspondence,' Lady Hardwicke said to her guests as her own and her daughters' letters were laid by her plate.

After a few minutes Isobel glanced up from her mother's recital of a very dull reception she had attended to see Giles working his way through half-a-dozen letters. He slit the seal on the last one and it seemed to her, as she watched him read, that his entire body tensed. But his face and voice were quite expressionless when he said, 'Will you excuse me, Lady Hardwicke, ladies? There is something that requires my attention.'

Isobel returned to her own correspondence as he left the room. It was to be hoped that whatever it was did not mean he would have to miss their ride. She told herself it was not that important, that she could take a groom with her, that it was ridiculous to feel so concerned about it, but she found she could not deceive herself: she wanted to be alone with Giles again.

The earl departed to the steward's office, Philip to his tutor and Cousin Elizabeth and Anne for a consultation with the dressmaker. Isobel followed behind them a little dreamily. Where would they ride this morning? Up to the folly and beyond, perhaps. Or—

'Lady Isobel.' Giles stepped out from the Yellow Drawing Room. 'Will you come to the library?'

It was not a request; more, from his tone and his unsmiling face, an order. 'I—' A footman walked across the hallway and Isobel closed her lips on a sharp retort. Whatever the matter was, privacy was desirable. 'Very well,' she said coolly and followed him through the intervening chambers into the room that was one of the wonders of Wimpole Hall.

But the towering bookcases built decades ago to house Lord Harley's fabled collection were no distraction from the sick feeling in the pit of her stomach. Isobel could not imagine what had so affected Giles, but the anger was radiating from him like heat from smouldering coals.

'What is this autocratic summons for?' she demanded, attacking first as he turned to face her.

'I should have trusted my first impressions,' Giles said. He propped one shoulder against the high library ladder and studied her with the same expression in his eyes as they had held when he had caught her staring at him in the hall. 'But you really are a very good little actress, are you not? Perhaps you should take part in one of her ladyship's dramas after all.'

'No. I am not a good actress,' Isobel snapped.

'But you are the slut who broke up Lady Penelope

Albright's betrothal. You do not deny that?' he asked with dangerous calm.

When she did not answer Giles glanced down at the letter he held in his right hand. 'Penelope is in a complete nervous collapse because you were found rutting with Andrew White. But I assume you do not care about her feelings?'

Isobel felt the blood ebbing from her cheeks. That foul slander…and Giles believed it. 'Yes, I care for her distress,' she said, holding her voice steady with an effort that hurt her throat. 'And I am very sorry that she chose such a man to ally herself with. But you must forgive me if I care even more that Lord Andrew mauled and assaulted me, ruined my reputation and that very few people, even those who I thought were my friends, believe me.'

'Oh, very nicely done! But you see, I have this from my very good friend James Albright, Penelope's brother—and he does not lie.'

'But he was not there, was he? He knows only what Penelope saw when she came into my room that night: four people engaged in a drunken romp. Only one of them, myself, was not willing and the other three—the men—were set on giving a stuck-up spinster a good lesson, a retaliation for snubbing their patronising flirtation.

'That is the truth and if you have not the perception to know it when you hear it, then I am sorry, but there is nothing I can do.' Isobel turned on her heel. One more minute and she was going to cry and she was *damned* if she would give Giles Harker the satisfaction of knowing he had reduced her to that. A fine friend he had turned out to be!

'Who would believe such a tale?' he scoffed as he caught her by the arm and spun her back to face him. 'No one there did and they were on the spot.'

'You think it improbable they would be deceived?' Yes, after all there *was* something she could do, something to shake that smug male complacency.

'Of course,' Giles began as Isobel threw herself on his chest, the suddenness of it knocking him off balance back against a bookcase full of leather-bound volumes. 'What the devil—'

As he tried to push her away she used the momentum of his own movement to swing around in his grip until she was pressed by his weight against the books, then she threw her arms around his neck, pulled his head down and kissed him hard, full on the mouth.

For a moment Giles resisted, then he opened his lips over hers and returned the kiss with a ruthless expertise that was shocking and, despite—or perhaps because of—her anger, deeply arousing. Isobel had been kissed passionately by her betrothed, but that was four years ago and she had loved him. The assault of Giles's tongue, his teeth, the fierce plundering exploration, fuelled both anger and the long-buried desire that had been stirring with every encounter they had shared. When he lifted his head—more, she thought dizzily, to breathe than for any other reason—Isobel slapped him hard across the cheek.

'Now, if someone comes in and I scream, what will they think?' she panted. His face was so close to hers that she could feel his breath, hot on her mouth. 'What will they have seen? Giles Harker, a rake on the edge of society, assaulting an innocent young lady who is struggling in his arms. Who will they believe? What if I tear my bodice and run out, calling for help? You would be damned, just as I was.

'I do not have to justify myself to you. But I was sitting in my room, reading by the fireside in my nightgown, and three men burst in. I thought I could reason with them. I did not want a scandal, so I did not scream—and that was my mistake. And for that I am condemned by self-righteous hypocrites like you, Giles Harker. So now will you please let me go?'

For a long moment he stared down at her, then those gorgeous, sinful lips twisted. 'Yes, I believe you, Isobel. I should never have doubted you.'

Kiss me again, a treacherous inner voice said. *Listen to your body. You want him.* 'You called me a slut. You just kissed me as though I was one.' She did not dare let go of her bitterness.

'I believe you now.' He looked at her, all the anger and heat gone from his face. 'I am sorry I doubted you. Sorry I called you… No, we won't repeat that word. But I am not certain I can be sorry for that kiss.'

'Unfortunately, neither can I,' Isobel admitted and felt the blood rise in her cheeks. 'You kiss very…nicely.' And as a result her body had sung into life in a way it had not done for a long time. 'No doubt you have had a great deal of practice. But kindly do not think that is why I…why I did what I did just now. I could think of no other way to prove my point.'

'Nicely?' Giles seemed a trifle put out by the description. 'We will not pursue that, I think. I should not make light of what has happened to you. I was wrong and you have been grievously slandered. What is your family doing about it?'

Isobel shrugged and moved away from him to spin one of the great globes that stood either side of the desk. It was easier to think away from all that intense masculinity. The man addled her brain. She had let herself be almost seduced into friendship and then he believed the worst of her on hearsay evidence. And instead of recoiling from her angry kiss he had returned it. He was not to be trusted. Not one inch.

'They denied it everywhere they could, of course. But my brother is a schoolboy, my father a martyr to gout. Neither of them is going to be taking up a rapier in my defence! Besides, my hostess threw me out the next morning, so the lie is widely believed. There is nothing to be done except take refuge where I am trusted—here with old friends of my parents.'

Chapter Nine

Giles paced down the length of the library to the other globe, the celestial one showing the heavens, and spun it viciously. 'Something should be done.' Hell's teeth, he had called an innocent woman a foul name, he had accused her on hearsay evidence. He was having trouble getting past his own self-loathing for that, and for wanting to kiss her again. Kiss her…and more. That made him a rutting beast like Andrew White and he was not. Please God, he was not that.

'Why is your old friend not calling out the man who betrayed his sister? Andrew White seems to be getting away scot-free,' Isobel demanded. It was a reasonable question.

'James is almost blind. He can see well enough to get around, but that is all. His sight was failing when we were at Harrow and it has deteriorated since.'

'Poor man. I had no idea. I was aware that he did not come into society, of course,' Isobel said, instantly compassionate. She was sweet when she was soft—pitying for James, tender with the child. He wanted that softness, but all she would give him was the fire.

'He is a scholar, a great mind. When we were children at school he held the bullies at bay because they were frightened of his rapier intelligence and his sharp tongue. He protected me with his wits when I was new, terrified and a victim because of my parentage. As I grew in size and confidence I defended him with my fists. Fortunately he can afford to keep secretaries and assistants so his studies are not affected by his sight. He is working on a new translation of the Greek myths.'

'A true friendship,' Isobel murmured, her head bent over the spinning globe, her long index finger tracing a route across continents. Was she imagining an escape from all this? 'Will you help me? Tell Lord James you believe me? If he can convince his parents and Penelope, then it might do some good.' She sounded doubtful that he would support her, even now.

'Of course.' *Of course. But that is not enough. You are mine. I saved your life so you are mine.* The anger boiling inside him became focused. He would tell James, of course, and Penelope, whom he had known since she was six, but there must be justice for Isobel. White and the other two had got off from this almost unscathed.

Out of the corner of his eye he saw Isobel put back her shoulders and straighten her back as if bracing herself to carry this burden of disgrace. Alone, she believed. But she was not alone any more. The fierce sense of possessiveness was unsettling, but he had never saved someone's life before—perhaps that accounted for the way he felt about Isobel now.

'You are very brave,' he said and her chin came up with a defiance that tugged at his heart.

'I refuse to go into hiding because I am the victim of an injustice, so what else can I do but carry on? Besides, if I was truly courageous I would be in London now, brazening it out, would I not?' Isobel threw at him.

'I think you are too much of a lady to be brazen about anything. And what well-bred virgin would not shy away from such behaviour?' Now, what had he said to make her blush so? 'It takes a wicked widow like my mother to carry off that kind of thing.'

She gave herself a little shake. 'There is nothing to be done about the situation beyond you telling your friend the truth. Look, the sun is shining—I think I will ride after all.'

'Then I hope the weather holds for you. I find I must go to London this morning.' There *was* more he could do and it seemed that Isobel had no one else to do it for her. Besides, Giles thought, the fierce possessiveness burning hot inside him, this would be both his right and a pleasure. The experience of defending a lady was not new, but it was an ironic twist that this time he would be on the side of innocence instead of mitigating his mother's latest outrages.

'It is not a problem with your business that takes you there, I see,' she said, watching him with narrowed eyes. 'That was the smile of a man who positively relishes what is in front of him.'

'Oh, yes,' Giles agreed. 'I am looking forward to it, although it is an unexpected development.' It was easy to resist the temptation to tell her what he was intend-

ing to do. This could all be covered by his willingness
to stand up for his friends the Albrights. Isobel's name
need not come into it.

'How mysterious! Or perhaps you are simply missing your mistress.'

'No.' He made himself smile at the jibe. 'It is a secret,
but I will tell you when I get back.' He would have to
do that, for she needed to know that the insult and the
calumny had been answered. Giles lifted a hand to
touch her cheek, pale and sweetly curved, but she
flinched away as though she feared even that caress.

He wanted to protect her, needed to possess her.
It seemed his wants might be satisfied, but never his
needs. Nor should they be, of course, he thought with
a stab of regret.

Behind them the library doors opened and he let his
hand fall away as Isobel pretended a renewed interest
in the globe.

'Ah! There you are, Harker.'

'My lord?'

'Excuse me, Isobel my dear—a matter of urgent business.'

'But of course. I hope your journey to London is uneventful, Mr Harker.' Isobel smiled politely and turned
from him. 'I will see if they can spare me a groom—the
morning is too fine to waste the opportunity of a ride.'

In the silence that followed the swish of her skirts
through the door the earl strode across the room and
half sat on the edge of the big desk.

'London? I need you here, Harker. My steward tells
me that my banker is due the day after tomorrow to

discuss how the financial affairs of the estate will be handled in my absence in Ireland. I need to confirm the figures Soane left with me for the further building work and to make a final decision on the Hill House and the other matters you were looking into for me. I must have the funds and authorities in place to allow matters to proceed without my agents having to endlessly send to Dublin for my agreement on every detail.'

'I will be back by then, my lord.' He could be in London by that night, have a day to do what he had to do and a day at most to travel back. 'I assure you of it.'

'You are certain? You will forgive me if I press you, but it would be extremely inconvenient if this were delayed and Delapoole had to return to town.'

'My word upon it, my lord.'

'Excellent. I will let you get on then. Safe journey, Harker.'

Giles walked up the steps into Brookes's, one hand unobtrusively under Lord James Albright's elbow. It was all the guidance his friend needed, other than a murmured word now and again to help him orientate himself in the blurred world he refused to allow to defeat him.

'Good evening, my lord, Mr Harker.' The porter came forwards for their hats and canes.

'Evening, Hitchin. Lord Andrew White in?'

'Yes, my lord. He is in the library with Mr Wrenne and Lord Halton, I believe.'

'Excellent,' James remarked as they made their way down the corridor. 'Three birds with one stone. I've never felt so helpless before—I wish I could get my hands on that swine White myself.'

'I'll hold him for you,' Giles offered with a grin as he opened the library door. The room was empty except for the three men lounging in deep leather armchairs by the fireside. They looked round as the friends entered and Giles saw the mixture of wariness and defiance on White's face when he realised who his companion was.

He guided James's hand to rest on the back of a chair, then walked across. The three got to their feet to face him. 'Harker. Do they let you in here? I thought this was a club for gentlemen.'

'Quite patently it is not,' Giles countered. 'They appear to have admitted the three of you and you are lying scum who think nothing of assaulting a lady and blackening her reputation. Or perhaps you crawled in here through the sewers like rats?'

'Wrenne, be so kind as to pull the bell, will you?' White drawled, but Giles could see the wariness in his eyes. The beginning of fear. 'Get a porter to throw out this bastard.'

'And what about me?' James asked. 'Do you expect the porters to expel two club members on no grounds whatsoever?'

'This is damned awkward, Albright.' White's bluff tone was at odds with the look of dislike he shot at James. 'Your sister took exception to a situation that was completely misinterpreted, made a scene, accused me of lord knows what, broke off the engagement— If I had been permitted to come and explain at the time, this could all have been put behind us.'

'You could hardly blame Penelope for her reaction,' Albright said with dangerous calm. 'You were found in another woman's bedchamber.'

'All a bit of fun that got out of hand. If Penelope had been a bit more sophisticated about it, we would still be betrothed.'

'And what a pity that would be,' James remarked. 'This is bad enough, but at least she discovered that you were a philandering cheat before she was irretrievably tied to you.'

'The devil!' White strode across the room until he stood immediately in front of James. Giles shifted his position so he could watch the other two—he did not want a brawl in the club, but if James lost hold of the threads of his temper, that is what they might well have. 'No one calls me a cheat! If you weren't as blind as a bat I would call you out for that, Albright.'

'And I would refuse your challenge, White. My grievance predates yours. You will apologise both to my sister and to the lady who you so grievously offended that night, or give me satisfaction.'

'I will do no such thing,' White blustered. 'And meet *you*? You couldn't hit a barn door with a blunderbuss.'

'I fear you are correct,' James said with such politeness that Giles felt his mouth twitch in amusement. 'However, as in all cases where a duellist cannot fight because of infirmity, my second will take my place.'

'And who is that?' White swung round as Giles cleared his throat. 'You? I'll not meet a bastard on the field of honour.'

'No?' Giles drawled. 'Then it will be all around town

within the day that you and your friends are cowards who will not fight, even when the odds are three to one. My friend did not make it clear, perhaps, that the challenge includes all of you. The choice of weapons is, of course, yours, as is the order in which you meet me. We stay at Grillon's tonight and I expect word from you as to place, time and weapons by nine tomorrow morning. I have no time to waste on you—the matter will be concluded by dawn the day after tomorrow.'

He took James's arm and guided him out of the door, closing it on an explosion of wrath. 'That went well, I think.' The picture of Isobel struggling in that lout's grip while he pawed at her was still painfully vivid in his imagination, but at least the gut-clenching anger had been replaced with the satisfying anticipation of revenge for her. He hoped they would choose rapiers; he would enjoy playing with them, making it last.

'Exceedingly well. I might not be able to see much, but I could tell that rat's face changed colour. Where shall we dine tonight?'

'We are being followed.' Giles took a firmer grip on James's arm. In the darkness with only occasional pools of light, or the wind-tossed flames of the torches carried by passing link-boys, his friend was completely blind.

'Who? How many?'

'Five, I think.' Giles turned a corner, aiming for King Street and the bright lights around the entrance to Almack's. They had been eating in a steak house in one of the back streets that criss-crossed the St James's area. Now they were only yards from some of the most exclusive clubs, gracious houses and the royal palace, but surrounded by brothels, drinking dens and gambling hells. It was not an area to fight in—not with a blind man at his side.

'As to who it is, I suspect our three friends and a pair of bully boys they've picked up.' He lengthened his stride. 'We rattled them, it seems. We're almost to King Street, James. If anything happens you'll be able to make out the lights if you just keep going down the slope and you'll be on the doorstep of Almack's.'

'And leave you? Be damned to that,' James said hotly.

'Go for help—hell, too late, here they come.'

There was a rush of feet behind them. Giles swung round, pulled the slim blade from the cane he carried and pushed James behind him as he let his sword arm fall to his side. The two big men, porters by the look of them, skidded to a halt on the cobbles, their shadowed faces blank and brutal.

Beyond three figures lurked, too wary to approach. Giles stepped back as though in alarm, flailed wildly with the cane and the big men laughed and rushed him. The rapier took the nearest through the shoulder, then was wrenched from Giles's hand as the man fell against his companion. As the second man fended off the slumped body Giles jabbed him in the solar plexus with the cane, kneed him in the groin as he folded up, then fetched him a sharp blow behind the ear as he went down.

'Stay behind,' he said sharply to James as his friend moved up to his side. The three men who had held back rushed them, so fast that he was only just aware as they reached him that they were masked. His fist hit cloth, but there was a satisfying crunch and a screech of pain as the man—White, he suspected—fell back. Then one of the others had him in a bear hug from behind and the other began to hit him.

Through the blows and the anger he kept control, somehow, and began to fend off the man in front of him with lashing feet and head butts when he got close enough. Dimly he was aware of the sound of breaking glass and James's voice, then he wrenched free and could use his fists.

James shouted again, there was a thud and swearing, a fast-moving shadow and pain in his face, sharp and overwhelming. Giles's fist connected with the chin of the man in front of him and he saw him fall. As he went down the alleyway was suddenly full of figures and the flare of light.

James was there at his side, gripping his arm, and a stranger who seemed strangely blurred, stood close, a torch in his hand. 'Gawd! They've made a right bloody mess of you, guv'nor.'

'Made more of a mess of them,' Giles said, his voice coming from a long way away. Then there was silence.

Giles had believed her. Isobel hugged that to herself through the rest of the day and into the next, allowing his faith to warm her like a mouthful of brandy. He believed her and he would convince Penelope's family of her innocence. Somehow that was less important than Giles's acceptance, although it should not have been.

She could not deceive herself: Giles Harker aroused

feelings in her that no unmarried lady should be feeling—anger and exasperation amongst them. But there was more, something between friendship and desire that every instinct of self-preservation told her was dangerous.

Perhaps it *was* simply desire. Isobel sat and sorted tangled embroidery silks for the countess without taking conscious note of the vivid colours sifting between her fingers. He aroused physical feelings in her and that, of course, was wrong and sinful.

If she was the unawakened innocent that he believed her, then perhaps she would not have recognised this ache, this unsettled feeling, for what it was. Or she would have been shocked at herself and put it out of her mind, convinced that she was simply attracted by a handsome face and fine figure.

But she was not innocent and not a virgin. She had made love with her betrothed twice and, although Lucas had been almost as shy and inexperienced as she, it had been intense and pleasurable and had left her body wanting more. In her grief, and through the heartrending decisions to be made after his death, those feelings had vanished. Unaroused and unimpressed by the men she met when she returned to society, Isobel had assumed that passion had died for her.

But it seemed that desire had only been sleeping and all it had taken was a kiss from the right man to awaken it. Giles Harker had not been the first man to kiss her since Lucas Needham's death, but he was the only man who made her feel like this.

What did that mean? Isobel held up two hanks of

orange silk and tried to focus on whether they were exactly the same shade. She knew how she felt: happy and apprehensive, warm and slightly shaky. Very restless. Her lips retained the feel of his, her tongue the taste of him.

Isobel shifted uncomfortably in the deep armchair. He was a rake, he had behaved disgracefully as well as heroically, and he made her want to cross verbal swords with him at every opportunity. She knew, none better, the dangers of giving in to physical passion—she should find an excuse and leave Wimpole before she was tempted any further.

Coward, an insidious little voice murmured in her head. *Why not enjoy being with him, even snatch a few kisses? You are far too sensible to—*

'Cousin Isobel, you are wool-gathering!' It was Anne, laughing at her. Isobel looked down at her lap and found greens carefully paired with blues, the orange arguing with a rich purple and pinks looped up with grass-green.

'So I am! Listen—is that a carriage arriving?' They were in the South Drawing Room and the sound of wheels and of the front doors opening came clear in the still of the house.

'Who on earth can that be?' Anne glanced at the clock. 'Past three. Too late for a call and we are expecting no one for dinner.'

'And Mr Harker is not due back until tomorrow.' Isobel dumped the silks unceremoniously into their basket and went to peep out of the window. 'Very unladylike of me, I know! Now who is that? I do not recognise him.'

'Neither do I.' Anne came to look over her shoulder. 'The groom is helping him down, even though he is quite a young man. I do believe he is blind—see his stick? But we do not know anyone who is blind, I am sure.'

'It must be Lord James Albright. Mr Harker mentioned that he had a blind friend of that name. But…' Her voice trailed off. If James Albright had heard from Giles of her innocence and had called to tell her so, surely he could not have arrived so speedily and uninvited by the Yorkes? Unless he had met Giles in town and had set out that morning without pausing to write.

'What on earth is going on?' Anne tugged her hand. 'Come on, we will find out better from the hallway— see, four footmen have gone out *and* Mama!'

'They are helping someone who is sick or injured,' Isobel said. Her feet did not want to move. Her stomach was possessed by a lump of ice. It was Giles, she was certain, and something was horribly wrong.

Chapter Ten

Isobel clutched the draped brocade at the window while Peter, the brawniest of the footmen, backed out of the carriage, supporting a tall figure. *At least he is alive.* Only then could she admit to herself the depth of her sudden irrational fear. With the thought her paralysis ended. It was Giles and he was injured. His head was swathed in bandages, his legs dragged as the men held him. *'Giles.'* She brushed past Anne, uncaring about the other girl's startled expression, and ran through the anteroom into the hall.

'Giles!'

'I can walk upstairs perfectly well,' he was saying to the footmen on either side of him. 'I do not need carrying up in a chair, I assure you.' His voice was slurred. As she ran forwards she saw his face was bruised. He did not seem to hear her, or see her.

'Giles.'

'Leave him.' Cousin Elizabeth caught her arm while she was still yards away. 'He is hurt, but the last thing he needs is women fussing over him. Peter and Michael will get him upstairs. The doctor has been sent for. I will go and have Mrs Harrison gather up salves and bandages and plenty of hot water.'

'But—'

'It is nothing mortal, I assure you, ma'am,' an unfamiliar voice said behind her. 'He is in a great deal of discomfort, but there are no deep wounds. Sore ribs, broken nose, bruising, cuts—so my doctor tells me. He should not have travelled today, but he said he had given the earl his word he would be here tomorrow and he's a stubborn devil.'

'You are Lord James Albright?' Giles had vanished unsteadily around the turn of the stair. The man who stood to one side, leaning on a light cane, wore thick spectacles on a pleasant face that showed both bruises and a graze along the jaw. When he held out his hand to her she saw his knuckles were raw. 'You have been in a fight? Is that what happened to Giles…Mr Harker?'

'The same fight,' he said with a grin. 'I might be nearly as blind as a bat, but when you put a big enough target in front of me, I can hit it.' As she took his hand he closed his fingers around hers, as if to detain her. 'I think you must be Lady Isobel?'

'Yes.'

'Then I have an apology to make to you on behalf of my sister.'

'There is no need. I understand why she thought as she did. But why have you and Giles been fighting?'

'Is there somewhere we can sit and talk?'

'Of course, forgive me. Lady Anne, do you think a

room could be prepared for Lord James, and some re-
freshments sent to the South Drawing Room?'

'Yes, of course. I'll arrange that and then go and help
Mama.' Anne hurried away.

'Through here, Lord James.' Uncertain how much
assistance he would need, Isobel laid her hand on his
arm and guided him to where she and Anne had been
sitting. 'Are you in need of any medical attention yourself?' The bruises seemed alarming as he settled into
the armchair with the last of the fading light on his face.

'It is nothing some arnica will not help,' he said with
a smile, then fell silent as the tea tray was brought in,
candles lit and the fire made up.

Isobel served him tea, then forced herself to wait patiently while he drank.

'You are wondering why I am here and what Harker
and I have been doing,' James Albright said after a
minute. 'He came to London yesterday to tell me the
truth of what occurred when my sister's engagement
was broken. At the time Penelope was adamant that
she did not want any action taken against White, that
in drink and high spirits he must have been entrapped
by—forgive me—a designing female. She just wanted
to put it all behind her.

'But once I heard the truth, that he had not only been
unfaithful to my sister but had plotted to assault another
woman in the process, then I knew I must challenge the
three men involved. My family honour was involved
twice over—once in the insult to Penelope and secondly
in the role we unwittingly played in your disgrace.'

'But, forgive me, you are—'

'Almost blind. Quite. But, as my second, Harker could legitimately take up the challenge on my behalf. He would have called them out in any case, but that would raise questions about his, er…relationship with you. This way we both achieved satisfaction and the matter appeared to be entirely related to the insult to my sister.'

'His relationship with me?' What had Giles said to this man? *What* relationship?

'You are friends, are you not?'

'Oh. Yes, of course.' Isobel's pulse settled back down again.

'We challenged them and they apparently decided it would be easier if we suffered an unpleasant accident and fell foul of some footpads. Foolish and dishonourable, and even more foolish in practice. They thought that two large bully boys would make mincemeat out of one blind man and an architect with a pretty face. Unfortunately for them they were not at school with us. I learned to defend myself in a number of thoroughly ungentlemanly ways and Giles, when he is angry, fights like a bruiser raised in Seven Dials.'

'And you beat them—five of them?'

'Almost. It turned nasty by the end, but then the noise brought out a crowd from the nearby ale houses and, er, another place of entertainment and they soon worked out who the aggressors were and the odds against us. White, Wrenne and Halton have been taken up by the watch for assault and affray and their two thugs proved to be wanted by the magistrates already.'

'But Giles—how badly is he hurt?'

'Sore ribs where he was kicked. He was kicked in the head, too, I suspect, so he is probably concussed. The broken nose. Bruises and grazes all over. But that will all heal.'

A chill ran down her spine. What was Albright not saying? 'And what will *not* heal?' Isobel demanded bluntly.

'Oh, it will all knit up again. It is just that his face… there was a broken bottle.'

It seemed it was possible to become colder, to feel even more dread. 'His eyes?' she managed to articulate.

'His sight is all right, I promise. As to the rest—I couldn't see well enough to judge.'

'No, of course not. Thank you for explaining it all to me so clearly.'

'Harker said you were not a young lady to have the vapours and that you would want the truth whole.'

'Indeed, yes. Please, allow me to pour you some more tea. Or would you prefer to go to your room now?' Giles expected her to be strong and sensible and so, of course, she would be.

The evening seemed interminable. The doctor came and went after speaking to the countess, the earl and Lord James. Dinner was served and eaten amidst conversation on general matters. The explanation that Mr Harker and Lord James had been set upon by footpads was accepted by the younger members of the family and everyone, once concern for Mr Harker's injuries had been expressed, seemed quite at ease. The earl was delighted with his intellectual guest and bore him off to the library after dinner to discuss the rarer books.

Isobel thought she would scream if she had to sit still any longer with a polite smile on her lips, attempting to pretend she had nothing more on her mind than helping Lady Anne with her tangled tatting. She wanted to go to Giles so badly that she curled her fingers into the arm of the chair as though to anchor herself.

Finally Cousin Elizabeth rose and shooed her elder daughters off to their beds. 'And you too, Isobel, my dear. You look quite pale.'

'Cousin Elizabeth.' She caught the older woman's hand as the girls disappeared, still chattering, upstairs. 'How is he? Please, tell me the truth.'

'Resting. He is in some pain—the doctor had to spend considerable time on the very small stitches on his face, which was exhausting for Mr Harker of course. He will be able to get up in a day or so.'

'I must see him.'

'Oh, no!' Lady Hardwicke's reaction was so sharp that Isobel's worst fears flooded back. 'He needs to rest. And, in any case, it would be most improper.'

'And those are the only reasons?'

'Yes, of course.' But the countess's gaze wavered, shifted for a second. 'Off to bed with you now.' As they reached the landing she hesitated. 'Isobel… You have not become unwisely fond of Mr Harker, have you? He is not…that is…'

'I know about his parentage. I hope we are friends, ma'am,' Isobel said with dignity. 'And he helped Lord

James clear my name, so I am grateful and anxious about him.'

'Of course.' Reassured, Cousin Elizabeth patted her hand. 'I should have known you would be far too sensible to do anything foolish. Goodnight, my dear.'

Anything foolish. She is worried that I have become attached to him in some way. And I have. I desire him, I worry about him. I want to be with him.

At her back was the door to his room. In front, her own with Dorothy waiting to put her to bed. Isobel walked across the landing and laid her right palm against the door panels of Giles's room for a moment, then turned on her heel and walked back to her own chamber.

'What an evening of excitements, Dorothy,' she remarked as she entered, stifling a yawn. 'I declare I am quite worn out.'

Half an hour later Isobel crept out of her room, her feet bare, her warmest wrapper tight around her over her nightgown. At Giles's door she did not knock, but turned the handle and slipped into the room on chilly, silent feet.

There was a green-shaded reading lamp set by the bed, but otherwise the room was in darkness, save for the red glow of the banked fire that was enough to show the long line of Giles's body under the covers. His left arm lay outside, the hand lax, and the sight of the powerful fingers, open and still, brought a catch to her breathing. It was unexpectedly moving to see him like this, so vulnerable.

On the pillow his head was still, with a bandage around the forehead, down over one cheek and around his neck. It was lighter than the heavy turban he had been swathed in when he arrived—Isobel tried to take comfort from that as she crept closer. The doctor had paid no attention to anything but getting his dressings right, it seemed—Giles's normally immaculate golden-brown hair stuck out incongruously between the linen strips.

She felt the need to smooth it, touch it and feel the rough silk, convince herself that he was alive and would soon be well, although he lay so immobile. Even as she thought it Giles moved, caught himself with a sharp breath. His ribs, or perhaps it was just the accumulation of bruised muscles.

'Lie still,' Isobel murmured and took the last few steps to the bedside. His unbandaged cheek was rough with stubble and unhealthily hot when she laid her palm against it. They had placed him in the centre of the wide bed and she had to lean over to touch him.

'Isobel?' His eyes opened, dark and wide in the lamplight, the pupils huge. 'Go 'way.'

'Did the doctor drug you?' It would account for the wide pupils, the slur in his speech. 'Are you thirsty?'

'Stubborn woman,' he managed. 'Yes, drug. Tasted foul...thirsty.'

There was a jug on the nightstand. Isobel poured what seemed to be barley water and held it to Giles's bruised lips. He winced as it touched, but drank deeply.

'Better. Thank you. Now go 'way.' His eyelids drooped shut.

'Are you warm enough?' There was no answer. She should go now and let him sleep. There was nothing she could do and yet she could not leave him. He had fought for her honour and for his friend who could not demand satisfaction for his sister. If she had only screamed when those men broke into her room, then none of this would have happened.

'Idiot man,' she murmured. 'You try to convince me that you are a rake and then you almost get yourself killed for honour.'

Giles shifted restlessly. He should not be left like this. There was a chair by the fireside, she could sit there and watch him through the night; she owed him that.

She eyed the bed. It was wide enough for her to lie beside him without disturbing him. Isobel eased on to the mattress, pulled the edge of the coverlet up and over herself. When Giles did not stir she edged closer, turned on her side so she could watch his shadowed face and let herself savour the warmth of his body.

It was very wrong to feel like this when he was injured, she knew that. It was not only wanton, it was unbefitting of a gentlewoman. She should be concerned only with nursing a sick man, not with wanting to touch every inch of him, kiss away every bruise and graze, caress him until he forgot how much he hurt.

She must not do it. But she could lie there, so close that their breath mingled, and send him strength through her presence and her thoughts. Tomorrow she must face the consequences of his defence of her, of the debt she now owed him and her own jumbled emotions, but not tonight.

* * *

'Oh, my Gawd!'

Giles woke with a jerk from a muddled, exhausting dream into pain that caught the breath in his throat and the sound of the valet's agitated voice. He must look bad to shake that well-trained individual.

He kept his eyes closed while he took stock. Ribs, back, a twisted shoulder, aching jaw, white-hot needles down the side of his face and a foul headache. Nothing lethal, then, only bruises, cuts and the effects of the good doctor's enthusiastic stitchery and drugs on top of a thoroughly dirty fist fight. But he had little inclination to move, let alone open his eyes. All that would hurt even more and, damn it, he had earned the right to ignore the world for a few minutes longer.

'My lady!'

That brought him awake with a vengeance as the bedding next to him was agitated and a figure sat upright.

'Oh, hush, Tompkins! Do you want to rouse the entire household?'

'No, my lady. That's the last thing I'd be wanting,' Tompkins said with real feeling. 'But you can't be in here, Lady Isobel! What would her ladyship say?'

'I was watching over Mr Harker last night and I fell asleep,' Isobel said with composure, sitting in the midst of the rumpled bedding in her nightgown and robe. Giles closed his eyes again. This had to be a nightmare. 'She would say I was very remiss to lie down when I became sleepy and we don't want to upset her, do we?'

'No, my lady,' said the valet weakly.

'So you will not mention this, will you, Tompkins?'

'No, my lady.'

Neither the valet nor the woman in bed with him—*in his bed*—were paying him the slightest attention. Giles gritted his teeth and pushed himself up on his elbows as the valet went to draw back the curtains. 'What the devil are you doing here, Isobel?'

'I wanted to make sure you were all right.' Her voice trailed away as she stared at him in the morning light and the colour ebbed out of her cheeks, leaving her white. 'Of all the insane things to do, to tackle five men like that!' She sounded furious.

'Insane? I did not have a great deal of options. I could have run away and left James, I suppose.' Damn it, he had fought for her and she was calling him an idiot?

'That is not what I meant.' Isobel slid from the bed and he turned his head away and tried to push himself upright, humiliated to find himself too weak to sit up and argue with her.

'Sir, you shouldn't try to sit up,' Tompkins said. By the sound of it he was trying to envelop Isobel in Giles's robe.

'Pillows,' Giles snapped, mustering his strength and hauling himself up. 'And a mirror.'

'Now I don't think that would be wise, sir.'

'Your opinion is not relevant, Tompkins. A mirror. At once.'

'Sir.' The valet piled pillows behind him, handed him a mirror and hovered by the bedside, his face miserable.

'Unfasten this bandage.'

'Giles—'

'Sir—' Giles lifted his hand to try to find the fastening and the man shook his head and leaned over. 'The doctor will have my guts for garters, sir.'

The process was unpleasant enough to make him feel queasy. When the dressing was finally unwrapped Giles lifted the glass and stared at the result. His nose had been broken, his mouth was bruised, but down the right side of his face where he had expected to find a single cut on his cheek, perhaps reaching to his cheekbone, were two savage parallel slashes from just above his eyebrow, down his cheek to his jaw.

'The swelling and the stitches made it look worse than it is, sir, I'm sure.' Tompkins rushed into speech. 'The doctor's very good, sir, lots of tiny stitches he took. Lucky it missed your eye, sir. A miracle, the doctor said that was.'

A miracle. A miracle that had changed his face for ever in seconds. Giles stared back at familiar eyes, a familiar mouth, eyebrows that still slanted slightly upwards. As for the rest… He had always taken his looks for granted. His glass had told him he was handsome. Some women called him beautiful. It was nothing to be proud of: his looks came from his parents and good fortune and had proved enough of a nuisance in the past. He would get used to the changes.

He had forgotten Isobel until she stammered, 'No… Giles…' She fled for the door, wrenched it open and, with the barest glance around to check outside, ran from the room.

So this new face sent a courageous young woman fleeing from the room in revulsion, a young woman who

was not a lover, but who had called him her friend. That
hurt, he discovered, more than the injuries themselves.
'Put back the bandage, Tompkins,' he said harshly.
'Then bring me hot water, coffee, food.'

'But, sir, you should be resting. Her ladyship told
Cook to prepare some gruel.'

'Tompkins, I have a job to do and I cannot do it
on gruel. His lordship requires my attendance today.
Either you bring me proper food or I will go down to
the kitchen myself and speak to Cook. And send for
the doctor. I cannot go about looking like an Egyptian
mummy.'

The valet left, shaking his head. Giles lay back
against the pillows and told himself that it did not matter. He would heal in time and scars and a crooked
nose were not the end of the world. But he could not
forget the look on Isobel's face when she had stared at
him, appalled. That felt as though something had broken inside him.

Chapter Eleven

By breakfast Isobel was no nearer overcoming the guilt. Giles's beautiful face was scarred for life and it was her fault. He had done it for her. The shock of how injured he was, her own helplessness, had made her angry—with herself as well as, irrationally, with him.

She should not have shouted at him, she thought penitently as she looked across the table to where James Albright sat, coping efficiently with bacon and eggs after a few moments' discreet exploration of the table around him with his fingertips. Giles had fought for him, too.

Cousin Elizabeth pressed Lord James to stay on, but he shook his head. 'You are very kind, but I will leave after luncheon if that is convenient. I must go and tell my family the truth of this matter.' He smiled in Isobel's direction before turning back to his hostess. 'I am sorry to trouble you for so long, but my groom tells me that one of the horses has cast a shoe and they must send to the village blacksmith. I thank you for your hospitality under such trying circumstances,' he added.

'Helping an injured man, and one who is a friend

of the family now, is no hardship, Lord James. And I know Mr Harker insisted that you bring him, although what on earth he was thinking about, I cannot imagine. Surely he did not think that he would be in any state to work with my husband and his advisers today—' She broke off and stared at the door. 'Mr Harker!'

'Good morning. I apologise for my appearance.' Giles walked into the room with a deliberation that Isobel realised must be the only alternative to limping. She found she was on her feet and sat down again. He did not spare her a glance.

Giles had discarded the swathes of bandage, although there was a professional-looking dressing across his injured cheek. The swelling around his nose was less, although the bruising was colourful. He sat down next to his friend and touched his hand briefly.

'Mr Harker, you should go back to bed immediately! What can you be thinking of?'

'Lady Hardwicke, I assure you I am quite capable of working with the earl and his advisers.' He accepted a cup of tea from Anne and reached for the cold meats.

The countess shook her head at him, but did not argue further, apparently recognising an impossible cause when she saw one. 'Benson, please tell his lordship that Mr Harker will be joining him and Mr Delapoole after breakfast.'

Isobel ate in silence, almost unaware of what food passed her lips. Giles not so much ignored her as managed to appear not to notice her presence. When he rose to leave she got to her feet with a murmured excuse to her hostess and followed him out, padding quietly behind him until he reached the Long Gallery.

'Giles! Please wait.'

He stopped and turned. 'Lady Isobel?' The beautiful voice was still slightly slurred.

'Don't. Don't be like that.' She caught up with him and laid her hand on his arm to detain him. 'Why are you angry with me? Because I have not thanked you for what you did for me? Or because I slept in your room? I am sorry if it was awkward with Tompkins. If you had to give him money, I will—'

'What were you doing in my room? In my bed?'

'I was not in it, I was on it.' She knew she was blushing and that her guilty conscience was the cause. She desired him. She had lusted after him. 'I was worried about you. I came to your room to make certain you were all right. You were thirsty so I gave you something to drink. You were drugged and I thought someone should watch over you. The bed was wide. I only expected to doze, not sleep so soundly that anyone would find me in the morning.'

'A pity you did not turn up the lamp and see at once just how repulsive I look now: then you could have fled there and then and not waited until Tompkins and daylight revealed the worst.' His bloodshot eyes fixed her with chilly disdain as she gaped at him. 'You have had time to pluck up the courage to look at me. Pretty, isn't it?'

'You thought I was repulsed? Giles, for goodness' sake! No, it isn't *pretty*, it is a mess. But it will get better when the bruises come out and the swelling subsides.

Your nose will be crooked, but surely you are not so vain that will concern you?'

'And the scars?' he asked harshly.

'Will they be very bad? The stitches will make it look and feel worse at first. My brother had them in his arm last year and they looked frightful. But now all there is to show is a thin white line.'

'Isobel, I am not a sixteen-year-old boy needing re-assurance.' Giles turned away, but she kept her grip on his sleeve.

'No, you are a—what?—twenty-nine-year-old man in need of just that! Physical imperfections are no great matter, especially not when they have been earned in such a way. You will look so much more dashing and rakish that your problems with amorous ladies will become even worse.'

'Then why did you look at me as you did this morning? Why did you flee from my room?' he demanded.

'Because it was my fault, of course! You had been hurt, you must have been in such pain, and it was all because of me. I know you felt you had to defend your friend's sister, but if I had not told you my story you would never have known. I was angry with myself, so I shouted at you.'

'Of all the idiotic—'

'I am not being idiotic,' she snapped, goaded. 'You could have been killed, or lost an eye.'

'Isobel, I could not let them do that to you and not try to defend you. How could I not fight?' Giles turned fully and caught her hands in his. The chill had gone from his expression, now there was heat and an intensity that made her forget her anger. But with it, her vehemence ebbed away.

'You hardly know me. We have been friends for such a short time,' Isobel stammered.

'Friends? Is that really what you think we are?' She could see the pulse beat in his temple, hard, just as her heart was beating. 'I saved your life—that makes you mine. I want to be so much more than friends with you, Isobel, did you not realise?'

'You do? But—'

'But it is quite impossible, of course,' he said with a harsh edge beneath the reasonable tone. 'You might be mine, but I can never have you. You do not have to say it. I am who I am—you are what you are. You must forgive me for speaking at all,' he added with a smile that did not reach his eyes. 'I have embarrassed you now.'

'No. No, you have not.' What did he really mean? What did he want, feel? She did not know, dared not ask. This was not some smooth attempt at seduction, this was bitter and heartfelt—the words seemed dragged from him against his will.

'I want you as more than a friend. I had hoped that I had hidden it. I knew I should not feel it. But I cannot help it,' she added despairingly.

'I should never have kissed you.'

'Two kisses are not what makes me feel like this.' She put her hand to her breast, instinctively laying it across the heart that ached for him.

'You fought very hard against what you feel?' he asked. His hands had come up to her shoulders. He was holding her so close that her skirts brushed his boots and she had to tip her head back a little to look into his face. The taut lines had relaxed into a wary watchfulness.

'Not as hard as I should have,' Isobel admitted. 'But I was afraid you would think me like the women you have to avoid, the ones who pursue you.'

'I doubt any of them would stand here, this close, with me looking like this,' Giles said with a return to the bitterness.

'I have seen better shaves,' Isobel admitted, seeing what humour might do. No good was going to come of this, she knew that. How could it? He was, as he said, who he was. But that was for tomorrow. Today she knew only that she was desired by this man. 'And I could wish your mouth was not so bruised.'

'Just my mouth?' He raised an eyebrow and winced.

'I would like to kiss you,' Isobel admitted, beyond shame at saying it. 'But I do not want to hurt you.'

'Kiss it better,' he suggested, pulling her closer and bending his head so his words whispered against her lips.

She slid her hands up to the nape of his neck to steady herself and trembled at the unexpected, vulnerable softness of the skin beneath her fingertips. With infinite care she met his lips with her own: the slightest pressure, the gentlest brush. He sighed and she opened to him and let him control the kiss.

This was so much more than that passionate exchange in the library, that foolish tumble in the shrubbery. So much more intimate, so much more trusting. Giles made a sound deep in his throat, a rumble of masculine satisfaction, and she met the thrust of his tongue with her own, learning the taste of him, the scent of his skin, the rhythm of his pulse. Their lips hardly moved as the silent mutual exploration went on, but Giles's hands travelled down her back until he held her by the waist, drew her tighter against his body.

He was lean and long and fit and Isobel pressed against him out of need and yearning and felt the heat and the hardness of his need for her. She wanted to get closer, to wrap herself around him, but she stopped herself in time, recalling his ribs.

'What is it?' Giles lifted his head.

'Your ribs. Lord James said you had been kicked.'

'If you can be thinking about my ribs while I am kissing you, it does not say much for my lovemaking.' Giles bent and brushed his uninjured cheek against hers, his mouth nuzzling at the warm angle of her neck and shoulder.

'You want to make love to me?' How brazen she was to ask such a thing. How wonderfully liberating it felt to do so.

'I would give a year of my life for one night in your arms.' His voice was muffled against her skin as she lifted her hand to touch his hair.

Isobel gasped. It was all her fantasies about Giles, all her wicked longings, offered to her to take. All she needed was the courage to reach out.

Almost as soon as he said it, she felt him hear his own words. The enchanted bubble that surrounded them shattered like thin glass. Giles's body tensed under her hands, then he released her and stepped back.

'I am sorry. I should never have spoken, never touched you.' His face was tight with a kind of pain that his physical injuries had not caused. 'I did not mean—Isobel, forgive me. I would not hurt you for the world.' He turned on his heel and walked away without looking back, up the gallery and into the book room that led to the library.

She stared after him, still shaking a little from the intensity of that kiss, unable to speak, unable to call him back.

He had only wanted a brief amorous encounter and his sense of honour had stopped him before they both were carried away. Isobel sank down on the nearest chair, stared unseeing at a landscape on the opposite wall and tried to tell herself she had just had a narrow escape.

The earl broke up the meeting shortly before noon. Giles suspected that such a short morning's work was on his behalf, but he could not feel sorry for it. Between the lingering effects of the doctor's potions, the pains in his body and his anger with himself over Isobel, it had been an effort to think straight at all, although the other men did not appear to notice anything amiss.

Of all the damnably stupid things to have done. But somehow he had not been able to forget that moment of waking to find her beside him in the big bed. All his good resolutions, all his self-deception that he could treat her as a friend, had fled to leave only a raw, aching need for her.

He could have controlled it, he told himself savagely,

as he turned left out of the steward's room and, on impulse, took the steps up from the basement. He emerged into the grey light of a blustery, cold day that threatened rain before nightfall. Giles jammed his hands into his breeches' pockets. He *would* have controlled it if she had not chosen that moment to come to him, her face full of hurt at the way he had coolly ignored her.

That vulnerability, that honesty, the way she confronted him so directly had somehow wrenched equal frankness from him. And because she was older than most of the unmarried girls he encountered, because he had been so open with her, he had let himself believe that they could have an affaire.

And of course she was too innocent to understand where their kisses were leading—even if she was not, it would have been wrong. By his own action he had cleared her name of all disgrace—now she could go back into society, find a husband, marry.

She was a lady and that meant marriage—but not to him, he told himself savagely. Not to him and she knew it, had remembered it when he had blurted out his desire for her. He had thought he had come to terms with his birth and with the limits it placed upon him: it seemed he was wrong.

'Idiot,' he muttered, kicking gravel. Of course a woman like her would not offer herself to a man she did not love. She had thought him her friend, nothing more, and he had betrayed her trust. 'Damnation.' What had he done?

'Harker, I could follow you across Cambridgeshire just from the muttered oaths.' He looked up to find

James, his cane in his hand, standing in front of him. 'What is the matter? Are you in pain?'

'Not as much as I deserve to be. What are you doing out here?' Giles took in his friend's thick greatcoat and muffler. 'It is no weather for a walk.'

'I went over to the stables to see how they were progressing in the search for a blacksmith. What's the matter with you? If you want to talk about it, that is.'

He could trust James, more than he could trust his own sense, just at the moment. 'Strictly between ourselves I've made a mull of things with Lady Isobel. More than a mull. Are you warm enough to walk? I don't want to risk being overheard.'

'Of course.' James fell in beside him as he walked past the stables and the church down the drive to the east. 'Have you told her you love her?'

'*What?* Of course not! I'm not in love with her. I do not fall in love with well-bred virgins. In fact, I do not fall in love with anyone.' James snorted. 'I want her, that's the trouble, and she caught me with my guard down and I damn nearly propositioned her.'

'Clumsy,' James remarked. 'And unlike you. But of course she, being female and having more intuition than the average male, presumably took your intentions to be honourable.'

'I don't know what she took them to be,' Giles retorted, goaded. 'She knows who I am, so how could she believe them to be anything but dishonourable? And what makes you think she wants me? Your fine understanding of female sensibility?'

'Not being able to see means I use my ears, my dear

Harker. And I listen to the silences between the words as well. You two are, as near as damn it, in love with each other. What are you going to do about it?'

'Nothing. Because you are wrong, and even if you were correct, even if I was fool enough to allow myself to fall in love, I would do nothing. I am not even going to apologise for what happened between us in the Long Gallery and perhaps that will bring her to her senses. And stop snorting, it is like having a conversation with a horse. I'll leave as soon as I can.'

'So you make love to her and then snub her. An excellent plan if you wish to break her heart, although I doubt Lady Isobel deserves that.'

'Then what do you suggest?' Giles demanded.

'Marry her.'

Chapter Twelve

'Marry her? Are you insane?' Giles slammed to a halt. 'Isobel is the daughter of an earl.'

'And so? She's a second daughter, she's perilously close to being on the shelf and she's had a brush with scandal. From what my sister tells me she was only doing the Season reluctantly in any case. Perhaps her father would be delighted for her to marry an up-and-coming architect with society connections, a nice little estate and a healthy amount in the bank.'

'You *are* insane,' Giles said with conviction.

'All right.' Albright shrugged. 'Go right ahead and break her heart because you won't risk a snub from the Earl of Bythorn.'

'Snub? I'd be lucky if he didn't come after me with a brace of Mantons and a blunt carving knife. I would in his shoes.'

'Coward,' James said.

'I am trying to do the honourable thing,' Giles said between gritted teeth. 'And that includes not knocking your teeth down your throat. You're the only man who can get away with calling me a coward and you know it.'

'If you want to do the honourable thing, then you want to marry her,' Albright persisted. 'Let's go back inside, it is raw out here and it must almost be time for luncheon.'

'Of course I do not.' Giles took the other man's arm and steered him down a path towards the back of the house. 'I am not in love. I have never been in love, I do not intend on falling in love. I intend,' he continued with more force when that declaration received no response, 'to make a sensible marriage to a well-dowered young woman from a good merchant family. Eventually.'

'That's three of you who'll be unhappy then,' James retorted as they went in through the garden door. 'Give me your arm as far as my room, there's a good fellow.'

Lord James was particularly pleasant to her over luncheon, Isobel thought. Perhaps he was trying to make up for the misunderstanding over the house-party incident. Sheer stubborn pride made her smile and follow all his conversational leads. She wished she could confide in him, for he seemed both intelligent and empathetic and he knew Giles so well. That was impossible, of course—he would have no more time for her foolish emotions than Giles had and, besides, she could not discuss Giles with anyone.

She had bathed her red eyes and dusted her nose with a little discreet rice powder. Giles would never guess she had been weeping, she decided, studying her own reflection in the overmantel glass.

'You think this new census is a good idea?' he was saying now in response to Lord James's speculation on how accurate the results of the government's latest scheme might be. He sounded not one wit discomforted by what had occurred that morning. Isobel tried to be glad of it.

'What do you think, Mr Harker?' she challenged him, frustrated by his impenetrable expression. He was treating her as though she was unwell, fragile, which was humiliating. It seemed to her that when he spoke to her his voice was muted. His face, when their eyes met, was politely bland. But she knew him too well now to believe he was indifferent to what had passed between them that morning. There were strong emotions working behind the green, shuttered eyes.

'I think that it will all depend on the competence of the parish priest entrusted to fill in the return in each place,' he said now. 'Better if each person was questioned individually. Or every householder, at least.'

'You think that would expose more of the truth?' Isobel asked. 'That people would reveal their circumstances honestly?'

'Perhaps not,' Giles said slowly. 'And perhaps it is a mistake ever to ask for too much honesty.' Isobel had no difficulty reading the meaning hidden in his words. He had been honest about his desires, had led her to the point of seduction and now he was regretting it.

'Sometimes people do not know the truth because they are too close to it,' Lord James observed, making her jump. She had forgotten that she and Giles were observer often sees more of the picture, ?'

and old maids like to say in order to jus-dling,' Giles said harshly.

d, Isobel glanced between the two men. Al-'s mouth twisted into a wry smile, but he did not appear to feel snubbed by what had sounded like a very personal remark. Giles, on the other hand, looked furious with his friend. Something had passed between them that morning, it was obvious.

The earl looked up from his plate of cold beef, unconscious of the undercurrents flowing around his luncheon table. 'The census? Very good idea in my view. I'd be glad if they did it in Ireland, then I might have a better idea of what to expect of conditions and problems there. I may suggest it when we see how this works out.'

The talk veered off into discussion of Irish politics, social conditions and, inevitably, sporting possibilities. Isobel placed her knife and fork neatly on her plate, folded her hands on her lap and watched Giles.

He guarded his feelings well at the best of times, except for his betraying eyes. But now, with his face so damaged and his eyes bruised, she was not at all sure she could read him at all. Except to know he was unhappy. *Good*, she thought, and went back to chasing a corner of pickled plum tart around her plate with no appetite at all.

In the general stir at the end of the meal Isobel found herself beside James Albright. 'I hope you have a safe journey home, Lord James.'

'Rest assured I will make your innocence k
to Penelope and all my family,' he said. 'And we
ensure the facts are spread far and wide. Unless,
course...' he lowered his voice '...you would prefer t
stay ruined?'

'Whatever can you mean, sir?'

'It might widen your choice of marriage partner, perhaps,' he suggested with a slight smile.

'Are you suggesting what I think you are?' Isobel
demanded. *Marriage?* 'There is no question of a match
between myself and...and anyone.'

'No? Of course *anyone* would say that, too, and, if...
er, *anyone's* defences were not down, he would never
have got himself into a position where he betrayed his
feelings to me quite so blatantly, as I am sure you realise.'

'As we are speaking very frankly, Lord James,' Isobel hissed, furious, 'the feelings betrayed to me were
not those which lead to a respectable marriage—quite
the opposite, in fact!'

'Oh, dear. Hard to believe that anyone could make
such a mull of it, let alone my friend. He is usually more
adroit,' Lord James observed. Isobel glanced round and
found they were alone in the room. His sharp hearing
must have told him that also, for he raised his voice
above the murmur he had been employing. 'If I am
mistaken in your sentiments, Lady Isobel, then pray
forgive me. But if I am not, then you are going to have
to fight for what you want. Not only fight your parents
and society, but fight Harker as well.'

'I have no intention of throwing myself at a man who

only wants me for one thing,' she said. 'And I do not want him at all, so the situation does not arise.'

'You know him better than that. Try to forgive him for his clumsiness this morning. If his feelings were not engaged he would have been…smoother.'

'How did you—?' She took a deep breath. 'My feelings are not engaged.'

'I found him in some agitation of mind. He told me he had erred and distressed you—I could fill in the rest. He let himself dream and hope and then woke up to the problems which are all for you, not for him. Giles Harker has a gallantry that will not allow him to harm you, so, if you want him, then you must take matters into your own hands.'

'Lord James—are you insinuating that I should seduce him?' Isobel felt quite dizzy. She could not be having this conversation with a man who was a virtual stranger to her.

The unfocused eyes turned in her direction. 'Just a suggestion, Lady Isobel. It all depends what you want, of course. Forgive me for putting you to the blush, but Giles Harker is an old and dear friend and I will happily scandalise an earl's daughter or two if it leads to his happiness. I wish you good day, ma'am.'

With Lord James's departure the men went back to their meeting and Lady Hardwicke swept up Catherine, Anne, Lizzie and Isobel, ordered them into bonnets, muffs and warm pelisses and set out for the vicarage to call on Mrs Bastable, the vicar's wife.

'I have sadly neglected my parish duties these past

few days and it is Sunday tomorrow,' she remarked as she led her party down the steps. 'What with Lizzie's drama and all our preparations for the move and the pleasure of having Isobel with us and now Mr Harker's accident, the Clothing Fund has been sadly neglected.'

'Was it an accident, Mama?' Lizzie demanded. 'Mr Harker, I mean. You said it was footpads who broke his nose and cut his face like that.'

'It was accidental in that he fell amongst criminals who tried to hurt him,' her mother said repressively.

'And Lord James was the Good Samaritan who rescued him?'

'I rather think he was rescuing himself quite effectively,' Isobel said, then closed her lips tight when Anne shot her a quizzical glance.

'And the bad men?'

'Have been taken up and will stand their trial, as all such wicked persons should,' her mother pronounced.

'The wages of sin is death,' Caroline quoted with gruesome relish.

'Really, Caro!'

'It is from the Bible, it was mentioned in last Sunday's sermon,' Caroline protested. 'Mr Harker is very brave, isn't he, Cousin Isobel?'

'Very, I am certain.'

'And he was very handsome. Miss Henderson said he's as handsome as sin. But will he still be so handsome when they take the bandages off?'

Lady Hardwicke's expression did not bode well for the governess, but she answered in a matter-of-fact tone, 'He will have scars and his nose will not be straight. But those things do not make a man handsome: his morals and character and intelligence are what matter.'

She pursued the improving lecture as they made their way across the churchyard and through the wicket gate into the vicarage garden. Isobel brought up the rear, her mind still whirling from that extraordinary conversation with James Albright.

Had he really meant that Giles was in love with her? Worse, he seemed to believe she shared those emotions.

The vicar's wife was grateful for help with the results of a recent clothing collection and, after serving tea, set her visitors to work that was familiar to Isobel from her own mother's charitable endeavours.

Isobel helped sort clothing into a pile that would be reusable by the parish poor after mending and laundering. The remaining heaps would be organised by the type of fabric so that when they had been washed the parish sewing circle could make up patchwork covers, rag-rugs or even suits for small boys from a man's worn-out coat.

It was worthy work and the kind of thing that she would be organising if she married a wealthy landowner, as she should. Lord James had spoken of marriage. An architect's wife would not have these responsibilities, although Giles had said he had a small country estate, so perhaps there were tenants. What would the duties of an architect's wife be? Not organising the parish charities, or giving great dinner parties or balls, that was certain. Nor the supervision of the staff of a house the size of Wimpole Hall, either. Not any of the things she had been raised to do, in fact.

This was madness. She would not marry save for love—on both sides—and Giles Harker wanted one thing, and one thing only.

'Cousin Isobel, you are daydreaming again,' Anne teased. Isobel saw she was waiting for her to take the corners of a sheet that needed folding. 'What on earth were you thinking of? It certainly made you smile.'

'Of freedom,' Isobel said and took the sheet. They tugged, snapping it taut between them, then came together to fold it, their movements as orderly as a formal minuet.

'Goodness, are you one of those blue-stockings?' Anne put the sheet in the basket and shook out a much-worn petticoat. 'I do not think this is any use for anything, except perhaps handkerchiefs.'

'Me, a blue-stocking? Oh, no. And I was not thinking of freedom from men so much as from expectations.' Anne looked blank. 'Oh, do not take any notice of me, I am wool-gathering.'

'I think everyone is behaving most strangely,' Anne said and tossed the petticoat onto the rag pile. 'There is the fight Mr Harker was involved in—and Lord James. I do not believe for a moment that it was simply bad luck with footpads, do you? Then you are daydreaming all the time and Mama is lecturing and there are peculiar conversations that seem to be about one thing, but I don't think are, not really. Like you and Mr Harker talking about the census and honesty.'

'Well, you know why I am here,' Isobel said. 'I have a lot on my mind, so I suppose that makes me seem absent-minded. And men are always getting into fights. It was probably over a game of cards or something. And I expect Cousin Elizabeth has a great deal to worry about with your father's new post, so that makes her a little short. And as for peculiar conversations, I cannot imagine what you mean.'

Anne looked unconvinced, but went back to sorting shirts while the countess tried to persuade the vicar's wife that she could take over judging the tenants' gardens for a prize, as Lady Hardwicke did every year.

Isobel picked up some scissors and began to unpick the seams of a bodice, letting Mrs Bastable's protestations that she knew nothing about vegetable marrows and even less about roses wash over her head.

Was she falling in love with Giles? Had Lord James, with whatever refined intuition his blindness had developed in him, sensed it when she could only deny it? Had Lord James really been serious when he had told her to take the initiative? Now Giles was no longer in shock, half-drugged and in so much pain, he would not take the first step—whatever his feelings, his defences were up.

I don't want to fall in love with him! That can't *be what I feel.* She had not felt like this over Lucas, so torn, so frightened and yet so excited. But then, Lucas had been completely eligible, there had been no obstacles, no secrets. No reasons to fight against it. Or was she simply in lust with the man and finding excuses for her desires?

* * *

'Cousin Elizabeth, I would like to speak to Mr Harker alone after dinner, if you will permit. He will not let me thank him properly for what he did—perhaps if I can corner him somewhere I can say what I need to.'

The countess put down her hairbrush and regarded Isobel with a frown. 'That will be all, Merrill.' Her dresser bobbed a curtsy and went out, leaving the two women alone in the countess's bedchamber.

'He has certainly put you in his debt and a lady should thank a gentleman for such an action, I agree,' Lady Hardwicke said, a crease between her brows. 'But a tête-à-tête is a trifle irregular.'

'I have been alone with him before,' Isobel pointed out.

But the countess was obviously uneasy. Perhaps she suspected, just as Lord James did, that there was something more between Isobel and Giles. 'A walk or a ride in the open are one thing, but in the house… Oh, dear. Perhaps one of the downstairs reception rooms would not be so bad—if you can persuade him to stand there long enough to be thanked! But for a man determined on escape there is a way out of all of them into another room. Unless you speak to him in the antechapel—there is no way out of that except into the gallery of the chapel and no one could object to a short conversation in such a setting.'

'Thank you, Cousin Elizabeth. Now all I have to do is lure him in there.'

Isobel left the countess shaking her head, but she did not forbid the meeting.

Chapter Thirteen

Giles schooled his face into an expressionless mask when Isobel, assisting the countess at the after-dinner tea tray, brought him a cup. He wanted to look at her, simply luxuriate in watching her, not have to guard every word in case he made things even worse.

He braced himself for murmured reproaches, or even hostility. 'Have you formed an opinion on the crack in the antechapel wall?' she asked without preamble. 'It sounds quite worrying, but perhaps the earl is refining too much upon it.'

'What crack?' It was the last thing he expected to hear from her lips. Giles put the cup down on a side table and the tea slopped into the saucer.

'Oh, he was saying something about it before dinner. I understood that he had asked you to look at it.' Isobel sat down beside him in a distracting flurry of pale pink gauze and a waft of some delicate scent. Now he did not want to look at all: he wanted to hold her, touch her. Did she not realise what she was doing to him? Was she trying to pretend nothing had happened in the Long Gallery?

'I was not aware of it,' he said, forcing his brain to deal with structural problems.

'Perhaps he did mention it and the blow to your head has made you forget it,' she suggested.

That was a disturbing thought. His memory was excellent, but then, he had believed his self-control to be so also and that episode with Isobel had proved him very wrong on that score.

'Or perhaps he meant to ask you, then decided it was not right while you feel so unwell,' she said with an air of bright helpfulness that made him feel like an invalid being patronised.

'I will go and look at it now.' Giles got to his feet and went into the hall. He took a branch of candles from the side table and opened the door into the chamber that led to the family gallery overlooking the chapel.

Once the room had been the State Bedchamber, but the great bed had long been dismantled and was somewhere up in the attics. Giles touched flame to the candles in the room and began to prowl round, trying to find cracks in the plaster, not think about Isobel's soft mouth, which seemed to be all he could focus on.

There in the left-hand corner was, indeed, a jagged crack. It would bear closer investigation in daylight, he decided, poking it with one finger and watching the plaster flake.

'Is it serious?'

'Isobel, you should not be in here.' In response she closed the door behind her, turned the key in the lock and slipped it into her bodice. 'What the devil are you doing?' Behind him was the double door into the gallery pew. Short of jumping fifteen feet to the chapel's marble floor, he was trapped, as she no doubt knew full well.

'I need to talk to you.' She was very pale in the candlelight and the composure she had shown over the tea cups had quite vanished. Giles saw with a pang that her hands were trembling a little. She followed his gaze and clasped them together tightly. 'About this morning.'

'I am sorry— I allowed my desires to run away with me. I had no right to kiss you, to hold you like that. It will not happen again.'

'That is a pity,' she said steadily. 'I would very much like you to do it again. I think I am in love with you, Giles. I am very sorry if it embarrasses you, but I cannot lie to you, I find. Not even to salve my pride.'

He stared at her, every bone in his body aching to go to her, to hold her, every instinct shouting at him to tell her… What? That he loved her? Damn James for even suggesting it. Of course he was not in love—he simply could not afford the luxury of hopeless emotion. But he did not want to hurt Isobel. 'I am very sorry, too,' he said, staying where he was. 'I never wanted to wound you.'

'I might be wrong, of course. I might not be. I thought perhaps…you…' Saying it brought the colour up under the delicate skin of her cheeks, soft pink to match her gown. He thought he had never seen her look lovelier or more courageous.

'No,' he said and kept his voice steady and regretful. He did not know what he felt, but surely it was only desire and friendship and liking. The emotion was stronger than any he had ever felt for a woman, but that was simply because he had never saved the life of one before, never fought for her honour, never met a woman like Isobel.

Isobel valued honesty above her own pride, but he could protect her from herself. 'No, I do not love you, Isobel. And that is a mercy, is it not? We could not possibly marry.'

'If you had not cleared my name and restored my reputation, and we did love each other, then perhaps we might have done.'

Hell, she's been talking to James, the interfering romantic idiot that he is.

'But not if I do not love you,' he pointed out. It felt like turning a knife in his chest, the pain of denying her, the knowledge that he was hurting her. 'And I do not think you love me, either. You feel desire, as I do, and it is easier for a woman to accept if you dress it up as love.'

'Do not patronise me! If I desire you I am not such a hypocrite as to pretend it is something else,' she flashed back at him. Her eyes were very bright, although if it was because they were full of tears, she did not shed them and he dared go no closer to see, in case she should read in his face how much he cared and took that for love. 'But you want me.'

'Oh, yes, and you know that too well for me to attempt to deny it. I want you so much it keeps me awake at night. So much that I ache and I cannot concentrate. But, Isobel, I might be many things, but I do not seduce virgins.'

'No,' she said, and smiled wryly. 'I am sure that you do not.'

'You will forget me soon enough,' he offered, flinching inwardly at the banality of the words.

'You think so? I thought we could talk this through with honesty, but it seems I misjudged you. Goodnight, Giles.'

She removed the key from her bodice, unlocked the door and walked away, leaving him, for once in his life, unable to think of a word to say.

Giles did not come back to the saloon afterwards. Isobel smiled and nodded to Cousin Elizabeth to reassure her that her mission to thank him had been successful, stayed to drink one cup of tea and then made her excuses and went up to bed.

He said he did not love her, but then he would say that whatever he felt, it was the honourable course of action in his position. And he said he wanted her—although he was quite correct and she hardly needed him to tell her that. If they made love, it would be hard for him to hide his true feelings, she was certain. She could try to seduce him, and if he made love to her then he would be trapped between a rock and a hard place—to marry her would be, in his eyes, dishonourable, but then not to marry her after sleeping with her would be equally bad.

And to put Giles in that position would be very wrong of her whether he loved her or not. Isobel wrestled with her conscience while Dorothy brushed out her hair and helped her into her nightgown. 'I cannot do it.'

'What, my lady?'

'Never mind. Something I had been wondering about.'

'You look sad, my lady. Aren't you pleased that Lord James knows the truth? It will be all over town in a twinkling, then you can go back and do the Season, just like all the other young ladies.'

'I do not want to, Dorothy.' It was the first time she had said it out loud, but it sounded so right. She had tried hard to please her parents, but the thought of entering the Marriage Mart again with this aching in her heart was agony. How could she even contemplate marriage to another man? She had thought she would never get over Lucas's death. Now that she had and had found Giles, it was impossible to believe she would recover from it. It must be love, she thought drearily. But love should make you happy, not confused and angry and scared.

'Now, my lady, that is foolishness indeed!' Dorothy bustled about tidying up until Isobel thought she would scream. 'All young ladies want to get married and have children.' An ivory hairpin snapped between Isobel's fingers. 'You had a nasty time at that horrid house party and then you almost drowned and then there's the shock of poor Mr Harker coming back with his face all ruined. No wonder you are feeling out of sorts, my lady. You'll find a nice titled gentleman with a big estate and live happily ever after with lots of babies.'

'I don't want lots of babies. I just want my—' Isobel caught herself in time. 'His face is not ruined,' she snapped. 'The bruises and swelling will go down, the scar will knit and fade in time.'

'Yes, but he was so handsome. Perfect, like a Greek

god.' The maid sighed gustily. 'Terrible blow to his pride, that will be.'

'He has more sense than to let such a thing affect him,' Isobel said, hoping it was true. Then a thought struck her. Surely Giles did not think she was saying she thought she loved him because she felt guilty that he had been wounded defending her good name? No, that was clutching at straws and she would go mad if she kept trying to guess at his motives. All she had was the bone-deep conviction that he did care for her and no idea how she could ever get him to admit it.

'I will go to bed and read awhile. Thank you, Dorothy, I will not need you again tonight.'

The maid took herself off, still talking about the joys of the London Season. Isobel stuffed another pillow behind her back and tried to read. *It might as well be in Chinese for all the sense it is making*, she thought, staring at the page and wondering why she had selected such a very gloomy novel in the first place.

The sound woke her from a light sleep that could only have lasted an hour at the most, for the candles were still burning. What was it? A log collapsing into fragments in the fire? No, there it was again, a scratch at the door panels. Isobel scrambled out of bed and went to open the door, half expecting Lizzie, intent on a midnight feast.

Giles stood on the threshold in the brown-and-gold brocade robe open over pantaloons and shirt, his feet in leather slippers. In the dim light his eyes sparked green from the flame of the candle he held.

'What on earth is wrong? Does Lady Hardwicke need me?'

'No. May I come in?' The clock on the landing struck one.

'Quickly. Before someone sees you.' Isobel pulled him inside and closed the door before the thought struck her that he was even more compromising on this side of the threshold. 'Giles, you should not be here.' How could he be so reckless? He spoke about her reputation and then he came to her room in the small hours. Isobel let her temper rise: it was safer than any of the other emotions Giles's presence aroused.

'I am aware of that.' He put down the candle and went to stand in front of the fire. 'I could not sleep because of you.'

'A cold bath is the usual remedy for what ails you, is it not?' she demanded.

He gave a short, humourless bark of laughter. 'Guilt, I find, trumps lust for creating insomnia.'

'What are you feeling guilty about and why, if I may be frank, should I care?' Isobel pulled on a warm robe and curled up in the armchair, her chilly feet tucked under her. There stood Giles, close enough to touch, and there was her bed, rumpled and warm, and if that was not temptation, she had no idea what was.

He stooped to throw a log on the fire and stirred it into flame with the poker. The firelight flickered across his bruised, grim face and made him look like something from a medieval painting of hell, a tormented sinner. 'You might care. I lied to you. I care for you very much, Isobel.'

It seemed she had been waiting to hear those words from him for days, but now all that filled her was a blank, hurt misery. Isobel blinked back the welling tears. 'I had not thought you so cruel as to mock me.' The heavy silk of the chair wing was rough against her cheek as she turned her head away from him.

'Isobel—no! I am not mocking you.' The poker landed in the hearth with a clatter as Giles took one long stride across to the chair to kneel in front of her.

'Then you are cynically attempting to make love to me.' She still would not look at him. If he had come to her room with a heartfelt declaration of love then he would not have looked so grim.

'That would make me no better than those three, tricking my way into your room.' His hands, strong and cold, closed over hers and she shivered and looked down at the battered knuckles. 'Isobel, my Isobel, look at me.'

With a sigh she lifted her eyes to meet his. 'Whatever your feelings, Giles, they do not seem to make you very happy.'

'That is true,' he agreed. 'And it is true that I care for you, and like you and want you, all those things. And it shakes me to my core that you might love me.'

'Then why deny it? Why hurt me, play with my feelings like this?'

He released her hands, rocked back on his heels and stood up to pace back to the fire. 'Because what I feel for you is not love and I dare not let either of us believe that it is. Because even if it was, I can see no way to find any happiness in this, however we twist and turn. I do not want to play with your feelings, I would never hurt you if I could help it. But we can do nothing about it. I believed it for the best if you thought I did not care—you might forget about me. Then I realised how much that wounded you and I could not bear not to tell you that I do care, that I want you, that in some way I do not understand, you are mine.'

The hard knot of misery inside her was untwisting, painfully, as hope warred with apprehension. *I am his, he wants me, he likes me, but he does not believe he loves me?* 'And what you feel for me is not love?' she asked.

'I do not think I know how to fall in love,' Giles said flatly. 'I have been with more women than I care to admit to you, Isobel. And I have never felt more than desire and a passing concern for them, pleasure in their company.'

How carefully he guards his heart, she realised with a flash of insight. *He knows he is ineligible for any of the women he meets socially, so he does not allow himself the pain of dreaming.*

'You think it is hopeless, then? My love for you, your…feelings for me?' *Yes*, she thought as she said it. *Yes, I do love him.*

'Of course it is hopeless. Even if I was a perfectly respectable second son, say, earning my own living as an architect, your father would consider it a poor match. As it is, he would never permit you to ally yourself to me. And you deserve a man who loves you. We can be strong about this, Isobel. Avoid each other, learn to live our separate lives.'

'Will you not even *try* to find some way we can be

together?' Isobel scrambled out of the chair and went to stand in front of him. The heat of the fire lapped at her legs, but every other part of her was cold and shivery. 'If we talk about it, perhaps we can see some way through.'

'No. It would be wrong to wed you.'

'I am of age, I can decide who to marry. Love grows. I would take a risk on yours.'

'Your father would cut you off,' Giles said. 'Disown you.'

'Do you want my money, then?' she jibed at him, wanting to hurt him as he was so unwillingly hurting her.

'No—but I do not want to deprive you of it.'

'As your wife I would hardly starve,' she pointed out. 'And I am not at all extravagant. We would not be invited to all the most exclusive events, so that would be a saving in clothes—'

'Do not jest,' Giles said, shaking his head at her. But she could see the reluctant curve of his mouth. Misery and pessimism did not come easily to him. 'A scandal would affect my business and then how could I support you?'

'You are imagining the worst.' Isobel shook his arm in exasperation. 'What if marriage to the daughter of an earl was good for your business? I would keep the other women at bay, I would entertain, I know all the people who might commission you. You say you do not think you will ever fall in love—well then, why not take the nearest thing to it?'

'Stop it, Isobel.' Giles put both hands on her shoulders and looked down into her face. 'You are talking yourself into an emotion you do not feel. I will go back to London. In a week or two you will go home and take part in the Season and you will find an eligible, titled husband and live the life you were born to live.'

'No. I will not,' she stated with conviction. 'I was waiting for a man to fall in love with. One who loved me. One I could confess my secret to and who might accept me despite it. I do love you, I know that now—this could not hurt so badly if it was simply desire. But I cannot believe that after Lucas, and now you, that I will find a third man to love, and one who feels the same. So I am resolved to give up on the Season. I will become a spinster, a country mouse who will dwindle quietly away as a good daughter and sister. One day, no doubt I will be an aunt and much in demand.'

'You are talking rubbish.' Giles's voice was rough. 'What secret?'

'That I am not a virgin.' There was the other thing as well, the thing that tore at her heart, but she could not tell him that, however much she loved and trusted him. 'Lucas and I were lovers in the weeks before he died, you see. Men seem to place such importance on that, in a bride. I could hope that someone who loved me would understand, but not a man who was making a marriage for other reasons. I could lie, I suppose, and hope he would not notice. I could pretend to be ignorant and innocent—but that is hardly the way to begin a marriage, by deceiving one's husband.'

She shrugged, his hands still heavy on her shoulders. The truth, but not the whole truth. But Giles, of all men, would not understand why she had done what she had done, why she had made the dangerous, desperate choice that she had.

He stood there silent and she wondered if she had shocked him. Was he like all the rest, the respectable ones who would condemn her for the sin of loving? 'I have disappointed you,' she stated, unable to wait for the condemnation on his tongue, the rejection on his face.

'Then you misjudge me,' Giles said. 'You were in love with him. He was a fortunate man. I can feel jealousy, I will admit that. But how can I condemn you? But you are right about one thing—it would have to be a deliberate act of deception to pretend to your husband that you are completely unawakened. Even holding you in my arms, kissing you, I felt the sensuality, the awareness of your own body's needs and of mine.'

'Giles?'

'Mmm?' He drew her in close and held her warm and safe against his bruised body and she felt his breathing as she slid her arms under his robe and around his waist. Suddenly it was all very simple.

'Make love to me.'

Chapter Fourteen

Giles's heartbeat kicked and his hands tightened. 'Isobel, think of the risk. You making love with the man you were going to marry is one thing. But I'll not chance getting you with child.'

'There are ways of making love that hold no risk,' she said. It was easier to be bold with her burning face hidden against his shirt front. 'We…Lucas and I, made love like that the first time.'

'You trust my self-control?' His voice rumbled in his chest against her ear and she felt the pressure as he rested his uninjured cheek against her hair. He had not rejected her out of hand. Her pulse quickened, the heaviness of desire settled low inside her. If he touched her intimately he would feel the evidence of her desire for him. And she wanted him to touch her, shamelessly.

'Yes.' The second time with Lucas, neither of them had had any self-control. But it had not mattered, they told themselves, lying tangled in a happy daze afterwards. They would be married within weeks. 'Am I asking too much of you?'

'There is nothing you could ask me that is too much, except to forget you. This is only going to make things worse for us, you know that?'

'I know. But it will not be worse until tomorrow.'

Giles gave a muffled snort of laughter. 'Feminine logic,' then gasped as she pulled a handful of shirt from his breeches and put her hands on his bare skin. 'Isobel, if we are found out—'

'Lock the door. Lock the door and make love to me, Giles.' Isobel stepped back out of his arms. 'Please. Make me yours, as much as we can.'

As he went to the door she blew out all but two of the candles.

'Isobel?' Giles turned back, the key in his hand.

'I am shy—a little,' she confessed and knew her blush added veracity to the half-truth. She did not want to risk what he might read from her body.

'There is no need,' he said, smiling at her as he let his robe drop then pulled his shirt over his head. 'It is all right,' he added as she ran forwards with a cry of distress at the sight of his ribs, marked black and blue with bruises. 'Bruised, not broken. Let me see you, Isobel.'

Her robe slithered to the floor. Under it all she wore was her nightgown, warm and sensible flannel for February. 'Ah. My little nun,' Giles teased and pulled it over her head before she could protest. 'Oh, no, not a nun. My Venus.'

'I am not that,' Isobel protested, her hands instinctively shielding her body, even as she warmed with shocked pleasure at Giles's expression as he looked at her in the shifting shadowlight.

'Slim and rounded and pale.' His hands traced down over her shoulders, down her arms, over her hips. His touch was warm now. 'When I first saw you I thought you were too thin and your nose was red from the cold. You seemed quite plain to me. I must have been blind.'

'And I thought you were a cold statue, too perfect to be real.' She let her hands stray to his chest and played with the dusting of dark hair. 'So cold.' His breath hitched as her fingernail scratched lightly at one nipple.

'No. Not cold,' Giles said thickly. 'Hot for you.' He kissed her, held her tight against him so her breasts were crushed against the flat planes of his chest and her thighs felt the heat of his through the black silk of his evening breeches. The thin fabric did nothing to disguise the hard thrust of his erection against her belly. This was no shy and tentative young lover, this was a mature, experienced man. Isobel moaned into his mouth, pressed herself against him.

She wanted him, needed him inside her so she could possess and be possessed, know that she was his. But they must not, she knew it. Whatever she did, she must not put Giles into a position where he felt honour-bound to marry her, come what may. Somehow—if only he would come to realise that he loved her—they would find a way, but not like that.

Giles slowed the kiss, gaining control after the first shock of their lips meeting. He edged her against the bed until she tumbled backwards and he followed her, rolling her into the centre of the mattress and coming to lie beside her.

'Your breeches.' Isobel felt for the fastenings, but

his hand stilled hers, pressing it down over the straining weight of his erection.

'Better leave them on.' He was having trouble controlling his breathing, she realised.

'No.' She shook her head and burrowed her fingers beneath his. 'I know what to do. Let me touch you, Giles.'

'You are— Oh, God.' He sank back as her determined hands pulled down his breeches and tossed them away.

'Oh.' He was…magnificent. The fight had battered and bruised his upper body, but below the waist the skin was unblemished, winter-pale. The dark hair that arrowed down from his waist added emphasis to a masculinity that did not need any enhancement. Isobel realised he was holding his breath and did what instinct was clamouring at her to do. She bent and kissed him there, her hands curved over the slim hips.

Satin over teak beneath her lips, the scent of aroused male musk in her nostrils, lithe muscles in tension beneath her hands, his sharply indrawn breath—every sense was filled with him as she trailed her lips upwards.

'Isobel.' He sounded in pain, but she knew enough to realise this was not agony. 'Not yet. Let me…'

She did not fight him as he pulled her up to lie beside him. She would let him lead because it was on him that the burden of control fell. But she would help, she would be rational and—

Giles took her right nipple between his lips and tugged and all rational thought vanished. Isobel pulled his head against her breast with a sob and the knowledge that he could do what he wished with her, she had absolutely no will to stop him.

His mouth, wicked and knowing, tormented each tight, aching nipple in turn, until she was writhing against his flank, gasping his name and some incoherent plea she did not even understand herself. Her body, the flesh she had thought immune to desire for so long, ached and clamoured and, as his fingers stroked down, laced into the damp curls, slipped between the swollen lips, she simply opened to him, quivering with need as he slipped into the tight heat that clenched around his fingers.

'I love you,' she managed and was silenced by his mouth, his tongue. Against her hip she could feel his straining body and reached for him, finding the rhythm as her fingers curled around him and his thumb worked wicked, knowing magic at her core. 'I love you,' she gasped, the words lost in his kiss as her body arched, pressing up into the heel of his hand, shuddering as the bliss that was almost pain took her.

'Isobel,' she heard through the firestorm and Giles thrust into her circling fingers, shuddered and was still.

How long they held each other afterwards, she did not know. She must have drowsed, for she woke to find him gently washing away the evidence of his passion, then he pulled the covers over them, snuggled her against his side and she felt the long body relax as he slid into sleep.

There was only one candle alight now, Isobel noticed hazily. And Giles had said nothing. Her body had not betrayed her as she feared. He had not realised she had borne a child and her secret was still safe from the man she loved.

'What time is it?'

'I can't tell with you wrapped round me like this,' Giles said, disentangling the clinging limbs that chained him so deliciously to the bed. He managed to raise himself on one elbow and lift the carriage clock that stood on the night table. It was almost completely dark and he had to bring it to his face to squint at the hands in the faint glow from the fire. 'Half past four. I must go soon.'

'Already?'

Isobel sounded peevish, he noted, amused, as she burrowed back against his side. The chuckle turned to a gasp as she slid one hand down and stroked. 'Ten minutes. Fifteen,' he amended as the caress tightened into a demanding grip.

'Only fifteen?' Isobel wriggled up to kiss his stubbled jawline. 'You are all bristles.'

'You would be amazed at what I can do in fifteen minutes with these bristles,' Giles said and burrowed down the bed, ignoring the twinges from his ribs.

'Oh, do mind your nose and the stitches,' Isobel said. Then, '*Oh*!' in quite another tone as he pressed her thighs apart and began to make love to her with mouth and tongue and, very gently, his teeth.

She was not shocked, he realised as he luxuriated in the scent and taste of warm, sleepy, aroused woman. Her fiancé must have made love to her like this as well. He half expected a twinge of jealousy, but surprised himself by feeling none, only pity for the other man. He would have married her if only he had lived, poor devil.

Then everything but the present moment and the pleasure of pleasuring Isobel was driven from his mind as she took his head in her hands and moaned, opening for him with complete trust, total abandon.

'Ten minutes,' Giles said with what even he recognised as smug masculine satisfaction when they lay panting in each other's arms, half inclined to laughter, completely relaxed.

'Fast is almost as good as slow,' Isobel murmured, kissing her way up from the tender skin just below his armpit to his collarbone. 'Giles, do you regret that your mother kept you instead of finding you a home where you would grow up with a family you thought were your own?'

'What on earth makes you ask that?' He sat up and struck a light for the candle beside them. Isobel rolled on to her back, her hair a tangled, wanton mass of shifting silk on the pillows. Giles bent and kissed her between her breasts.

'I don't know. Do you regret it? It cannot have been easy, being known as the Scarlet Widow's illegitimate son. It sounds as though you were bullied at school and there are some in society who shun you.'

'I would probably have been bullied anyway,' he said with a shrug. 'I was far too pretty—a real little blond cherub until I started to grow and my hair darkened. And if Geraldine had tried to give me away my grandfather would have had something to say about it, so I would have ended up with him and been an illegitimate gardener's boy instead of having the education and the opportunities I have had. No, I do not regret it. I know who I am, where I came from. I am myself and there is no pretence, no lies.'

'You call your mother by her first name?'

'The last thing she wants is an almost-thirty-year-old man calling her "Mama." It makes people do the arithmetic and I doubt she'll admit to forty, let alone fifty.'

'I suppose her position protected her at the time, made it easier for her to keep you.'

'No.' At first he had assumed that, but with maturity had come understanding. 'It was anything but easy. I picked up some of the story from her, some from my grandfather, but she kept me when it would have been an obvious thing for her to have pretended she was with child by her late husband. All she had to do was to apparently suffer a miscarriage late on, then retire from sight to recover, give birth and hand me to Grandfather.

'But she brazened it out and never pretended I was anything but my true father's son. I remember that whenever she is at her most outrageous. She is a very difficult woman.'

'She must have loved him very much,' Isobel ventured. She was pale and seemed distressed. Perhaps this was bringing back memories of her fiancé's death.

'She had been in a loveless, if indulgent, marriage to a man old enough to be her father for four years. She must have needed youth, heat, strength.' Had it been love? Or, as he suspected, had Geraldine simply needed to feel the emotion as she did with every lover since? It was such an easy excuse, love. But how did you learn to feel it genuinely?

'My father was young, handsome, off to fight in his scarlet uniform. Perhaps he was a little scared under all the bravado. By all accounts it was not some wanton seduction by an experienced older woman or some village stud taking advantage of a vulnerable widow.'

'How brave she was.'

'It cut her off from her own family, from her in-laws and, for a long time, from society. But she fought her way back because I think she realised that my future depended upon it.' Giles got out of bed and began to dress. 'Not that she was ever the conventional maternal figure. And the shocking behaviour is probably a search for the love and affection she experienced for such a short time. Not that she would ever talk about it.' What had she felt when she heard of his father's death in battle? He had never wondered about that before. Now with someone to care about himself, the thought of his mother's pain was uncomfortably real.

Isobel still looked pensive. 'Giles, what are we going to do?'

'I am going to my own bed and you are going back to sleep. And check the pillow for hairs when you wake.' He rummaged under the bed for a missing slipper, determinedly practical.

'Our hair is close enough in colour for Dorothy not to notice. You have had a lot of practice at this sort of thing,' she said slowly. 'Only I presume it is suspicious husbands you need to deceive, not protective ladies' maids.'

'Complacent, neglectful husbands—a few in my time,' he confessed. 'I do not make a habit of it. Are you jealous?'

'Of course.' Isobel sat up straight and shook her hair back. It seemed her brooding mood had changed. The sight of her naked body filled him with the desire to rip his clothes off and get back into bed again.

'Yes, of course I am jealous even though I have no right to be,' she said with a half smile. 'My brain is all over the place—I am not thinking straight. When I asked what we are going to do, I did not mean now. I meant afterwards. In the morning.'

'And for the rest of our lives?' Giles pulled on his robe and made himself meet her eyes, too shadowed to read. 'I do not know, Isobel. I honestly do not know anything, except that this has no future.'

He turned the key in the lock and eased the door ajar. 'The servants are beginning to stir, I can hear them moving about on the landing above.' He looked back at her, upright, shivering a little in the morning air, her lips red and swollen from his kisses, her eyes dark. What he wanted was to drag her from the bed, bundle her in to her clothes and flee with her, take her home to Norfolk and be damned to the consequences. Was that love? If it was, it was selfish, for nothing would more surely destroy her.

'Go back to sleep,' Giles said instead and went out into the darkness.

What she wanted to do was to get up, get dressed, throw her things into a portmanteau and follow him, beg him to take her away, to his home and his grandfather and let the world say what it would. Because this was love, however much she might fight it. Love was too precious, too rare, to deny.

But it was impossible to act like that, as though she had only her own happiness to think of. Her parents would be appalled and distressed. Cousin Elizabeth and the earl would be mortified that such a scandal had occurred while she was under their roof. Giles's business, his whole future, would suffer from the scandal.

He cared for her and that was a miracle. He had shown her love, all through the night, as much by his care and restraint as by the skill of his lovemaking. Perhaps he would come to realise that he loved her, but some deep feminine instinct told her that he would be wary of admitting it, even if his upbringing, his past, the constraints upon him, allowed him to recognise it.

She had given him everything she could, except that one deep, precious secret. Annabelle. Lucas's child was being raised as a legitimate Needham, believed by all the world to be the twin of little Nathaniel, the child of her friend Jane and Jane's husband Ralph Needham, Lucas's half-brother. The two men were drowned together when their carriage overturned into a storm-swollen Welsh mountain beck late one winter's night.

No one knew except Jane, her small, devoted household in their remote manor and the family doctor. Annabelle was growing up secure and happy with all the prospects of a gentleman's daughter before her and Isobel dared not risk that future in any way. She saw her child once or twice a year and lived, for the rest, on

Jane's letters and Annabelle's messages to *Aunt Isobel*. Her parents would never know their own grandchild. She had not heard her daughter's first words nor seen her first steps.

If she married again Isobel knew her conscience would tear her apart. How could she take her marriage vows while hiding such a thing from her husband? But how could she risk telling a man when he proposed? If he spurned her and then could not be trusted with the secret it would be a disaster.

Giles had said he was glad he had stayed with his mother, that he knew who he was. No pretence, no lies, he had said and he obviously admired and loved the Dowager for the decision she had taken. He would not understand why Isobel gave her child away; he would think she did not have the courage of his own mother to keep Annabelle and defy the world.

There was a very large lump in her throat and her face was wet, Isobel realised. She dared not let Dorothy find her like this. She slid out of bed, her legs still treacherously weak at the knees from Giles's lovemaking, and splashed her cheeks in the cold water on the washstand. Then she smoothed the right-hand side of the bed, tucked it in and got back in, tossing and turning enough to account for the creases.

A clock struck six and Isobel knew she had been lying, half asleep, half waking and worrying, since Giles had left her. In an hour and a half Dorothy would bring her chocolate and hot water. She must try to sleep properly despite the warm tingling of her body and the agitation of her mind. Whatever the day brought, she would need her wits about her.

Chapter Fifteen

There was no sign of Giles at breakfast, nor was he with the earl, Isobel discovered after some carefully casual questions. Lizzie finally gave her a clue.

'I think it is such a pity,' she was protesting to Anne as they entered the breakfast room. 'Good morning, Cousin Isobel. Have you heard the awful news? Mr Harker is conspiring with Papa to demolish the Hill House.'

'Really, Lizzie! You are dramatising ridiculously,' Anne chided as she sat down. 'Papa has decided it is not worth reconstructing, that is all. Much better that it is safely demolished.'

'But Mr Repton said—'

'Mr Repton is not always right and it is Papa's decision. Anyway, we would not be here to use it for ages, even if it was rebuilt.'

'Well, I am very disappointed in Mr Harker,' Lizzie announced darkly. 'He had better not try to knock down my castle.'

'I believe he is going to see what can be saved of the

stonework to go to strengthening the Gothic folly,' her sister soothed. 'I expect that is what he is doing today. I heard him say something to Papa about good dressed stone not going to waste.' Lizzie subsided, somewhat mollified.

'Is Cousin Elizabeth coming down to breakfast or have I missed her?' Isobel asked. 'I was going to ask her if I might ride this morning.' If Giles was not at the Hill House, then she would ride over the entire estate to find him, if necessary.

'Oh, Mama left early to drive into Cambridge to take Caroline to the dentist,' Anne said. 'I know it is Sunday, but she woke with the most terrible toothache. Mama says we can all go to evensong instead of matins. But I know she will not mind you taking her mare. Benson, please send round to the stables and have them saddle up Firefly for Lady Isobel.' As the butler bowed and crooked a finger for a footman to take the message, Anne added, 'I do not think this sunshine will last— my woman predicts a storm coming and she is a great weather prophet.'

The sky was certainly dark to the west as the groom tossed Isobel up into the saddle of the countess's pretty little chestnut mare. 'Shall I come with you, my lady? She's a lively one.'

'No, thank you. I can manage her.' She held the mare under firm control as they crossed in front of the house and then gave her her head up the hill towards the derelict prospect house.

Giles's big grey was tied up outside and whickered a

greeting as Isobel reined Firefly in. A movement caught her eye and she glanced up to find Giles sitting at the window over the portico. One foot up on the sill, his back against the frame, he turned his head from the distant view he had been contemplating and looked down.

'Isobel. You should not be here.' But he smiled as he said it and a tremor of remembered pleasure ran through her.

She brought the mare up next to the grey and slid down to the steps, managing to avoid the mud. 'But we need to talk,' she said, tilting her face to look at him as she tied the reins to the same makeshift hitching post.

'Come up, then.' Giles disappeared from sight and met her at the top of the staircase.

'This feels so right. So safe,' she said and walked into his arms without hesitation. 'I do love you so, I know that now.'

Giles's reply was muffled in her hair, but she heard the words and the happiness was so intense it made her shiver. 'Last night was very special for me, Isobel.' Then he put her away from him and the look on his face turned the frisson into one of apprehension. 'But I have been up here for hours thinking—without any conclusion other than this is wrong and we must part.'

'No! No,' she repeated more calmly as she walked past him into the chamber. 'We are meant to be, meant for each other. I refuse to give up.'

'There is no way. We cannot change who I am and that is that.' The bruises on his face were yellowing now, the swelling subsiding. Isobel stood biting her lip and looking at his profile as Giles stared out of the window, his mouth fixed in a hard line.

'Your nose is not so very crooked,' she said after a moment. 'It is not as bad as when it was so swollen. Now it just looks interesting. Perhaps this—us—is not so bad either if we give it time and think.'

'The only thing that would make our marriage acceptable is your ruin, and you know it as well as I do. And there is no alternative for you other than marriage.'

'Then what is to become of us?' she said, her voice cracking on the edge of despair.

'We will learn to live without each other,' Giles said harshly. 'Just as you learned to live without Lucas when he died.'

'I would not call it living,' Isobel whispered. At first, despite the bitter grief, it had been bearable. That year when she had been with Jane, their pregnancies advancing together, the month after the births when she could hold Annabelle, truly be a mother to her—that had been a time of happiness mixed with the mourning. It was only after she had returned home, doubly bereaved of both fiancé and child, that Isobel had plunged into deep sadness.

'I do not think I realised how depressed I was,' she said, looking back over the past four years. 'Even when I felt better I did not want to mix socially, look for another man to love, because I did not believe there was one. I could not see what the future held for me. Now—'

'Now you must start afresh,' Giles said and turned from the window to look at her. 'You have the courage and the strength, you know you have. And you are

eside her, lower his mouth to hers and kiss
nguorous slowness while his hands caressed
g her to the brink, then pulling back, build-
pleasure until Isobel thought every nerve must
ble as they quivered under the skin, then leaving
again teetering on the edge of the abyss.

'Oh, you wretch,' she sobbed, her fingers tight on
the hard muscle of his shoulders as she arched, seeking
his touch. 'You torturer.'

'Touch me,' Giles said, bringing her hand to clasp
around him. 'Take me with you.' Then he held nothing back, his body at her mercy, his hands demanding,
demanding, until Isobel lost all sense of what was her
and what was Giles and surrendered to the mindless
oblivion of pleasure.

She came to herself to find him slumped across her,
relaxed into sleep. 'Giles?'

'Mmm.' His lids fluttered, the dark lashes tickling
her cheek, then he was still again.

Isobel tugged the greatcoat more securely over them,
curled her arms around him and lay, cheek to cheek,
thinking. Nothing lasted for ever. She had him now
and for a few days and precious nights even though
she did not have his words of love. She would not waste
those moments by anticipating the inevitable parting;
she would live them and revel in them and then do her
best to live without him. *I will not pine. I will find some
purpose, some joy in life. I will not allow something so
precious to destroy me*. In the distance thunder rumbled.

An hour later they approached the house from different directions, Giles from the western drive, Isobel

better off without me, even ignoring my birth. I have
been—I am—a rake, Isobel. I have never courted a respectable young woman.'

'So will you forget me easily?' He had made love
with her, slept with her, been thinking about her for
hours—and he still did not know if he loved her, she
thought, her confidence shaken.

'No.' He shook his head. 'You have marked my heart
as surely as these scars will mark my face. I will never
forget you, never cease to want you. You are, in some
way I do not understand, mine.'

'But you will find a wife and marry and have children.' She could see it now. He would find an intelligent,
socially adept daughter of some wealthy city merchant
and she would love him and he would be kind to her
and together they would raise a family and Isobel would
see them sometimes and smile even though her heart
was cracked in two…

'Yes. And you will find a husband. We will find con-
tentment in that, Isobel.'

How the sob escaped her, she did not know; she
thought she could control her grief. 'It sounds so dreary,'
she said and bit her lip.

'You will make a wonderful mother,' Giles said. 'You
will have your children.'

'Oh, no. Do not say that. Do not.' And then the tears
did finally escape, pouring down her face as she thought
of Annabelle and the children she would never have
with Giles.

'Sweetheart.' Giles pulled her into his arms, kissing

away the tears. 'Please don't cry. Please. I am sorry I cannot be what you want me to be.'

She turned her head, blindly seeking his mouth, tasted her own tears, salt on his lips. 'Love me again, Giles. Now and every night while we are both here.' He went so still she caught herself with a pang of guilt. 'I'm sorry, that is selfish, isn't it?' She searched his face, looking for the truth she had learned to read in his eyes. 'It isn't fair to expect you not to make love fully.'

'I would want to be with you even if all I could do was kiss your fingertips,' Giles said, his voice husky. 'You gave me so much pleasure last night, Isobel. But I have no right to let you risk everything by coming to your chamber again.'

'If that is all we have, just the time we are both here, then surely we can take that, make memories from it to last for ever? We will not be found out, not if we are careful as we were last night.' It was Sunday, so perhaps it made what she was asking even more sinful. But how could loving a man like this be a sin?

'Memories?' He held her away from him, studying her face, and then he smiled. It was a little lopsided, but perhaps that was simply because of the stitches in his cheek. 'Yes. We will make one of those memories here and now and use that little chamber one last time for the purpose for which it was intended.'

There was a rug thrown over the chair at the desk he had been using to write his notes. Giles spread it over the frame and ropes that were all that remained of the daybed in the painted chamber and while he closed the battered shutters Isobel shed her riding habit, pulled off

her boots and was standing ...
chemise and stockings, wh...

'Goose bumps,' she a...
over her chilled upper a...

'I'll warm them away. ...
too cold.' He wrapped his grea...
eased her on to the bed before strippi...

Isobel lay cocooned in the Giles-smell...
of the big coat and feasted her eyes on him. He w...
be embarrassed if she told him how beautiful his b...
was, she guessed, and besides, many other women ha...
told him that, she was sure. Instead she wriggled her
arms free to hold them out to him. 'Giles, come into
the warm.'

'I am warm.' He wrapped her up snugly again, then
parted the bottom of the coat so he could take her feet
in his hands, stroking and caressing them through her
stockings, teasing and warming and arousing as he
worked his way up. Then he flipped the coat back over
her lower legs and proceeded to kiss and lick and nib-
ble her knees until Isobel was torn between laughter
and desperation.

'Giles!'

'Impatience will be punished.' He covered her knees,
then shifting up the bed, left precisely the part she
wanted him to touch shrouded. He pushed up her chemise to lick his way over the slight swell of her belly,
into her navel, up between her breasts without once
touching the curve of them, the hard nipples that ached
for his touch.

Only when he reached her chin and she was whim-
pering with desire and delicious frustration did he lie

retracing her route, bringing Firefly across the wide
sweep of gravel before the house to the stables. They
met, as if by chance, outside the stable arch.

'Mr Harker! Good morning.' Isobel let the groom
help her dismount and waited while Giles swung down
from the grey. The sound of bustling activity made her
look through into the inner yard where the back of a
chaise was just visible.

'Visitors,' Giles observed. 'Have you had a pleasant
ride, Lady Isobel?'

'Very stimulating, thank you. But I fear it is about
to rain.' She caught up the long skirt of her habit and
walked with him across to the front door. Benson
opened it as they approached and Isobel stepped into
the hall to find the callers had only just been admitted.
A grey-haired man of medium height with a commanding nose turned at the sound of their entrance, leaning
heavily on a stick. Beside him a thin lady in an exqui-
sitely fashionable bonnet started forwards.

'Isobel, my darling! What good news! We had to
come at once even if it did mean travelling on a Sunday.'

She stopped dead on the threshold. 'Mama. Papa.'
Her mother caught her in her arms as Isobel felt the
room begin to spin. There was a crash of thunder and
behind her the footman slammed the door closed on the
downpour. *No escape.*

'Darling! Are you ill? You have gone so pale—sit
down immediately.'

'I…I am all right. It was just the shock of seeing you,
Mama. Thank you, Mr Harker.'

Giles slid a hall chair behind her knees and Isobel
sat down with an undignified thump. 'Lord Bythorn,

Lady Bythorn.' He bowed and stepped away towards the foot of the steps.

'Wait—you are Harker?'

'My lord.' Giles turned. His face had gone pale and the bruises stood out in painful contrast.

'Lord James Albright tells me that you were injured standing with him to bring to account those scum who compromised my daughter. And I hear from her own letters that you rescued Isobel and young Lizzie from the lake.'

'The lake was nothing—anyone passing would have done the same. And Lord James is an old friend, my lord. I merely did what I could to assist him.' Giles made no move to offer his hand or to come closer. Isobel realised her mother had not addressed him and she was looking a trifle flustered now. Of course, they knew who he was, what he was, and Giles had expected that, should he ever meet them, he would receive this reaction.

'You have my heartfelt thanks.' The earl paused, a frown creasing his brow. 'You are a resident in this house?'

'I am undertaking architectural work for the earl. Excuse me, my lord. Ladies.' He bowed and was gone.

'Well, I'm glad to have the opportunity to thank the fellow in person,' her father said, wincing from his gout as he shifted back to face her. 'But I must say I'm surprised to find him a guest in the house.'

'Lady Hardwicke always gives rooms to the architects and landscape designers,' Isobel said indifferently. 'The earl works so closely with them, I believe he finds it more convenient. I met Mr Soane when I arrived, but I have not yet met Mr Repton.'

'Soane? Well, he's a gentleman, at least. I hear rumours of a knighthood,' her father said. Isobel opened her mouth to retort that Giles was a gentleman, and a brave and gallant one at that, then shut it with a snap. To defend him would only arouse suspicion.

'The man looks a complete brigand with his face in that state,' her mother remarked with distaste.

'He was injured in the fight defending Lord James and, by extension, me.'

'Well, he might be less of a menace to women now he has lost his looks. The man was a positive Adonis, so I hear—and there are enough foolish ladies with the instincts of lightskirts to encourage men like that,' Lady Bythorn added with a sniff.

'Perhaps he is only a menace to married ladies,' Isobel said sweetly, her hands clenched so tightly that a seam in her glove split. 'Cousin Elizabeth has no qualms about allowing him to socialise with her daughters or myself. Suitably chaperoned, of course.'

'I am glad to hear about the chaperonage, at least! But that is all academic—I expect your woman can have your things all packed by the time we have finished luncheon.'

'Packed?

'Well, of course.' Her mother beamed at her fondly. 'Now everyone knows the truth of what happened, there is no reason for you to be hiding in the country. You can come home and do the Season just as we planned.'

'But—' Isobel could hear Cousin Elizabeth's voice

coming closer. And the butler and footmen were still standing in the background, having stood to attention with blank faces throughout Lady Bythorn's opinions on Giles's morals. This was no place to start arguing with her parents about her future.

'Margaret! Bythorn! What a pleasant surprise.' The countess sailed into the hall, beaming. 'You've come to collect dear Isobel, of course. We are going to miss her sadly.' She ushered them towards the Yellow Drawing Room. 'Margaret, would you like to go up with Isobel to her room? I will ring for her woman to bring you whatever you need after your journey. You must have set out at the crack of dawn to make such good time.'

'I will go up in a moment, Elizabeth—it is so good just to see Isobel again! We left as soon as we received Lord James's letter and put up overnight at the Bell at Buntingford. I could not wait to get my dear girl home again. Thank heavens we have not missed anything of the Season.'

'I imagine Isobel is more glad about the restoration of her reputation than the opportunity to take part in social events,' Cousin Elizabeth said with a glance at Isobel. There was understanding in the look and a kind of rueful sympathy. She, at least, had some inkling of how reluctant Isobel was to plunge back into the social whirl that she so disliked and the imagination to understand what gossip and snide remarks would still follow her.

'I would prefer to stay here, Mama,' Isobel said. She folded her hands on her lap and sat up straight, as though perfect deportment would somehow be a barricade against this disaster. If she let her shoulders droop, if she relaxed in the slightest, she did not think she would be able to stop herself either sobbing in despair or running to find Giles.

Chapter Sixteen

'Stay here?' said Lady Bythorn, turning her gaze on Isobel. For a moment she thought there was hope, then her mother shook her head. 'But you cannot impose on Lady Hardwicke's hospitality now it is not necessary. Really, Isobel, it is about time you shook off this pose of indifference to society. We should never have allowed you to stay with Mrs Needham for over a year in that remote place as we did. I declare you came back a positive stranger to us.'

'I am sorry, Mama.'

'It would be best for you to go back to London, Isobel,' Cousin Elizabeth said. 'We will miss you, but there is the risk that rumours may begin again if you do not make an appearance. It might seem that you have something to hide after all.'

So there was no help there. Where else could she go? If she ran away to Jane and Annabelle, then Papa would fetch her back and she did not think she could face him meeting his granddaughter all unawares. Without her allowance she had no money. To throw herself into Giles's arms would be to embroil him in a scandal that might wreck his career.

It seemed very hard to think coherently. Isobel felt she was running through a darkened house, banging on doors that all proved to be locked, twisting and turning in a maze of corridors.

She had thought she had a few more precious days with Giles—now those had been snatched away from her. She had to speak to him. When he left the hall he had turned towards the stairs. He must have gone up to his chamber to change.

'Mama, shall I show you to my rooms? I can set Dorothy to packing.' From somewhere she dredged up the courage to smile and stand and pretend composure.

'Of course.' Her mother linked arms with her as they went up the stairs. 'Now, you only have to overcome this indifferent shyness you seem to feel and all will be well. The country air has done you good—your cheeks are rosy, your lips look fuller and there is such a sparkle in your eyes.'

All the consequence of Giles's lovemaking, if her mother did but know it. It seemed she had no suspicion that anything untoward had occurred, even though they had entered the house together. Perhaps it seemed impossible to Mama that her daughter would even think of flirting with someone in his position, let alone anything else.

'Here we are. It is a lovely view, is it not? Dorothy, please can you pack all my things as soon as possible—I am sure you can ask for help if you need it. We will be leaving after luncheon, so do not neglect your own meal. But first, please fetch hot water for her ladyship.'

'Yes, my lady.' The maid bobbed a curtsy to the countess. 'I am so glad Lady Isobel is going home, my lady, if I may be so bold.'

'Thank you, Dorothy. We are all delighted,' Lady Bythorn said and the maid hurried out.

'Mama, would you excuse me while I run up to the nursery and schoolroom and say goodbye to the children? I have become very fond of them.'

'Of course. I will just sit here and admire the prospect from the window and rest a little.'

Isobel dropped a kiss on her mother's cheek and went out of the door leading to the back stairs. As soon as she was out of sight she ran up to the attics and into the schoolroom.

'Cousin Isobel!' Lizzie jumped up beaming from her seat beside Caroline, who had her head wrapped in a shawl and was looking very woebegone.

'Excuse me, Miss Henderson, for interrupting your lesson, but I have to say goodbye to the children. My mama and papa have come to collect me, Lizzie.'

'Oh.' Her face fell. 'Can you not stay a little longer?'

'No, I am sorry. I promise I will write to you all. Is Charles in the nursery? I must kiss him as well,' she said as she disentangled herself from the children's hugs.

'If you are all very good, we will wrap up warmly and go out on the leads to wave Lady Isobel goodbye,' the governess suggested.

'That will be lovely. Thank you. Now, I will be going

to London, so I will send you all a present. Would you like that?'

She left them agog at the thought of gifts arriving when it was not even their birthdays or Christmas and whisked down the stairs and along the passage leading to Giles's bedchamber. There would be just time, if he was only still there.

Isobel pressed her ear to the panels, but she could hear no voices, so the valet was not with him. Without knocking she opened the door and slipped inside.

'Isobel!' Giles strode out of his dressing room and shut the door behind her.

'Your face—why have you taken the dressing off? The doctor hasn't even removed the stitches. Oh, it looks so sore!'

'It looks thoroughly unsightly and will, I hope, convince your parents that no daughter of theirs would look twice at its owner.' He gave her a little shake. 'What on earth are you doing here? There will be hell to pay if you are found with me.'

'I had to talk to you,' she protested. 'And I do not know when we could have snatched even a moment alone. Papa intends to return home immediately after luncheon. Giles, what are we going to do?'

'Nothing, except come to our senses,' he said, his face harsh. 'This is a blessing in disguise—the longer we were together, the more chance there was of this being discovered.'

'But we have no chance to plan now—'

'There is nothing to plan for. You are not a romantic young girl, Isobel. You knew this was hopeless, just as I did, but we let ourselves daydream and now it is time to wake up.'

'Just like that?' She stared at him. The cold, aloof man of their first meeting was back and her tender lover was quite vanished. 'No regrets, no sadness, just a *blessing in disguise*? I love you, Giles.'

'And I let myself think I could dally with an earl's daughter.' He cupped his hand around her cheek. 'Sunshine in February. I should have known there would be a frost to follow. *Wake up*, Isobel—it is over.'

'So you really do not love me?' she asked painfully. He thought of what had happened as just a dalliance? The rain drumming on the window echoed the frantic beating of her heart.

'I told you that. And you have not fallen in love with me, if you will only be honest with yourself. You had been hurt and rejected by people you thought were your friends. You wanted affection and you wanted to rebel, too.'

'You think so? After we made love as we have, you can still say it was all a delusion, an act of rebellion? It must have been, because I thought I knew you and now I do not think I do, not at all.'

She turned away, unable to bear his touch any longer, then swung back. 'Why did you fight for me if I was not important to you?'

'It was the right thing to do, for my friends and for any lady who had been betrayed in that way.'

'Gallantry, in effect. Just like rescuing two drowning people from the lake. I thought I was your friend.'

It sounded forlorn, but however much it hurt her pride, she could not help herself. 'You said I belonged to you.'

'It was wrong of me to think I could make a friend of an unmarried lady and what I said about you being mine was foolish sentimentality.'

'So there is nothing between us?' It was like sticking pins into her flesh, but she had to have the truth from him. 'You were gallant and then deluded. We made love, but that was merely lust.'

'I admire your courage and your generosity, your wit and your elegance. I was privileged to share your bed, and my lips will be for ever sealed about that. You need have no fear I would ever give the slightest hint that so much as a kiss had passed between us.'

Isobel stared up at the scarred, battered face and tried to find her friend, her lover, her love, somewhere behind the hard mask. But there was nothing, just a faint pity, the hint of a smile. 'I trusted you, Giles.'

'I never lied to you. I never told you I loved you. I am sorry it went as far as it did.'

'But not as sorry as I am, Giles.' Isobel turned on her heel and walked out. She wanted to hesitate at the threshold, to stand there a moment, for surely he would call her back, but she made her feet keep walking, closed the door behind her with care and went back to her own room. He did not speak.

Her mother, hair tidied and complexion restored with the judicious use of rice powder, was sitting with her feet on a stool while Dorothy bustled about packing.

'Isobel dear—have you been crying?' Her mother sat up straighter and stared at her.

'No… Well, a little. I was upset at leaving the children, they are very sweet. I suppose it has made my eyes a trifle watery, that is all. There is the gong—shall we go down?'

They descended the stairs arm in arm again. Her mother had relaxed now, Isobel sensed. Her unaccountable daughter had yielded, the Season could be exploited in every possible way and, by the end of it she, Isobel, would have come to her senses and be betrothed to a well-connected, wealthy man who would father a brood of admirable children. All would be well.

Cousin Elizabeth and her three eldest children were already in the dining room. Lord Hardwicke and her father followed them in and then, on their heels, Giles entered.

Lady Bythorn took one look at his face, gasped audibly and plunged into conversation with Lady Anne. Cousin Elizabeth frowned, more in anxiety about the effects of leaving off the dressing than from any revulsion at the scar, Isobel thought. Her father stared, then resumed his discussion of tenancy issues with the earl. Giles, apparently oblivious, thanked Lady Caroline for the bread, passed her the butter and addressed himself to his meal.

'Some brawn, my lady?' Benson produced the platter. Isobel stared at it quivering gently in its jelly and lost what little appetite she had left.

'Thank you, no, Benson. Just some bread and butter, if you please.'

It was strange, she thought as she nibbled stoically through two slices of bread and butter and, to stem her mother's urgings, a sliver of cheese. She had not expected a broken heart to feel like this. She was numb, almost as if she no longer cared. Perhaps it was shock; they said that people in shock did not feel pain despite dreadful injuries.

Over the rim of her glass she watched Giles and felt nothing, just a huge emptiness where only a few hours ago there had been a turmoil of feelings and emotions. Hope, love, desire, fear, uncertainty, happiness, confusion, tenderness, worry—they had all been there. Now, nothing.

She found she could smile, shake her head over Cousin Elizabeth's praise of her courage in rescuing Lizzie, tell her mother of the interesting recipe for plum jam the vicar's wife had given her. When her eyes met Giles's down the length of the table she could keep her expression politely neutral, even smile a bright, social smile.

It was only as they were gathered in the formal elegance of the Yellow Drawing Room to make their final farewells that Isobel realised what she felt like. She had visited Merlin's Mechanical Museum in Princes Street once and had marvelled over the automata jerkily going about their business with every appearance of life and yet with nothing inside them but cogs and wheels where there should have been a brain and a heart and soul.

She shook hands, and exchanged kisses, and smiled and said everything that was proper in thanks and when she saw a shadow fall across the threshold, and Giles stood there for a moment looking in, she inclined her head graciously. 'Goodbye, Mr Harker.'

But when her parents turned to look he was gone. Like a dream, she thought. Just like a daydream. Not a memory at all.

Chapter Seventeen

'I have absolutely no expectation of finding anyone I wish to marry, Mama,' Isobel said, striving for an acceptable mixture of firmness and reasonableness in her tone. 'I fear it is a sad waste of money to equip me for yet another Season.' For four days she had tacitly accepted all her mother's plans, now she felt she had to say something to make her understand how she really felt.

Lady Bythorn turned back from her scrutiny of Old Bond Street as the carriage made its slow way past the shops. 'Why ever not?' she demanded with what Isobel knew was quite justified annoyance. She was doing her best to see her second daughter suitably established and any dutiful daughter would be co-operating to the full and be suitably grateful. 'You are not, surely, still pining for young Needham?'

'No, Mama.'

'Then there is no reason in the world—' She broke off and eyed Isobel closely. 'You have not lost your heart to someone unsuitable, have you?'

'Mama—'

'Never tell me that frightful Harker man has inveigled his way into your affections!'

'Very well, Mama.'

'Very well what?'

'I will not tell you that Mr Harker has inveigled in any way.'

'Do not be pert, Isobel. It ill becomes a young woman of your age.'

'Yes, Mama. There is no illicit romance for you to worry about.' *Not now.*

'We are at Madame le Clare's. Now kindly do not make an exhibition of yourself complaining about fittings.'

'No, Mama. I will co-operate and I will enter into this Season, fully. But this is the last time. After this summer, if I am not betrothed, I will not undertake another.'

'Oh!' Lady Bythorn threw up her hands in exasperation. 'Ungrateful girl! Do you expect me to wait for grandchildren until Frederick is finally old enough to marry?'

The guilt clutched like a hand around her heart. Mama would be a perfect grandmother, she loved small children. She would adore Annabelle and Annabelle would love her. 'I am afraid so, Mama. Thank you, Travis,' she added to the groom who was putting the steps down and remaining impassive in the face of his mistress's indiscreet complaints.

Isobel followed her mother into the dress shop, sat down and proceeded to show every interest in the fashion plates laid out in front of her, the swatches fanned out on the table and the lists of essential gowns her mother had drawn up.

'You have lost weight, my lady,' Madame declared with the licence of someone who had been measuring the Jarvis ladies for almost ten years.

'Then make everything with ample seams and I will do my best to eat my fill at all the dinner parties,' Isobel said lightly. 'Do you think three is a sufficient number of ballgowns, Mama?'

'I thought you were not—that is, order more if you like, my dear.' Her mother blinked at her, obviously confused by this sudden change of heart.

One way or another it would be her last Season—either a miracle would occur and she would be courted by a man who proved to be outstandingly tolerant, deeply understanding *and* eligible enough to please her parents or she would be lying in a stock of gowns she could adapt for the years of spinsterhood to come.

'Aha! All is explained! Lady Isobel is in love,' the Frenchwoman cried, delighted with this deduction.

Isobel simply said, 'And two riding habits.' She felt empty of emotion. That had to be a good thing. It meant she could lead a hollow life and indulge in all its superficial pleasures for a few months: clothes, entertainment, flirtation. It would satisfy Mama, at least for a while, and it would be something to do, something to fill the void that opened in front of her.

'I am not certain I quite approve of Lady Leamington,' Lady Bythorn remarked two weeks later as the queue of carriages inched a few feet closer to the red carpet on the pavement outside the large mansion in Cavendish Square. 'She strikes me as being altogether too lax in the people she invites to her balls, but, on the other hand, there is no doubt it will be a squeeze and all the most fashionable gentlemen will be there.'

Isobel contented herself with smoothing the silver net that draped her pale blue silk skirts. A shocking squeeze would mean plenty of partners to dance with, many fleeting opportunities for superficial, meaningless flirtation to give the illusion of obedience to her mother. In large, crowded events she felt safe, hidden in the multitude like one minnow in a school of fish.

Following the scandal of Lord Andrew's arrest and subsequent disappearance to his country estates, she found herself of interest to virtually everyone she met. Men she had snubbed before seemed eager to try their luck with her again, young ladies gasped and fluttered and wanted to know all about how *ghastly* it had been. The matrons nodded wisely over the sins of modern young men and how well dear Lady Isobel was bearing up.

'I do not care any more, so I have suddenly become attractive,' she said wryly to Pamela Monsom who stopped for a gossip when they met in the ladies' retiring room. Pamela had been one of the few friends who had stood by her in the aftermath of the scandal, writing fiercely to say that she did not believe a word of it and that men were beasts.

'It is not just that,' Pamela said as she studied her,

head on one side. 'Although you are thinner you also look more… I don't know. More grown up. Sophisticated.'

'Older,' Isobel countered.

'Oh, look.' Pamela dropped her voice to a whisper. 'See who has just come in!'

'Who?' Isobel pretended to check her hem so she could turn a little and observe the doorway. 'Who is that?'

The lady who had just entered was exceedingly beautiful in a manner that Isobel could only describe as *well preserved*. She might have been any age above thirty-five at that distance—tall, magnificently proportioned, with a mass of golden-brown hair caught up with diamond pins to match the necklace that lay on her creamy bosom.

She swept round, catching up the skirts of her black gown, and surveyed the room. The colour was funereal, but Isobel had never seen anything less like mourning. The satin was figured with a subtle pattern and shimmered like the night sky with the diamonds its stars.

'That, my dear, is the Scarlet Widow,' Miss Monsom hissed. 'I have never been this close before—Mama always rushes off in the opposite direction whenever she is sighted. I think she must have had a fling with Papa at some point.' She narrowed her eyes speculatively. 'One can quite see what he saw in her.'

For the first time in days Isobel felt something: recognition, apprehension and a flutter very like fear. The wide green eyes found her and she knew Pamela was right: this was the Dowager Marchioness of Faversham, Giles's mother.

The lush crimson lips set into a hard line and the Widow stalked into the room.

'She is coming over here!' Pamela squeaked. 'Mama will have kittens!'

Isobel found she was on her feet. Her own mother would be the one needing the smelling bottle when she heard about this. 'Lady Faversham.' She dropped a curtsy suitable for the widow's rank.

'Are you Lady Isobel Jarvis?' The older woman kept her voice low. It throbbed with emotion and Isobel felt every eye in the retiring room turn in their direction as ladies strained to hear.

'I am.'

'Then you are the little hussy responsible for the damage to my son's face.'

'I shall ignore your insulting words, ma'am,' Isobel said, clasping her hands together tightly so they could not shake. 'But Mr Harker was injured in the course of assisting Lord James Albright to deal with his sister's errant fiancé who had assaulted me.'

'You got your claws into him, you convinced him that he must defend your honour and look what happened!' The Widow leaned closer, the magnificent green eyes so like Giles's that a stab of longing for him lanced through Isobel. 'He was *beautiful* and you have scarred him. You foolish little virgin—you are playing with fire and I'll not have him embroiled in some scandal because of you.'

No, I do not want to feel, I do not want to remember… 'I should imagine that Mr Harker has far more likelihood of encountering scandal in your company than in mine, ma'am,' Isobel said, putting up her chin. 'If a gentleman obeys an honourable impulse on my behalf I am very grateful, but as I did not request that he act for me, I fail to see how I am responsible.'

'You scheming jade—'

'The pot calling the kettle black,' Isobel murmured. Her knees were knocking, but at least her voice was steady. She had never been so rude to anyone in her entire life.

'I am warning you—keep your hands off my son.' By a miracle the Widow was still hissing her insults; except for Pamela beside her, no one else could hear what they were talking about.

'I have no intention of so much as setting eyes on your son, ma'am, let alone laying a finger on him,' Isobel retorted.

'See that is the truth or I can assure you, you will suffer for it.' Lady Faversham swept round and out of the room, leaving a stunned silence behind her.

'What dramatics,' Isobel said with a light laugh. 'I have never met Lady Faversham before and I cannot say I wish to keep up the acquaintance!'

That produced a ripple of amusement from the handful of ladies who had been staring agog from the other end of the room. 'What on earth is the matter with her?' Lady Mountstead demanded as she came across to join them.

'Her son was injured assisting Lord James Albright to put right an unpleasant situation—I am sure you know to what I refer. The Dowager blames me for some reason.' But not as much as she blamed herself.

Isobel lingered, working to dampen down the speculation, turn it towards gossip about the scandalous Widow and away from her own affairs. She felt reasonably confident she had succeeded when she left the retiring room, but her mother would be aghast, she knew it.

'I had best go and find Mama and warn her of that little incident,' she said to Pamela. 'If we do not see each other again tonight, you must call, very soon.'

'I will most certainly do that.' Pamela was still wide-eyed with speculation. 'And I expect to hear all about the shocking Mr Harker. But now I suppose I had better go and rejoin my party in the supper room.' She hurried off.

Thoroughly flustered, Isobel took the other right-hand corridor. It was deserted, badly lit, but she thought it might lead to the end of the ballroom where she had last seen her mother. The temptation to tell her nothing at all was strong, but the gossip would be certain to reach her ears, so she had no choice but to warn her.

She hurried on, head down, trying to think of a way to break the news that she had been accosted, in public, by the Scarlet Widow. 'Ough!' The man she had walked right into caught her by both arms to steady her, then, as she looked up, the grip tightened. 'You!'

'Me,' Giles agreed. He did not release her and she stood still in his grasp, not knowing whether that was because she wanted to have his hands on her or because struggling would be undignified.

'Your face is healing well.' It was the first thing that came into her head that she dared say out loud. *I love you* or *You abandoned me* or *Take me away with you* or *I hate you* were all impossible. 'How long have the stitches been out?' The scars were still red, but the swelling and bruising had gone—soon they would begin to fade.

'Two weeks.'

'You look…it makes you look dangerous.'

'So I have been told.' Something in his tone suggested that whoever had said so had been female. 'You appear to be enjoying yourself, Isobel.'

'Do I? You have been watching me?'

'You are hard to miss in that gown and when you are so ubiquitous. Dancing every dance, flirting with so many gentlemen. Your heart has quite recovered, I see.'

'And also whatever of yours was engaged.' Isobel twisted her right hand out of his light grip and flicked at the trace of face powder on his lapel. 'The lady favours Attar of Roses, I think.'

'One of them, as I recall, yes.' He sounded bored, like a tomcat who could hardly be bothered with the hunt. With his newly broken nose and the scars above the immaculate white linen and complicated neckcloth, he looked like a pirate playing at being a gentleman.

'Such a bore for you, all these women throwing themselves at you,' Isobel said, her voice dripping with false sympathy. 'Still, I suppose you can hardly afford to neglect your admirers—who knows, one of them might be about to persuade her complaisant spouse that she needs her boudoir remodelled.'

'The lady with the Attar of Roses wants a new library as a present for her husband.'

'And I am sure she will be at home the entire time to supervise.'

'Probably.' He was angry at her jibes. The colour was touching his cheekbones and the green eyes were cold, but the drawl was as casual and as insolent as before. 'What are you doing in town, Isobel?'

'The Season. What else?' She shrugged.

'I thought that was the last thing you wanted.'

'That was before a certain gentleman reminded me about the pleasures of the flesh,' she said, smiling at him when his brows snapped together in a frown. A demon seemed to have taken control of her tongue. 'I thought perhaps I might be…entertained if I came to London.'

'And I thought you did not want to marry again.'

'Were we discussing marriage, Giles?'

'You little witch. If it is fleshly pleasure you want—' He tugged on the wrist he still held captive, pulling her against his exquisite silk waistcoat. The lingering scent of roses warred with his citrus cologne in her nostrils and under it was the faint musk of a man who was hot with temper.

And lust, she realised as his mouth came down and his hands trapped her and his lips punished her for defiance. She knew his body and he knew hers. She found she had clenched one hand on his buttock, holding him tight against her. The pressure of his erection sent tongues of flame to the core of her as his mouth left hers and he began to pull at the neckline of her gown, his lips seeking the nipple, his tongue and teeth wreaking havoc with her senses.

They were crushed into a corner now, his hand under

her skirts as she lifted her leg to hook it around his hip to give him access. It was mad, insane, they were both so angry, both so—

The sharp clip of heels on marble was like a bucket of cold water thrown in her face. Isobel gasped, found her feet, pushed at Giles even as he spun round instinctively to shield her.

'Geraldine,' Giles said. His mother.

From behind him Isobel could see the dark sheen of black satin, the glitter of diamonds. She pushed her way free to stand at his side and confront the other woman, her chin up.

'You little fool,' the Dowager hissed. 'So you lied to me. You will be sorry for this. Very sorry.'

Isobel simply turned on her heel and walked away. Neither of them made the slightest attempt to stop her.

The passage turned and she jumped at the sight of someone coming towards her, then she saw it was her own reflection in a long glass. Her bodice was awry, her hair half-down, her skirts crumpled. With hands that shook Isobel righted her gown, twisted the loose ringlets back into order, fanned her face with her hands until the hectic colour began to subside, then went out into the ballroom before she had time to think about what had just happened.

'Mama.' Lady Bythorn was deep in conversation with the Dowager Lady Darvil, but she turned with a smile that became rigid when she saw Isobel's face.

'Are you unwell, my dear? You look quite—'

'Flustered,' Isobel hissed. 'I know. Mama, I must speak with you alone. Urgently.'

'You have the migraine?' Lady Bythorn said clearly as she got to her feet. 'Do excuse us, Georgiana, I fear Isobel is suffering from the heat—we had best go home. Come, dear.'

With a suitably wan smile for Lady Darvil, Isobel let herself be led to the hallway and fanned while their cloaks were found and the carriage called.

'What is it?' her mother demanded the moment they were inside. 'Has someone been referring to the scandal?'

'No. Mama, the Dowager Lady Faversham found me in the retiring room and said the most horrible things. She blames me for the injuries Mr Harker suffered.'

'Oh, my heavens! That frightful creature. I knew Frederica Leamington could not be trusted not to invite the wrong sort of people. Did anyone hear her?'

'Only Pamela Monsom and she is very discreet. There were other people in the room, but they did not hear exactly what she said and when she left I explained that she was upset about Mr Harker's scars and they were very sympathetic. But they are sure to gossip.'

'And now your name will be linked with his,' her mother observed grimly. 'There is nothing to be done but brazen it out—thank goodness he was not there tonight!'

Isobel bit her lower lip. She did not feel capable of confessing to her mother that Giles Harker had indeed been at the ball. Her body still quivered from his touch and from the anger that had flashed between them.

'There, there.' Her mother leaned over in the shadowed interior to pat her hand. 'It will be all right. That woman has such a dreadful reputation that no respect-able person would believe a word she has to say.'

But I do. She said I would be sorry, and she meant it.

Chapter Eighteen

'What the devil are you about?' Giles planted himself squarely in the corridor to block his mother's furious, impetuous path. She was quite capable of sweeping out into the ballroom on Isobel's heels and continuing this scene there.

'You fool,' she snapped at him, eyes flashing. 'You aren't content with having your face ruined for the sake of that little madam, but now you are getting yourself entangled with her. She'll be the ruin of you! She's an earl's daughter—Bythorn won't stand for it and he has influence.'

'And he never slept with you, so you can't play that card,' Giles drawled, hanging on to his temper by a hair's breadth. 'I am not entangled with Isobel Jarvis—'

'Hah!'

'We were merely continuing an argument.'

'An argument? I have heard it called many things, Giles, but never that!'

'I am not having an affair with the girl.'

'No,' the Widow said grimly. 'You fancy yourself in love with her.'

'I am not in love with her. I am considering strangling her.'

'Listen to me! I have found you the perfect wife, Giles,' she said as he turned on his heel.

'Really?' he threw back over his shoulder. 'Some plain daughter of a Cit?'

'No. Caroline Holt, the daughter of Sir Joshua Holt.'

'And what is wrong with her? Or the family, that they should consider allying themselves with us?'

'There is absolutely nothing wrong with Miss Holt who is tolerably pretty, intelligent and twenty-three years old. What is wrong with her father is a series of investments that have gone badly wrong, an estate mortgaged to the hilt and four unmarried daughters on his hands.'

Giles turned round fully to face his mother. 'So Caroline is the sacrificial lamb. You buy her for me, Holt pays off the debts and the other girls can enter the Marriage Mart with some hope of attracting respectable husbands. Provided they aren't seen with their brother-in law, that is.'

'Exactly. And you get a well-bred wife who will be grateful for all we have done for her family.'

'How did you find her?' he asked even as he wondered how he was managing to keep his temper, and the urge to storm into the ballroom and drag Isobel out of it, under control.

'I have excellent enquiry agents.'

Of course, Geraldine had always prided herself on

being able to find out anything about anyone. It was how she made such good choices in her lovers, avoided blackmailers, kept away from men with wives who had connections that would be dangerous to her and always found the right place to invest her money.

'I hope you have not made the Holts any promises.' His body was throbbing with frustrated desire. He felt as though he had been kicked in the gut and he had an overwhelming need to break something. 'Because I am not marrying the girl, for which she should be profoundly grateful. I have told you before, there is nothing you can buy me, least of all a wife.'

A dismissive flick of Geraldine's hand was all the acknowledgement she gave that she had heard him. 'Caroline Holt is not going anywhere far from her home in the wilds of Suffolk,' the Widow said with a thin smile. 'She will wait until you come to your senses about the Jervis chit.'

'My senses are perfectly in order, ma'am. My refusal to marry Miss Holt has nothing to do with Lady Isobel.'

'Liar!' she threw at him. 'She ruined your looks and yet you lust after her like a—'

'Mother,' Giles said. It stopped her in midrant. He never called her that unless he was deeply angered and she knew it. 'I have it on good authority that a broken nose and a couple of scars gives me an interesting air of danger. Really, I should thank Lady Isobel.'

The Widow took a deep breath. 'I would sacrifice everything for you, Giles. I would do anything to ensure your future.'

It was guilt, he knew, although she would never

admit it, or probably even recognise it. Her actions had made him a bastard—now she would fight tooth and nail to force society to accept him.

'I can look after my own future,' he said, not unkindly. He hated it when her voice shook like that. 'Society accepts me for who I am and I make my own way in it. Go back to Carstairs and stop plotting: I'll not have Lady Isobel insulted.' Knowing Jack Carstairs, her current youthful lover, he would be scouring the house trying to discover where Geraldine had got to, well aware that he would probably have to extricate her from some scrape or another when he did find her.

Giles walked away with the firm intention of getting drunk. Behind him he thought he heard Geraldine repeat, 'Anything,' but he was not certain. Besides, there was no need to worry—there was nothing that she could do to harm Isobel. He was her only dark secret and Geraldine would not risk involving him in further scandal.

'Who is your letter from, Isobel?' Lady Bythorn glanced up from her own correspondence. 'You've been staring at the same page for minutes. Is the handwriting bad?'

'No. No it is from Jane Needham. I am just…thinking.'

We are all in the best of health and the children are flourishing despite being cooped up with the dreadful weather, Jane had written. *Nathaniel wants a puppy and Annabelle wants a kitten, so I foresee scratches all round before much longer. The oddest thing happened the other day: there was a stranger staying at the Needham Arms—we heard all about him because, as you know, we hardly ever get any strangers in the parish and the rumour was he looked like a Bow Street Runner. Which is pure fancy of course, because no one here has ever seen a Runner!*

But he came to the house asking for you and when I saw him and told him he was mistaken, that you do not live here, he just brushed it aside and said he's heard you stayed here sometimes. I demanded to know his business and he said he had been sent by a distant relative of yours, a sea captain, who was estranged from the family and was trying to make contact again, but who did not want to go directly to your parents. It sounded the most perfect nonsense to me and I said as much and he bowed himself off. But the thing that worries me is, when Molly went out for firewood yesterday afternoon she found him talking to the children in the yard—they had gone to look at the puppies.

She sent him about his business and I have had young Wally Hoskins go with them everywhere since then, just in case. But if he was intending to kidnap them—why these children? We are not wealthy, he must have realised that.

I thought I had better tell you—because of him asking for you by name. Perhaps I am worrying too much and he is just what he said. Or slightly mad. But I must confess to being anxious.

'Mama, do we have any relative who is, or was, a sea captain? Or any relative who is estranged from the family?'

'A sea captain? Or someone estranged? Goodness, no, I do not think so. In fact I am certain. Why?'

'Oh, Jane met someone who said something that puzzled her. She must have misunderstood.'

'No doubt she did. I cannot help but think that living so secluded as she does cannot be good for her.'

Isobel folded the letter, then opened it again. The mysterious man had been asking for her and then he was found with the children. *Annabelle.* Lady Faversham's words came back to her like a curse, even though it had been almost a month since they were uttered. *You will be sorry for this. Very sorry.*

She could not possibly know and Isobel had seen neither her nor Giles since that night. And yet Annabelle was Isobel's only weak spot, the only secret she was desperate to keep. She tried to tell herself it was pure fancy, yet she could not be easy in her mind.

Three days later there was another letter. It began, *Do not leave this lying around, for I cannot write in such a way that would disarm suspicion if your mother reads it and yet convey my anxiety adequately. The strange man is still hanging around the neighbourhood—and still asking questions about us. When you were here, how long you stayed, what happened to Ralph, how old the children are—he has looked at the parish registers, I am certain, for Mr Arnold found him right by the cupboard where they are stored and it was not locked.*

He is very subtle about it, which, I confess, worries me most of all, for it seems professional somehow. It is only by piecing together bits of gossip that I can see a pattern in his questions, for he never interrogates the same person for long. I have spoken to the few servants who were with us that year and who know the truth so they are on the alert. I cannot see how he would approach Dr Jameson, who, besides, would never say anything.

Can you make any sense of this, dearest Isobel? I vow I cannot. I have hired two of the Foster brothers— you recall what a size they are—and they patrol the house and yard at night and one of them is always with the children by day. It is doing dreadful things to Nathaniel's vocabulary!

It would not take much effort for anyone to find out where she had spent that year after Lucas's death—they had made no secret of it at the time, quite deliberately. Isobel's refusal to allow any friends or relatives to visit had been lamented by Lady Bythorn to all her circle and had been attributed to hysterical grief followed by a sad decline. The very openness of her mother's complaints seemed to disarm all suspicion that there was anything to hide and Isobel's reluctance to socialise since her return had contributed to the diagnosis of a melancholic temperament.

'Jane is unwell,' she said to her parents, the letter tight in her hand. 'I must go to Hereford.'

'Now?' Her father put down the copy of *The Times* he had been muttering over and frowned at her. 'In the middle of the Season? All that way?'

'It would take me only twenty-four hours, even if I go

by the Mail, but if I might take a chaise, Papa, I could do it in less time and more comfortably.'

'Certainly not the Mail,' her mother said firmly. 'And a chaise? Oh, dear, you know how those things bring on my migraine and they do your father's gout no good at all.'

'I can go with Dorothy, Mama, there is no need for either of you to disturb yourselves. If we leave before luncheon and take a basket with some food we can go right through to Oxford for the night with only stops for changes—and there are any number of most respectable inns where I could find a private parlour.'

It took almost an hour of wrangling to convince her parents that she could not possibly abandon her friend when she was unwell and worried about the children. That, yes, of course she would come home just as soon as she could and not miss the Lavenhams' ridotto which promised to be the event of the Season. And yes, she would take the greatest care on the road and not speak to anyone unless absolutely necessary and certainly no gentlemen.

It was only then, as she organised her packing, that the apprehension churning in her stomach turned to real fear. If she was ruined, then that was just too bad, although she was very sorry that the disgrace would distress her parents. But for Annabelle to be exposed as an illegitimate child would destroy all her prospects as well. And what of Jane? There might be penalties for allowing a false record to be entered in the registers. Would it even cast a shadow over little Nathaniel's legitimacy?

It had to be Lady Faversham behind this, for surely Giles would not do anything to hurt her, however angry she made him. It was only as she climbed into the chaise and waved goodbye that she realised she had no idea what she could do when she reached Hereford. But she could not sit in London while her child was in peril and leave Jane to face whatever this was alone.

'You were right—Geraldine's up to something and she's planning to go to Hereford of all places.'

'Are you certain?' *Hereford.* Giles put down his knife and fork and stared at Jack Carstairs over his half-eaten breakfast. His mother's lover had arrived at his Albany chambers without warning and seemed decidedly put out.

Since the confrontation at the Leamingtons' ball Giles had been at pains to avoid Isobel. It would do her reputation no good to be seen with him and it seemed he could not trust himself to keep his hands off her. There were two things he could do to protect her: stay out of her way and make certain his mother did her no harm.

Before Jack's arrival, it had occurred to him after a night of tossing and turning that the best way to circumvent Geraldine was to discover where Isobel was vulnerable. He was certain there was something, something more to her past than the simple loss of her virginity to her fiancé.

Unable to sleep, his remedies had been either a cold bath or distraction. Shrugging into his robe he had taken a candle and pulled the *Peerage* off the shelves. He might as well start by getting the family straight: Isobel's family, the Jervises—no, after ten minutes he could see nothing out of the ordinary there.

Then, on impulse, he looked under Needham. The current viscount was a half-brother of Lucas who had drowned in January 1797. He looked at the other entries for the same name. *The Hon. Ralph Needham decd.* Lucas's other half-brother, he worked out. And he had died on the same day as Lucas, Giles realised, flicking back to check. *Married Miss Jane Barrymore, by whom issue Nathaniel and Annabelle.* Twins born posthumously in September 1797. *Longmere Manor, Gaston, Hereford.*

Hereford rang a bell. Isobel had mentioned it with a note of longing in her voice and then, when he would have questioned her about it, for the area was unknown to him, she had abruptly changed the subject.

Giles had stared at the entry, working out the relationships. Ralph was Lucas's younger half-brother. That was a close connection to Isobel, but what did it signify and how could it harm her? *Lucas and I were lovers*, she had confessed. But what of it? She had been betrothed to the man. He ran a finger over the close-packed black lines of type, half-formed ideas worrying at the edges of his mind.

Giles dragged himself back to the present and the other man. He had taken Carstairs into his confidence to a degree, putting it to him that it was in Geraldine's interests if they could stop her embarking on a destructive feud with Lady Isobel.

'I'm certain. But I've no idea why, she won't tell me. Threw the coffee pot at my head when I wouldn't go with her. Damn it, Harker,' Carstairs said, pulling out a chair and sitting down, 'I'm not trailing half across the country in support of one of her vendettas and I told her so. Told her you wouldn't like it, either. Is there any fresh coffee?'

'Hicks! Coffee for Mr Carstairs.' Giles picked up his own cup and frowned into the dregs. They held no answers. 'Any more letters?'

The other man nodded. 'She's been getting letters daily that have been pleasing her inordinately, as I told you, and then this one arrived and she said, *Hah! I've got the little hussy now* and ordered her woman to pack and sent her footman out to hire a chaise.

'Thought you ought to know, because I'm pretty certain it has some connection with Lady Isobel. Or, at least, something to do with you. When she got these letters she'd stare at that portrait of you over the fireplace with such a look in her eyes. Brrr.' He shuddered theatrically and peered at Giles more closely.

'How's the face? Looks as though it is healing well. Thought they'd carved half of it off, the way Geraldine was carrying on at first.'

Giles shrugged. 'Healing. There will always be scars. Geraldine attaches too much importance to looks.' What the devil had the woman discovered about Isobel?

He was prepared to go to any lengths to protect her, he realised, even though he was not willing to put a name to his feelings. Her hints at the ball that she might take a lover had made him jealous, furiously jealous, even while he knew she was deliberately provoking him and would no more do such a thing than fly. With disastrous honesty she had told him she loved him and she had meant it. His attempts to reject her for her own good had made her angry, but it had not changed her love for him, he sensed that.

'I'm going to Herefordshire to find out what is going on. But I'll see Geraldine first and make damned certain she stops this nonsense.'

'The best of luck, old chap,' Carstairs said with a rueful grin.

Isobel got down from the chaise at the Bell in Oxford at seven in the evening, nine hours after she had finished reading Jane's letter at breakfast that morning. They had made better time than she had expected, but even so she felt exhausted already and there were another fourteen or fifteen hours travelling ahead of her.

'Looks a decent enough place,' Dorothy conceded with a sniff as one of the porters came forward, touched his forelock and took their bags.

'We will require two adjoining bedchambers and a private parlour,' Isobel said. 'The quieter the better.'

'Yes, ma'am, there's just the thing free, if you'll come this way.'

'And hot water and tea and a good supper,' Dorothy chimed in, clutching the dressing case that she insisted on keeping with her even though Isobel had brought no jewellery.

'We're famous for our suppers, at the Bell.' The man halted. 'Just mind this chaise coming in, ma'am.'

The vehicle with four horses sweating in the traces swept into the yard and pulled up in front of them. Isobel stepped back to take a new path to the inn entrance.

The door opened in her face, the porter hurried forwards. 'Here, mind the lady!' Dorothy took her arm and a tall figure dropped down onto the cobbles.

'Giles!'

'What the devil are you doing here?' He slammed the carriage door shut and confronted her, for all the world as if he had a right to know of her movements, she thought, feeding her temper to keep the treacherous delight at seeing him at bay.

'Never you mind my lady's business and watch your tongue, you rogue.' Dorothy planted her hands on her hips and confronted him, bristling. 'A respectable lady ought to be able to travel the country without being accosted in inn yards by the likes of you!'

Heads were turning, more carriages were pulling in. 'I think we would draw less attention if we go inside,' Isobel said, tugging at her stalwart defender's arm. 'Come, Dorothy.'

'I'll have them fetch the parish constable, I will,' the maid scolded as she marched into the inn on Isobel's heels. 'I told you he was no gentleman. What's he doing here, I'd like to know!'

Chapter Nineteen

'I, too, would like to know what Giles Harker is doing in Oxford,' Isobel said with feeling. She felt queasy with surprise and nerves, her pulse was all over the place and her thoughts were in turmoil. After that initial shock, the delight of thinking that, somehow, he had come for her, common sense reasserted itself.

What *was* Giles doing here? It was too much of a co-incidence that they should both find themselves in an Oxford inn. Had she been wrong and he was the one behind the mysterious stranger who was probing the secrets of Longmere? But if that was the case it could only be out of some twisted desire to hurt her, to expose her secrets, and surely she had done nothing to deserve that? It was hard to believe she had been so far awry in her assessment of his character.

'Welcome, my lady.' The landlord appeared and ushered them farther in. 'If a nice pair of rooms with a parlour on the quiet side of the house is what is wanted, we have just the thing. If you will follow me, ma'am.

'I'll have hot water sent up directly, my lady, and

supper will be on the table within the half hour. Here you are, ma'am.'

'That looks very satisfactory, thank you.' He could have shown them into a prison cell for all Isobel cared, or noticed. The man bowed himself out and Dorothy threw herself dramatically in front of the door, her back pressed to the panels.

'He'll not get in here, the vile seducer!'

'Oh, for goodness' sake, Dorothy, Mr Harker is no such thing, although what he is doing here I have no idea.' A rap on the door made Dorothy jump. She emitted a small scream and flung it open to reveal a startled maid with a jug. 'Your hot water, ma'am.'

'Thank you.' Isobel waited until the girl had gone before she turned back to Dorothy. 'There is no need for alarm. Please be less melodramatic! There is absolutely no call for all this shrieking—oh!' She pressed her hand to her thudding heart as the door swung open on the knock and Giles stepped into the room.

'Lady Isobel. Will you join me for supper?'

'Certainly not. I have no intention of dining with a man in an inn, and most definitely not with you.' She looked at him with painful intensity. The scars were paler and thinner now. His expression was politely neutral, but his eyes were wary. *As well they might be*, she thought as she strove to settle her breathing.

'The middle of the Season seems an unusual time to be taking a long coach journey, Lady Isobel,' Giles observed. 'Your admirers will be missing you.'

She did not attempt to cover her snort of derision. 'I hardly think so. A friend needs me for a few days, then I will be returning.'

'A friend in Oxford?' He leant a shoulder against the door frame and frowned at her.

'No. If that was the case I would hardly be staying in an inn.'

'Where my lady is going is none of your business,' Dorothy interjected. 'Shall I go and get a couple of pot boys and have him thrown out, ma'am?'

'I do not think that is necessary, thank you, Dorothy.' Isobel doubted two lads would be capable of ejecting Giles in any case. She knew he was strong and fit, but now he looked leaner—and tougher with those scars and his dark brows drawn together into a frown. 'Mr Harker will be leaving immediately, I am certain.'

'If I might have a word with you first—alone.' He straightened up and held the door open for Dorothy.

Isobel opened her mouth to protest, then thought better of it. If five minutes of painful intimacy meant she discovered what he was about, then it would be worth it. 'Dorothy, go downstairs, please. No,' she said as the maid began to launch into a protest. 'Either you go or Mr Harker and I will have to. I wish to speak to him confidentially.'

'But, my lady—'

Giles bundled the maid out of the room, closed the door and locked it before she could get another word out.

'It is a strange thing if a lady may not visit a friend without being waylaid and interrogated,' Isobel snapped.

'Yes. I wonder that you stand for it,' he said musingly, his eyes focused on her face. 'I would have expected a cool *good evening* on seeing me and then for you to refuse to receive me. It is very shocking for us to be alone like this.'

'I am well aware of that, Mr Harker! I want to know why you are here.'

'In Oxford? Why should I not be?'

'In Oxford, in this inn, at this time? I was foolish enough to fall in love with you, Giles Harker. Even more foolish to trust you. This is too much of a coincidence for my liking.'

'That trust certainly appears to have vanished. Isobel, you know full well you could trust me to take only what was offered to me.'

'I am not talking about—' She could feel herself growing pink, whether from anger, embarrassment or sheer anxiety she could not tell.

'Sex?'

'Yes, *sex*.' She was blushing, she knew it, and it was more from desire and anger at herself than embarrassment. 'I am talking about the way you abandoned me, washed your hands of me the moment my parents appeared.'

His eyebrows rose. 'You wanted me to treat you as a friend in front of your parents? You wanted to risk your reputation by acknowledging a liaison with me?'

'No, I did not want that and you know it! But there was no word of affection or regret, no acknowledgement that I was distressed or of what we had shared. You had your amusement—and yes, I am aware of your self-control, I thank you—and then, when it all became difficult, you shrug me and my feelings aside.'

Giles pushed away from the door, all pretence of casualness gone. 'Isobel, I only did what was practical. It would not have helped to have drawn out our parting, merely added to your unhappiness.'

'Practical? Giles, there was nothing practical about my feelings for you.'

'Was? Past tense?' He came so close that the hem of her skirts brushed his boots, but she would not retreat. 'I thought that when you loved, you would love for ever.'

'Then I cannot have been in love with you, can I? Just another foolish woman fascinated by your handsome face.'

'We did not make love until after this.' He gestured towards his scarred cheek.

'Guilt, then. Gratitude. Lust. Call it what you like. It was certainly lust, those few mad moments in the passageway at the Leamingtons' ball!' Only her anxiety for Annabelle and Jane, only the price of misplaced trust, kept her from falling into his arms. 'What do my feelings for you matter? I want to know why you are here. Are you following me?'

'No,' Giles said. 'I am not following you and our meeting here is a genuine coincidence.' Truth? Lies? How could she tell? She had thought he had fallen in love with her and he had not. Obviously she could not understand him at all.

If she did not love him, he would not make her so angry. If she only dared trust him—but he would be disgusted when he realised she had given away her child, had not had the courage to raise her as his own mother had raised him. Whatever she thought of the Scarlet Widow, the woman's fierce love for her son could not be mistaken.

'You are very agitated for a woman who is merely going to visit a friend for a few days,' he remarked, cutting through her thoughts and sending her tumbling into unconsidered speech.

'If I am agitated, then it is because I cannot get free from you. It seems I cannot keep even my secrets—' She stumbled to a halt.

'So,' Giles said slowly, his eyes never leaving her face with its betraying colour, 'I am right. You have a secret, one greater than the loss of your virginity, one that you would not trust to me even though you tell me you loved me, even though then you had no reason to mistrust me. You are afraid. Is it a secret that lays you open to blackmail, perhaps?'

'Blackmail?' Isobel went cold. 'No, of course not.' Was that what the prying stranger was about? But who had sent him? 'You may leap to whatever conclusions you wish, Giles Harker. You have made me so angry I scarce know what I am saying.'

'No, you are not angry.' He caught her hands in his and held them even when she tugged. 'Or, rather, anger is not the main emotion here. You are afraid.'

Unable to free herself without a struggle, Isobel turned her face away. What she was going to do when he left her alone—if he ever did—she had no idea. She dared not let him know where she was going or she might lead him to Annabelle. All she could do was to get to Jane and try, somehow, to work out how to protect her daughter and her friend.

'Of course I am afraid—I am locked in a room and being manhandled. Am I your prisoner while you interrogate me?' she demanded. Defiance was the only weapon she had against the fear and the awful weakness of her love for him. And that love would betray Annabelle.

Giles released her wrists and she stood rubbing them, although he had not held her tight enough to hurt. The touch of his hands, the fingers that had orchestrated such pleasure in her, seemed to burn like ice. 'This has gone too far for me to walk away from it now, Isobel, whether you want me or trust me or not. You are in trouble, more trouble than you know.'

He turned the key in the lock and walked out, letting the door slam behind him. Isobel sank down in the chair behind her, her knees suddenly like warm wax.

'My lady? I passed him on the stairs and he looked like thunder—are you all right, my lady? I should never have left you alone with him.'

'I am perfectly fine, Dorothy,' Isobel said with a calm that was intended to steady herself as much as the maid. 'Mr Harker and I had unfinished business, that is all. I did not have the opportunity to say everything I wanted to when we left Wimpole.'

She had not convinced her, but there was nothing to be done about it now. 'Dinner will be here soon and neither of us have so much as washed our hands.'

But what had those parting words meant? How did he know she was in trouble?

'Just you stop right there, my bullies.'
The chaise juddered to a halt and Isobel let down the

window. 'Ned! Ned Foster, it is I, Lady Isobel. Please open the gate.'

'Yes, my lady!' the big man called back and swung open the heavy gate that barred the entrance into the manor courtyard. Chickens ran flapping in panic as the postilions brought the chaise in and Isobel heard the clang of the gate thudding back into its catches. It felt as though she was in a besieged castle. Isobel fought back the melodramatic image and gathered her things.

She was paying off the men and Dorothy was carrying the bags around to the back entrance as Jane came running down the steps, a big shawl bundled around her shoulders against the raw air. 'Isobel! I did not dare hope you'd come. How long can you stay?'

'For as long as it takes,' Isobel said grimly as she hugged her friend. 'I am so glad to be here. The weather was bad after Oxford and there was a landslip about sixty miles from Oxford so we had to spend another day on the road. Oh, Jane,' she confessed as they entered the hallway, out of earshot of the servants. 'I do not know what is going on here, or who is to blame for it, but I have been so foolish. I fell in love with the most impossible man and I think this is a consequence. I am so sorry.'

'Foolish to fall in love?' Jane smiled. 'That is never foolish.'

'It is when the man in question is the illegitimate son of the Scarlet Widow.'

Her friend's eyes widened. 'Oh, my, I have heard of her. But how on earth did you meet him? Does he know you love him?'

'Unfortunately, yes. We made love, Jane,' she added as the drawing-room door shut safely behind them. Best to get the entire confession over as quickly as possible.

'You aren't—'

'No. But it all ended badly—I thought he felt the same for me, but it is quite obvious that he does not, and, in any case, there is no way we can ever be together. His mother sees me as a threat to him and I think she must be behind whatever is going on here. But how she ever found out, I do not know.'

'You did not tell him?'

'That I had a child? No. He knows that Lucas and I anticipated our marriage, but that is all.' Isobel paced to the window and stood staring out at the darkening gardens. 'Perhaps I am worrying unduly after all, for unless one of your people betrays us, there is no reason anyone might suspect Annabelle is not exactly who you say she is.'

'And I trust them implicitly,' Jane said, nodding. 'There might be a danger if she resembled you closely, but as it is, she is very obviously a Needham. It is seven months since you saw her, isn't it? She is growing.'

'Yes.' It seemed like seven years. 'May I see her now? I did not want to speak of this unless we were alone, but now, I cannot wait. Is she much changed?'

'I think she is perfect, but you will judge for yourself.' Her friend's smile was warm and once again Isobel was filled with gratitude that Jane had taken her child, loved her like her own and yet was prepared to share her so unselfishly. 'She is bright, quick and very lovely.

Come and see—they are in the kitchen with old Rosemary, hindering her efforts to make cakes.'

Isobel almost ran down the stone-flagged passageway and into the kitchen. Two small children were perched on the edge of the big table, legs dangling, their eyes glued to the big bowl of fruit cake mixture the cook was stirring.

'More plums,' Nathanial demanded, but Isobel could only focus on the little girl.

She scooped her up, warm and sweet and slightly sticky around the mouth from stealing batter. 'Surprise!'

'Aunt Ishbel,' Annabelle said with a crow of delight and a kiss. She had never been able to get her tongue around Isobel's name.

'How pretty you look—and how sticky you are.' Isobel whirled her round in her arms and everything in the world was right again. Then she stopped at the sight of their reflection in the battered mirror propped at one end of the dresser. Annabelle, female to her chubby fingertips, examined her own image with interest. Two heads of tumbled hair, soft and slippery, sliding out of its pins, but Annabelle's was blonde while Isobel's was brown. Two rather determined little chins, but very different noses. Two pairs of wide grey eyes.

'Pretty,' Annabelle said with a crow of delight.

'Pretty,' Isobel agreed. *Oh, thank you, Lucas, for giving me this child*. And anyone who saw them together would not pick up any significant likeness, she was sure. She turned to see Jane smiling as she watched them.

'She grew so quickly,' Jane said. 'One minute she was still a chubby little baby and the next, there she is—a little girl. Now I think we can see what they will be like when they grow up. They are both going to have the Needham height, don't you think?'

'Yes,' Isobel agreed, swallowing the tears that threatened to well up. It was ridiculous to weep because she was so happy to be here and it would frighten Annabelle. 'I cannot believe how she has grown.'

She had dreamed of the experiences she and her 'niece' would share as Annabelle grew up. They would go shopping together, she would be there at her first parties, her first dance. She would hear her whispered confidences about first love.

'Isn't it bath time?' she asked, grinning at little Nathaniel as he stuck out his lower lip mutinously. 'Come along, I'll tell you stories about Wimpole Hall where I have been staying and about London and I'll tuck you up in bed.'

'Cake,' Annabelle said. 'Cake and bath and stories and bed.'

'Bath and bed and stories now, cake in the morning,' Isobel countered, holding out her hand to the little boy. 'How many stairs is it up to bed? I'll wager you cannot count them yet.'

'I can!' He was off at a run and Isobel followed him, her cheek pressed against Annabelle's soft one. *Oh, Lucas, what a lovely child we made. I'll protect her, I promise.* Even if the danger was from the man she now loved.

'Come and see the kittens.' Annabelle stood beside the breakfast table and hopped from one foot to the other while Isobel spread honey on her last piece of toast. 'Mama says I may have a kitten.'

'A puppy,' Nathaniel contradicted.

'Both,' Jane said, rolling her eyes. 'But by the time they decide which they are going to have they'll be grown cats and dogs.'

'Shall I help choose?' Both heads nodded as one—this was obviously the solution to an intractable problem.

'Come along, then.' Isobel put down her napkin. 'And wrap up warmly.'

The farmyard was enclosed, with high arches in the walls to east and west. The walls kept out the wind and the stall-fed cattle and the horses kept the barns and stables surprisingly warm, so it was no hardship to sit on a bale outside the cowshed while the children brought out the kittens and puppies for inspection.

'I think the little boy with the white tip to his tail,' she said to Nathaniel. The pup was big and bold and looked as though he would cope well with the rough and tumble of life with Nathaniel. 'And the black-and-white kitten with the white tip for Annabelle—and then they will match.'

Delighted, the children reached for their new pets and Annabelle promptly had her knuckles swiped by the mother cat who had stalked out to see what was going on. Isobel hauled the crying child onto her lap and hugged her and the kitten equally while she wrapped a handkerchief around the scratched hand. 'It is all right, she was only cross because—'

'What a charming picture. Maternal love. I thought

that must be the secret, from the timing of things.' The deep, familiar voice cut through the sounds of the farm-yard, the child's sobs, the barking of the sheepdog on its chain.

Chapter Twenty

Isobel froze and Annabelle stopped wailing to inspect the new arrival.

'Go—' With an effort Isobel moderated her tone so as not to frighten the children. 'Nathaniel, Annabelle, go inside and ask Cook to find a proper bandage for Annabelle's hand and tell her I said you may have a slice of cake each.'

They ran, tears and strange men forgotten, before she changed her mind about cake directly after breakfast. Isobel stood up, the kitten unregarded in her hands. 'You are not welcome here, Giles. How did you get in?'

'The brawny yokel outside is guarding the front gate, but he does not appear to have the wit to work out that there is a perfectly obvious track leading to this one.' Giles strode across the straw-strewn yard and stopped by the mounting block.

'What do you want?' Isobel demanded.

'To discover if what I suspect, what my mother believes she has discovered, is true.'

'Your mother discovered? So this is blackmail?' *Is*

it a secret that lays you open to blackmail, perhaps?
Giles had asked. *He knows,* she thought, a sort of bleak
misery settling over her, eclipsing even the fear.

'It would have been if I had not caught Geraldine in
time and made her tell me exactly what she had discovered about you. She's as protective as that mother
cat and has about as many scruples.'

'What do you think you know?' Isobel asked. Her
lips felt stiff, the question almost choked her, but she
had to know what she was fighting.

'That you have a love child whom you gave away to
your friend to raise as her own.'

'I did not want to let her go!' The kitten gave a squeak
of protest and Isobel set it down next to its mother who
promptly began to wash it. 'It was the only thing to do.
I suppose you think I have no courage because your
mother kept you.'

'I have to thank her for that,' Giles said.

'It seems she had no scruples about shaming her
family or taking you from your grandfather's care. You
grew up with a mother who had a scandalous reputation,
and, apparently, she had no concerns about bringing
you up to have to fight every day of your life because
of who you are.'

'She gave me life and she gave me, I hope, some of
her courage. But she had to fight for so long that she
does not know how to stop. When I discovered that
she had found out something to your detriment and
was coming here to threaten you with it, I stopped her.'

'How? Are you telling me you can control that
woman?'

'Oh, yes. She believed me when I told her that if she tried to hurt you I would take her back to the Dower House, lock her in and keep the key. I have done it before when she went beyond the limit and I'll do it again if I have to.'

'Then I must thank you for that, at least,' she threw at him. 'But if you have the situation under control, what are you doing here?'

'I wanted to make sure you were safe here, that her agents had gone. I knew you had a secret before she discovered what it was.'

'How?' She had been so careful...

'Just putting together things that you said. I realised it was something here, in Herefordshire, something to do with Needham.' He took a step towards her, then shook his head and turned back to hitch one hip on the mounting block. 'I must have gone over every word you have said to me, Isobel. Every silence, every moment when there was such sadness in your eyes. Until I realised she was on your trail all I wanted to do was protect you by keeping away.'

'Why, Giles? Why did you care so much? Are you—?' Isobel broke off, her courage almost failing. But she had to know. 'Are you telling me you love me after all?' she asked flatly.

'No,' he said, his face tight and stark. 'Nothing has changed, Isobel. I care for you, I want to keep you safe. And I am every bit as ineligible for you as I ever was.'

Her pride would not let her weep or plead. 'What a good thing,' she said. 'Of course, I have realised that I do not love you—it was a foolish infatuation when

I was lonely and miserable. Now I am doing the Season and looking for a husband—I will be delighted if I never see you again.'

'I was a foolish infatuation, was I, Isobel? In that case either your acting skill is incredible or you have equally good powers of self-deception. You fell in love with me and I believe your current protestations as much as I did those at Oxford or at the ball.'

'I am not a good actress, merely someone telling the truth,' she said forcing the words out between numb lips. 'I needed what you could give me at Wimpole. I needed heat and warmth and…affection.' One brow slanted up satirically at the euphemism. She felt her cheeks burn red. 'You do not care for me now, so why are you concerning yourself? I told you at Oxford that I did not want you.'

'On the contrary, at Oxford you told me I had betrayed your trust and your feelings.' He stood up and took one step towards her before her upflung hand stopped him.

'I would say anything to get rid of you,' she threw at him, desperate to hang on to the last shreds of her self-control. 'I do not want you, I do not need you—all I need is your silence and for you to keep your blackmailing mother silent also.'

'So the little girl is your daughter and your friend is raising her as the twin of her son.' He glanced down at the Border Collie puppy that was attempting to chew the heel of his boot, picked it up by the scruff and handed it to Isobel. She caught it up without taking her eyes from his face and clutched the warm squirming bundle to her bosom like a shield. 'She has your eyes. May I see her?'

'No! I have told you, I do not want anything more to do with you. Go back to London and marry a wife your mama will buy you. She will purchase your heirs in the same way as she bought your accent and your education and your smooth society manners.'

'No one controls my life.' There was anger in his voice. 'Not since I was a child. Do you condemn my mother for wanting the best upbringing she could get for me? What do you buy for your child, Isobel? Do you pay for her clothes and her nurse? Will you pay for her governess? Will you search for the right husband for her when she is old enough to make her come-out, even if you do it from behind the walls of your own home? Or will you wash your hands of her and leave it all to Mrs Needham so you can walk away and find this husband you seek?'

'Between us Jane and I will do everything we can for the children. I thought this would be best for Annabelle. I did not want her to grow up as...'

'A bastard?' Giles enquired in a tone that made her wince. 'I manage.'

'I do not want her to have to *manage*. And it is different for a woman and you know it,' she threw at him.

'Isobel, are you all right?' She turned and there was Jane, a shotgun in the crook of her arm. 'Don't you dare lay a finger on her,' she said fiercely to Giles.

Giles took a reckless step towards the woman with the gun. A woman who Isobel knew was perfectly capable of taking a shot at a cattle thief. And now it was the children under threat. 'There is no call to shoot anyone.'

'None at all if you leave,' Jane agreed. 'And are silent about this.'

'I will tell no one,' Giles said. Then, ignoring both Jane and the gun, he went to stand in front of Isobel. He lifted the puppy from her arms and set it down before catching her hands in his. 'Isobel, I thought you loved me.' He spoke directly to her as though they were alone, so close she could feel his warmth, smell his familiar scent of clean linen and citrus and something that was simply Giles.

'I—' She stared into the green eyes and the farmyard seemed to vanish. Jane, the animals, everything faded away and there was only the two of them, handfast. She could not lie to him, not about this. 'Yes, I love you. I try not to, but I cannot lie to you about it.' And in his eyes she thought she read an answering love and all the doubt and fear vanished. 'I love you, I trust you and I am sorry that my faith in you wavered for a while.'

She waited for the words, but they did not come, only a shadow that clouded the clear green eyes and a twist of the mouth that she so much wanted to kiss. 'Do you truly not love me?' she had to ask at last when he did not speak. 'Can I be so wrong in what I feel from you?'

'I cannot allow myself to love you, Isobel. There is no future for us. Nothing has changed except that now I know you are too vulnerable with this secret to risk the slightest breath of scandal. The secret is safe, I promise you. There will be no risk, Isobel, because this ends here. This is where we part.'

'I know.' She had faced that finally on the long drive. There had never been any hope because a scandal would ruin him, would break her parents' hearts, might even compromise Annabelle's future in ways she could not foresee. 'I know that. I give up.' Her voice cracked and she controlled it somehow. 'I just need you to tell me how you feel, Giles.'

'No.' His face was stark as he bent his head. 'No, I will not say I love you, Isobel. Only that I care too much to make this worse than it already is.' The kiss was gentle, achingly tender. His lips lingered on hers and she could taste the heat and the passion that he was holding in check, feel the tremor that ran through him when she raised her arms and curled them around his neck to hold him for just a moment longer.

'Goodbye, Isobel.' He turned and strode out of the yard and when she sank down onto the bale, her legs too weak to hold her, and looked around, she was alone. Jane had gone. Distantly there was the sound of carriage wheels, then silence.

Something wet touched her hand and she looked down. The puppy that had been chewing Giles's boot was licking her hand. It wasn't the pup Nathaniel had chosen, but a skinny little female with a comical white patch over one eye. Isobel scooped her up and the puppy licked her nose.

'Hello,' Isobel said, her voice sounding thready in her own ears. Then she got up and walked inside with the dog in her arms. 'One more day and then we are going to London,' she said to it as it wriggled.

'Isobel.' Jane stood just inside the empty kitchen and

hugged her and the pup together. 'Oh, my dear.' When Isobel just shook her head she said, 'I would not have shot him, you know. Not the man you love.'

'Thank you,' Isobel said, her smile hurting. 'I will go home tomorrow. May I take the puppy? I don't expect trying to housetrain a dog in a post-chaise is easy, but I will manage. We will be fine.'

'Of course you will,' Jane said and her face showed that she knew it was not the puppy that Isobel was talking about. 'Come and let Annabelle choose a name for it.'

A puppy in a post-chaise was certainly an excellent distraction. Maude, as Annabelle inexplicably named the black-and-white bundle, proved to be ravenously hungry and ate and drank everything put in the dishes on the floor for her—with inevitable consequences. Jane had the forcsight to give them a small sack of sawdust and a large roasting dish, so Dorothy climbed out to empty it at every stop, complaining vociferously.

But Isobel would not let her chastise Maude, even when she started to chew shoes and the edge of the carriage rug. 'She's only a baby, Dorothy,' she said, picking up the puppy and receiving a wet slurp on the nose for her pains. With a contented sigh the little dog went to sleep on her lap, worn out by her adventure.

Which left all the stages from Gloucester still to sit through. They would not arrive in London until past ten that night after a six o'clock start in the morning. Dorothy started to doze, wedged in one corner against the jolting, but Isobel sat upright, cradled the puppy on her lap and let her mind wander where it might. She was too tired and too hurt to try to think sensibly. And besides, what was there to think about?

Other than Annabelle, she realised with a smile that faded as the guilt took over once more. Her parents would adore her and yet they would never know they had a granddaughter.

She realised she was about to drift off, and did not fight it. It would bring dreams, she supposed, but dreams were all she had left now.

Trust...I trust you. The words she had said to Giles. But it was not his face in the dream, it was her parents, watching her anxiously. She woke, but the image did not fade. They had trusted her when she had fled to Hereford, loved her enough to leave her there a year when she wrote and begged not to be asked to come home. They had believed her when she was sent home in disgrace after the house party when virtually no one else had. If she could trust anyone, she could trust her parents, she realised. Perhaps, after all, some good could come of this unhappiness.

Isobel curled into the corner of the chaise and went back to sleep.

'God, she has courage, my Isobel,' Giles said to himself as he sat at the writing table in his inn bedchamber.

Isobel, so frank, so brave, so direct with the truth and with her love. She had known he would never act on his true feelings, never show her what was in his heart. The most she could hope for was his flirtation and his idle, thoughtless kisses. So she had shown him what love was.

He screwed up what he had been writing and threw the paper on the fire. A letter would only do more damage. He had written the words he had wanted to say, the true words. But they were better as ashes—it would do Isobel no good to tell her he loved her.

What was he going to do now? He was not going to marry Miss Holt, that was certain. Somehow he would have to make Geraldine accept that. She only wanted him to be happy and she found his independence infuriating. She wanted to arrange everything to her satisfaction, including his happiness.

He would be happy again, one day, he supposed. One day.

Chapter Twenty-One

'Mama. Papa. May I speak with you?'

'We have been speaking to each other for the last half hour,' Lord Bythorn pointed out. But he folded his copy of the *Morning Chronicle*, laid it beside his breakfast plate and waited.

'I mean, in private. In your study.' Isobel's chest felt tight, her breakfast—what little of it she had managed to eat—was sitting uneasily in her stomach and she was all too aware of her parents' anxious attention.

'Very well, if you can keep that confounded puppy of yours out of it. It has already destroyed my slippers and it has only been in the house twelve hours.'

'Thank you, Papa.' He was making a joke out of it, bless him.

'Now, what is this about, eh, Isobel?' He sat behind his big desk, Isobel and her mother in the two wing chairs in front of it. 'This looks uncommonly like a confession.'

'It is.' *Trust*, she reminded herself. *Too late to back*

out now. Just trust them, they love you. 'In the last few weeks before Lucas was killed, we were lovers.'

She heard her mother's sharply indrawn breath. Her father's face went blank, then, to her surprise, he said, 'Shocking, but not so very unusual.' There was the very faintest suspicion of a smile in the fleeting look he sent her mother. Isobel opened her mouth to blurt out a question and shut it hurriedly.

'After he died, I discovered I was pregnant.' This time the breath was a gasp and her father's face lost its smile as the colour ebbed out of his cheeks. 'That was why I stayed with Jane. She is not the mother of twins: her daughter is mine. Your grandchild.'

The silence was broken only by her mother's sob, quickly stifled with her hand. Isobel reached out her own hand, hesitated, then withdrew it.

'You could not trust us to look after you?' her father asked with a gentleness that warned her he was keeping a tight rein on his emotions.

'No,' Isobel admitted. Only the truth would serve now. 'I was not thinking very clearly. I wanted Lucas and he was gone—I was frightened that the child would be taken from me. I could not trust anyone except Jane.' The tears were running down her mother's face now. This was as bad as she feared it would be—she had hurt them dreadfully. 'I am so sorry. I did it for the best.'

She turned and this time took her mother's hand. It stayed in hers and, after a moment, the fingers curled around her own. 'Her name is Annabelle.' It was her grandmother's name.

'Why now? Why are you telling us now? Is something wrong with her?' Her mother clutched her hand with a desperate urgency.

'She is perfect and she is well. No, it is not that. I realised I am never going to marry and have a family. And I saw that I was depriving you of your grandchild and that was wrong. And I have been thinking a lot about trust, these past few days—and I knew I should have trusted you from the beginning.'

'Who knows about the child?' her father asked.

'Jane's old family retainers, but they would never betray her secrets and they adore Annabelle. The doctor, and he is a family friend.' She saw their relief and knew she had to shatter it. 'And the Dowager Marchioness of Faversham and her son, Giles Harker.'

'What! That wanton creature? How in blazes did she discover this?'

'She feared I would marry Giles and that there would be a great scandal which would harm him. She uses enquiry agents all the time, it seems, so she set a man to find what secrets I might have. Her intention was to blackmail me into giving up Giles.'

'Marry him? Give him up?' Her mother stared, aghast. 'You are not having a liaison with that man?'

'I am in love with that man,' Isobel corrected gently. 'But, no, we are not lovers and I will not marry him—she is quite right, the scandal would ruin him. He will not admit he loves me because he thinks it would ruin *me*.'

'You love him? He is a—'

'So is our granddaughter,' Lord Bythorn said and her

mother gave a gasp of dismay. 'Will he and that woman hold their tongues?'

'Oh, yes. She had no other motive than to protect her son, she will wish me no harm once Giles has convinced her I am no threat to his standing or his career.'

'Hah!' Lady Bythorn said, swiping ineffectually at her eyes with a tiny scrap of lace.

'Mama, he saved my life when I would have drowned. He was scarred defending my honour.'

'True enough,' her father admitted. 'Can we see Annabelle? Or must you keep her from us?'

'No! Of course I will not. But we cannot acknowledge who she is, you must see that. Her prospects are good now—her birth seems perfectly respectable, she will grow up without any stain, a Needham. And her supposed father was Lucas's half-brother, after all.

'But we can visit. She calls me "Aunt," so it is only natural that you should take an interest in her. Jane can visit us here and bring the children.'

'Oh, yes.' Lady Bythorn brightened, sat up and rubbed her palms over her wet cheeks. 'My *granddaughter*! Oh, my goodness.'

'And what of you, Isobel?' her father asked.

She shook her head. 'I cannot marry. I cannot hide this from my husband and even if I did find someone, I dare not risk Annabelle's reputation by telling him before I am wed.' She added, 'I will finish this Season, I do not wish to cause any further talk.'

'Oh, my dear.' He sighed and shook his head, but when he looked at her there was a smile lurking under the heavy dark brows. 'But thank you for my grandchild.' As she got up he rose too and came round the desk to embrace her. 'I had hoped, after Needham's death, you could have found a good man who would love you.'

'I did, Papa,' she said. 'But it seems I cannot have him. I must write to Jane.'

The Season was in full swing now. Isobel hurled herself into it as though the sea of frivolity and pleasure could wash away the pain and the longing. Only her parents' delight in hearing about Annabelle kept her spirits up and the arrival of some portrait sketches that Jane had asked the village schoolmaster to make had them in a frenzy of planning for a visit just as soon as the summer came.

Taking tea after dinner a week after her return, Isobel overheard her father in conversation with their host. '...remodelling the entire West Wing of the Priory,' Lord Roehampton said. 'Got a very promising young architect working on it—Harker. But I was forgetting,' he added, lowering his voice. 'He's the man who stood up for Albright over that wretched business your daughter fell victim to. Good show, that. His mother's a menace in society, but he can't help that and, to do him credit, he stands by her. Loyal, as I said to Lady Roehampton when she was cavilling about employing him. The man's got the instincts of a gentleman.'

'Yes,' Lord Bythorn said slowly. 'It seems he has.'

Isobel stared at her father, a hope forming in her mind so improbable, she hardly dared try to think it through. As the three of them sat in the carriage on the short ride home through the streets of Mayfair she said abruptly, before she could give herself time to lose courage, 'Papa, if Giles Harker came to you now and asked for my hand in marriage, what would you say?'

'My love, he would not do such a thing. He knows it would cause a scandal. I think I've discovered enough about the man by now to know he won't hurt you,' her father said gruffly.

'But if he did, would it cause a scandal if you said *yes*?' she asked. 'I know it would if you forbade the match and we ran away together. But if it was seen that you approved, would that not make all the difference?'

'Isobel!' her mother interjected. 'You cannot marry a man born out of wedlock.'

'Why not? I am not going to marry any other man and it seems to me that if it does not hurt anyone else, then I may as well be happy as not! It is not as though I wish to be received at court again or spend my time at Almack's. Papa—if you gave us your blessing, *would* there be a scandal? One that would hurt you and Mama, be difficult for Frederick at school? One that would ruin Giles's business?'

Her mother moaned again at the word *business*, but her father said, after a pause, 'You heard me talking to Roehampton? I must confess, I see Harker in a different light now, with all that has happened. No, I do not think it would cause more than a seven-day wonder, not if I gave it my blessing and your mother received him. You have enough of a reputation for eccentricity already, my dear.'

'Oh, Papa!' She launched herself across the carriage and hugged him, squashing his silk hat. 'Thank you!'

'But he will not ask me, will he?' Lord Bythorn said gently, setting her back on her seat. 'The more he cares for you, the less likely he is to approach you again.'

'No,' Isobel agreed. 'So I will just have to ask him.'

Her mother subsided against the squabs with a moan. 'I knew I should have brought my smelling bottle!'

The first thing was to find out where Giles was, Isobel decided as she sat up in bed the next morning nursing a cup of chocolate in her hands. The work at Wimpole could not have been completed yet, but she assumed that, like Mr Soane, he would have several commissions in hand at any one time. Some she knew about, such as Lord Roehampton's West Wing, but Giles could be anywhere.

There was only one person in London who might know, and Mama would have the vapours if she thought her daughter was going anywhere near her. It did not seem to have occurred to her parents that if she married Giles then the Scarlet Widow would be her mother-in-law, which was probably a sign that they believed there was little chance that such a thing would ever happen. Well, time to worry about that later, she thought philosophically. Just at the moment it was the least of her worries.

'Will you fetch me a London directory please, Dorothy?' she called.

'Yes, my lady. Just one moment. This dratted dog has chewed the tassel on the curtain tie.' The maid sounded exasperated, but Isobel knew full well that she doted on Maude and sneaked biscuits to her in her basket.

'Here we are.' Dorothy bustled out of the dressing room with the book in her hands. 'Heard about an interesting shop, have you, my lady?'

'Er…no. I am just looking up the address of a new acquaintance.'

Lady Faversham lived not so very far away in Bruton Street. Close enough, in fact, not to need the carriage. 'My blue walking dress and the dark blue pelisse and the velvet hat this morning, Dorothy. I have some calls to make, but I can take one of the footmen with me, so you can carry on with those alterations.'

An hour and a half later, at an unconscionably early hour to be making a call, Isobel was admitted to Lady Faversham's elegant hall by her equally elegant butler.

'I am sure that if it is a matter concerning Mr Harker her ladyship will wish to receive you,' he said, admirably concealing any trace of speculation. 'If you would care to wait in here, my lady, I will enquire.'

Giles's name did indeed open doors. Isobel was received by her ladyship who was reclining on a chaise in her boudoir in a confection of lace and sea-green gauze that roused a pang of envy in Isobel's breast.

'What do you want with my son now?' the Widow demanded, narrowing ice-green eyes at her.

There did not seem to be any point beating about the bush. Isobel took a deep breath and said, 'To tell him that if he asks for my hand my father will give it to him willingly. There will be no scandal, he will be welcomed into the family.'

'What?' The Widow stared at her.

'My parents have accepted that I will never marry anyone else. They are grateful to Giles for what he has done for me. And,' she added as the Widow opened her mouth, 'they know about my daughter.

'And also—' she slipped in before Lady Faversham could speak. 'I am well dowered, well connected and perfectly placed to help Giles's career. All I need to know is where he is and I will go and propose to him.'

'Propose? You have courage, I will say that for you. And if I object?'

'Why should you be so spiteful?' A hint of colour touched the older woman's cheekbones under the powder. 'If he does not want me, he can always refuse. If this is some sort of trick, you have the instrument of revenge in your own hands.'

'I only want him to be happy,' Lady Faversham said and to her horror Isobel saw one tear roll down her cheek. 'And he is so stubbornly independent. Will you make him happy?'

'Oh, yes,' Isobel said. 'I promise.'

'Excellent.' With a dab of lace the tear was gone, taking the momentary weakness with it, and the green eyes defied Isobel to ever recall she had seen it. 'He is at Wimpole Hall.'

'Thank you.' She turned to go, then on an impulse swung round. 'Where did you purchase that exquisite robe?'

'Mirabelle's,' the Widow said and, to her amazement, smiled. 'Buy blue, not green. Blue and silver.'

Giles floated on his back in the plunge pool, ears below water, the steam coiling and rising around him. It had been a long, hard, damp day up at the Hill House supervising the demolition and the salvaging of the best stone and he had become chilled to the marrow.

The heat soothed his body, but the more he relaxed physically, the more his imagination could work and the worse the pain in his heart was. The gentle lap of the water made him think of Isobel's caressing fingers, the silence gave her voice space to echo in his mind. *I love you, Giles.*

He had done the only thing he could for her and her daughter, he told himself for the thousandth time. He had left her, he had silenced his mother and he had refused to tell Isobel what was in his heart. *Cruel to be kind.* The easy cliché mocked him. Cruel to be perhaps less cruel in the long run, that was the best he could hope for.

Before Isobel had come into his life he had never felt lonely. Now he ached with it. Here at Wimpole, as the bustle of the family's preparations for their departure to Ireland gathered momentum, he could have company every hour of the day and evening if he chose. But he knew he would feel this alone in the midst of thousands without Isobel.

It seemed that to deny love, the emotion he had never believed he could feel, required as much courage and resolution as facing a fellow duellist. The pain certainly lasted longer, bad enough to force him to admit that the emotion was true and would never leave him. He loved her. He could admit it now he was no longer a danger to her, now he would never see her again, except, perhaps, across a crowded ballroom.

He wanted to write to her, tell her how he felt, tell her why this was so impossible. He wrote the letters every night and every morning burned them. How long was it going to be before he could shake off this sensation that without her he was merely a hollow shell, going through the actions of life? Or perhaps he never would be free of it. Perhaps the heart could not heal as the body did.

But doing the honourable thing, the right thing, was never going to be easy. He was not a gentleman, but, for Isobel's sake, he was going to behave like one. He could cope with physical pain, he just had to learn to deal with mental torment, too, or go mad.

A ripple of water splashed his face and his floating body rocked. Someone else had got into the pool. Lord Hardwicke or young Philip, he supposed, opening his eyes and staring up at the vault of the ceiling, wishing they would go away. The other bather said nothing. Giles raised his head and saw something on the curving edge at the end of the pool.

A small black-and-white puppy was sitting on its haunches watching him. Its tongue lolled out, its tail thrashed back and forth—it was obviously delighted to see him. A long blue leash curled onto the damp brown marble where it had been dropped.

Giles surged to his feet, turned and found Isobel, as

naked as a water nymph, her wet hair on her shoulders, standing behind him.

'Isobel.' She smiled, that warm, open trusting smile. 'No! No, go away, damn it! I do not want you.' And he turned to forge his way through the water to the steps.

Chapter Twenty-Two

'Giles.' Her voice stopped him for a second, two, three, then he summoned up all his will and began to walk away again. 'Giles. Please. If you feel anything at all for me, answer one question.'

He should keep going, deny his feelings for her sake, but he found he could not lie to her. 'What is it?' He did not turn around: to see her face, those wide eyes, would be too much to bear.

'If you had not only my father's agreement, but his blessing, his public acceptance, would you marry me?'

'If wishes were horses, beggars might ride,' he said, still looking at the steps that rose out of the water, then twisted steeply to the changing area. Escape. His voice was choked in his throat.

'It is not a wish, it is a fact.'

It could not be. It was impossible. He was dreaming.

'Giles,' the voice from his dreams persisted, 'I wish you would turn around. I am trying to propose to you and it is very difficult talking to the back of your head.'

That brought him round in a spin that created waves.

The puppy retreated with a yap of alarm as water sloshed over the sides. The naked nymph was still there, her wet hair almost black, plastered over the curves of her breast. Not a dream, not an hallucination. The real woman.

'Isobel…' He sank his pride and tried an appeal. 'This is not fair. Not to you, not to me, to pretend this is possible.'

'I have only ever lied to you to protect my daughter,' she said, her gaze locked with his. 'I swear on her life that I am not lying to you now. I am not delusional. My father accepts I will marry no one else, ever. I told my parents all about Annabelle, you see, so finally they understand. And once my father thought about it, once he began to hear about you from other people, he realised that he respected you.'

She made no move to come closer to him, only waited patiently, watching his face as he worked painfully through what she was telling him. 'You told them about Annabelle—risked that, for me?'

'No.' She shook her head, painfully honest as ever. 'But it is because of you that I told them. You made me think about trust and honour and what I was withholding from them because I dared not take a chance on their love. So I told them. It was later that I realised that, now they have given up all hope of me making a conventional match, they might consent if they thought you would make me happy.'

'There is a lesson for me in that, you do not have to spell it out,' Giles said. *Trust and the withholding of love.* He had not trusted her to be strong enough to cope with his impossible love as well as her own. 'I thought I was doing the right thing, making the right sacrifice.'

'So it was a sacrifice?' For the first time he saw her fear and her uncertainty in the wide grey eyes and the way she had caught her lower lip between her teeth.

Still the words would not come. How could he risk her regretting it as soon as the knot was tied? So much of her life that she took completely for granted would be lost to her. But if Isobel could trust him, then he must trust her. 'Yes, it was a sacrifice,' Giles admitted.

Her smile was radiant. 'Oh, thank goodness.' It was an ungainly business, splashing towards each other through water that was more than waist-deep. Giles found he was laughing when he finally had Isobel in his arms and so was she, and crying, and the puppy was yapping.

'This is so bizarre it has to be true,' Giles said, his arms full of wet woman. His pulse was racing, he felt dizzy. 'I thought I was dreaming. How on earth did you get here?'

'Never mind that! Will you marry me?' Isobel demanded, her arms twined round his waist.

'Are you sure?' This time he knew she saw his hesitation clearly, realised he had not said those words that mattered to her so much.

'Not if you are not.' All the animation drained away, leaving her naked and vulnerable. 'I am sorry if I misunderstood. I thought it was only the fear of scandal that stopped you and if that was no longer there, it would be all right.' Isobel pushed away from him and splashed to the steps. She climbed out, dripping and naked, the puppy gambolling around her feet until it sensed her unhappiness and crouched, whining.

'Isobel!' Giles took three long strokes and climbed the steps beside her. 'You do not realise what it would mean to be married to me.' He caught her, blocked her escape up the narrow twist of steps that led to the changing area.

'You are used to a great house, a London home, dozens of servants. You are received at Court, you are invited to the most fashionable functions.

'I cannot give you that. You won't be received at Court any longer, there will be people who will snub us, my country home is a tenth the size of this and if we want to live in London we must rent, at least at first. I don't own a carriage. I—'

'Is that all?' she demanded. 'What do you think I want, Giles?' When he just stood and looked at her, she prodded him in the ribs.

'Me?' Isobel nodded. 'Our children?' Another nod.

'That is all and that is everything. I have a perfectly good dowry which will keep me in all the fashionable frivolity I want—if I want it. The rest can go to the children if you are too stiff-necked to take it to buy a town house or a carriage or whatever you want to improve the estate.'

'Truly?'

'Truly. Now, tell me why you will not marry me, because the only reason that I am prepared to accept is that you do not love me.'

It was like shackles breaking or a dam bursting inside. There was only one thing between him and having the woman he loved and that was his stubborn fear of believing what Isobel was telling him.

Giles took a deep breath. 'I love you.' He found he was grinning. 'I love you. I never thought I would be able to say it to you.' He picked her up, slippery as a fish, and started to climb as she wrapped her arms around his neck and buried her face against him. Apparently his love had run out of words.

Giles stood her on her feet when they reached the little changing room. His brocade robe hung neatly on one of the hooks on the wall that was warmed by the boiler. His slippers equally tidy below. 'My dear love,' he said mildly as he surveyed the scattered feminine clothing that strewed the floor. 'Am I to expect our home to be in this much of a muddle?'

'I was in a hurry,' Isobel said with dignity. She ran her hands over his body. 'I still am. You love me,' she murmured, as if she could still not quite believe it.

Giles caught her wrists as her fingers descended lower. 'And I will prove it to you. But I refuse to make love to you on the floor.' *Not here and not now, anyway.* There was a large bearskin rug in front of his dressing-room fire at home that had fed a particularly delicious and tormenting fantasy about Isobel.

'In my bedchamber, then. Or yours?'

'Neither.' Reluctantly he let her go and pulled on his robe, stuffed his feet into his slippers. There was something respectable about slippers. Wicked rakes did not make passionate love in slippers.

'Why not? You want me.' She slanted a look that was pure provocation from beneath her wet lashes.

'Of course I want you, you witch. I love you. But I am going to marry you.' *Marry you.* He repeated the words in his head, trying to convince himself that this was really going to happen. 'So I am going to do this properly. Respectably.' Isobel opened her mouth to protest. 'I am going to go and get dressed. So are you and you will then find Lady Hardwicke.

'I will ask the earl if he can spare me for a few days. We will drive back to London, in separate chaises, where I will formally ask your father for your hand. We will then proceed to do whatever it is that respectable people do for the duration of a respectable betrothal before they are respectably married.'

'Giles, that will take *weeks*.' Isobel rescued a stocking from the puppy and began to pull it on. Giles studied the way the walls had been painted with minute attention while the rustling and flapping of her dressing went on.

'Precisely. Our wedding is going to be the exact opposite of an elopement.'

'I am dressed. You may stop looking at the architraves or whatever it is you are pretending such interest in.'

'Soffits,' he said vaguely. 'God, you are beautiful.'

'No, I am not. I am—'

'Beautiful. I love you.'

'Then kiss me, Giles. You haven't kissed me since you told me you loved me.'

'Not here.' He watched as she wrapped her wet hair into a towel. 'I will walk you to your room and I will kiss you at your door because I cannot trust myself to touch you here.' He looked down. 'Why is there a puppy chewing my slipper?'

'It is the same one from the farmyard. You gave her to me to hold. She is the only thing you ever gave me— except my life and my honour and a broken heart—so I had to keep her.'

'Oh, hell,' he said, appalled to find his vision blurring. 'Come here.'

Isobel melted into his arms and Giles wondered why he had not realised from the first moment that he touched her that this was where she belonged. Her body was slender and strong in his embrace and her mouth hesitant, soft, as though she was shy and this was the first time.

So he kissed her as though it was, as though this was new for both of them. And it was true, he realised, because this was love and he had never loved before. So he did not demand or plunder, only explored and tasted gently, leisurely, until she was sighing, melting in his arms and he realised that he was more simply happy than he had ever been in his life.

'What was your favourite thing about the wedding breakfast?' Giles asked Isobel as she curled up against him on the wide and opulent seat of the carriage that had been his mother's wedding present to them.

'My father plotting a new shrubbery with your grandfather's advice and your mother and mine circling each other like wary cats and then deciding their mutual curiosity about each other's gowns was too much to resist. I have to say, it does help that Papa never had an affaire with her. Did you notice Pamela Monsom's father dodging about the room to avoid her? Pamela is convinced there was something between them.'

'Oh, Lord,' Giles groaned.

'It doesn't matter. Or rather, it does to Lady Monsom, of course, but we can't help that now. I like your mama—she says what she thinks and she is very kind to me now she doesn't regard me as a menace to your well-being.'

'She has had eight weeks to get used to the fact,' Giles said.

'And we have had eight weeks of blameless respectability.' She snuggled closer and nibbled his earlobe.

'I am not going to make love to you in the carriage,' he ground out. 'There is a big bed waiting for us. After that you may assault me where and when you please.' She curled her tongue-tip into his ear. 'Within reason!'

'Very well.' With an effort Isobel stopped teasing him, sat back and watched the countryside rolling past in the sunshine of the late afternoon. 'Wasn't Annabelle lovely? The children were so well behaved. I am so glad Jane brought them down.'

'We will have them to stay whenever she can come,' Giles promised. Isobel had watched him, seen how he was with both the children, how careful he was not to single Annabelle out. He would make a wonderful father.

'We are here.'

She craned to look at the grounds as they rolled up the carriage drive. The house when they reached it was perfect, the brick and dressed stone still crisp with newness, but the garden already embraced it, softened it. 'I love it,' she said and felt his pleasure at hers. 'Where is the room with the big bed?'

'At the back, overlooking the lake. Don't you want to eat first?'

'No, I want to make love,' she whispered in his ear as he swung her down from the carriage. 'Where is everyone?'

'I told them you would meet them in the morning. You see, I guessed you might want to inspect the bed-chamber first—there should be a cold meal laid out.'

The front door opened as if by magic as he swept her up into his arms and carried her up the steps, but there was no one to be seen in the hall with its wide staircase. Giles carried on up to the first floor to where double doors stood open on to a room decorated all in palest grey and in blue silk with a wide Venetian window framing the landscape and, as he had promised her, a very big bed.

'Lady Isobel Harker,' Giles said as he set her on her feet. 'There is something in the marriage service about worshipping you with my body and I take promises very seriously.'

'I hope so, Mr Harker,' she murmured as he began to unfasten her gown. Silk and lawn whispered to the ground, her stays followed with a facility that she would tease him about later. But now this felt too important for levity, only for deep happiness.

Giles carried her to the bed and stripped off his own clothing. 'I have never seen you without all those bruises,' she murmured, running her hands over the flat planes of his chest, the ridged muscle of his stomach. 'I was too nervous to notice in the pool that they had gone.'

He lowered himself over her, his scarred cheek resting next to her smooth one and she twisted so she could kiss it, then his nose with its new bump.

'I love you,' he told her as his hands began to caress her. Every time he said the words it seemed to her that it was never just a phrase. Each time he seemed to find it wonderful and new, a surprise to love and be loved.

'Show me,' she whispered back, curling her legs around his waist, cradling him between her thighs where she had wanted him for so long.

'Eight weeks of respectability is all very well,' Giles said, his voice husky. 'But it makes a man very, very impatient.'

'So am I,' Isobel told him, and lifted her hips to press against him, took his mouth and thrust with her tongue to tell him it was all right to be urgent, to take her. It had been a long time since Lucas, but for all his scarce-controlled desire Giles was gentle. She opened to him when he entered her, as he slid home deep and sure to make her his, and then she lost every trace of apprehension in the heat and the joy of their merging and the pleasure that he spun out of caresses and kisses to send her wild and desperate for release.

They cried out together and sank into sleep together. When she woke Giles was watching her and lifted his hand to trace where his eyes had been roaming, across her brow, down her cheek, softly over her lips.

'You were meant for me,' Isobel told him.

'I know. I think I knew from the moment I caught your hand in the lake and feared I was too late. Mine,' Giles said. 'Mine for ever.' And he began to prove it all over again.

* * * * *

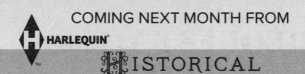

COMING NEXT MONTH FROM

HARLEQUIN®

HISTORICAL

Available September 17, 2013

CHRISTMAS COWBOY KISSES
by Carolyn Davidson, Carol Arens and Lauri Robinson
(Western)

Wrap up warm with these three Christmas tales from Carolyn Davidson, Carol Arens and Lauri Robinson. Three cowboys see just how far a little Christmas magic can go in the West!

ENGAGEMENT OF CONVENIENCE
by Georgie Lee
(Regency)

Julia Howard needs a most *convenient* engagement to find the freedom her inheritance will bring her.... And so an encounter in the woods with a dashing stranger couldn't be more timely.

A DATE WITH DISHONOR
by Mary Brendan
(Regency)

When a mysterious lady advertizes her charms in the newspaper, Viscount Blackthorne has his doubts. But the reluctant beauty who appears is far from the scheming courtesan he was expecting....

DEFIANT IN THE VIKING'S BED
Victorious Vikings
by Joanna Fulford
(Viking)

Captured and chained, Leif Egilsson has one thought in his mind: *revenge*. He's determined that Lady Astrid's innocence will finally be his, but will she be tamed as easily as he believes?

YOU CAN FIND MORE INFORMATION ON UPCOMING HARLEQUIN® TITLES, FREE EXCERPTS AND MORE AT WWW.HARLEQUIN.COM.

HHCNM0913

REQUEST YOUR
FREE BOOKS!

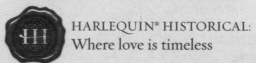

HARLEQUIN® HISTORICAL:
Where love is timeless

2 FREE NOVELS PLUS 2 **FREE GIFTS!**

YES! Please send me 2 FREE Harlequin® Historical novels and my 2 FREE gifts (gifts are worth about $10). After receiving them, if I don't wish to receive any more books, I can return the shipping statement marked "cancel." If I don't cancel, I will receive 6 brand-new novels every month and be billed just $5.44 per book in the U.S. or $5.74 per book in Canada. That's a savings of at least 16% off the cover price! It's quite a bargain! Shipping and handling is just 50¢ per book in the U.S. and 75¢ per book in Canada.* I understand that accepting the 2 free books and gifts places me under no obligation to buy anything. I can always return a shipment and cancel at any time. Even if I never buy another book, the two free books and gifts are mine to keep forever.

246/349 HDN F4ZY

Name (PLEASE PRINT)

Address Apt. #

City State/Prov. Zip/Postal Code

Signature (if under 18, a parent or guardian must sign)

Mail to the **Harlequin® Reader Service:**
IN U.S.A.: P.O. Box 1867, Buffalo, NY 14240-1867
IN CANADA: P.O. Box 609, Fort Erie, Ontario L2A 5X3

Want to try two free books from another line?
Call 1-800-873-8635 or visit www.ReaderService.com.

* Terms and prices subject to change without notice. Prices do not include applicable taxes. Sales tax applicable in N.Y. Canadian residents will be charged applicable taxes. Offer not valid in Quebec. This offer is limited to one order per household. Not valid for current subscribers to Harlequin Historical books. All orders subject to credit approval. Credit or debit balances in a customer's account(s) may be offset by any other outstanding balance owed by or to the customer. Please allow 4 to 6 weeks for delivery. Offer available while quantities last.

Your Privacy—The Harlequin® Reader Service is committed to protecting your privacy. Our Privacy Policy is available online at www.ReaderService.com or upon request from the Harlequin Reader Service.

We make a portion of our mailing list available to reputable third parties that offer products we believe may interest you. If you prefer that we not exchange your name with third parties, or if you wish to clarify or modify your communication preferences, please visit us at www.ReaderService.com/consumerchoice or write to us at Harlequin Reader Service Preference Service, P.O. Box 9062, Buffalo, NY 14269. Include your complete name and address.

HH13R

*Join Georgie Lee for sizzling scandal, intense passion and
the biggest adventure of all—marriage—in*
ENGAGEMENT OF CONVENIENCE

"Excellent shot, Artemis," Captain Covington congratulated
from behind her.

She whirled to face him, her chest tight with fear. A meeting
was inevitable, but she hadn't expected it so soon.

A smile graced his features, but it fell when Julia pinned him
with a hard glare. He stood near the equipment table, arranging
the arrows, his tousled hair falling over his forehead. She longed
to run her fingers through the dark locks then caress the smooth
skin of his face. Plucking the bowstring, she willed the urge away
and forced herself to remain calm. This constant craving for him
made her feel like a runaway carriage no one could stop, and she
hated it.

"There is a slight wind, otherwise I would have hit the mark."
She tried to sound nonchalant, but it came out more irritable than
intended.

"Yes, I see the wind has definitely increased," the captain
observed drily.

Julia stepped aside, sweeping her arm toward the range.
"Please, take a shot. Being a sailor, you must know a great deal
about how the wind blows."

"I do, though I'm not always correct." He knocked his arrow,
pulled back the bow and let it fly. The arrow stuck in the outer
ring of the target.

"It appears you judged wrong this time." Selecting an arrow, she stepped forward, aimed and hit the target dead center.

"You seem to have a much better grasp of how it blows. Perhaps you can advise me?"

"A gentleman of your experience hardly needs my advice."

"My experience is not quite as developed as you believe."

Julia chose another arrow and moved toward the range, but Captain Covington stepped in front of her, his eyes pointed. She smiled up at him, refusing to betray the fluttering in the pit of her stomach at his commanding presence. Despite her anger and embarrassment, having him so close only made her think of his hands on her bare skin, the strength and weight of his chest, the hot feel of his lips and tongue playing with hers. She turned away, fingering the leather strap of her arm guard. She did not want to have feelings for a man who only feigned interest in her or who might abandon her as he had another.

"Let us be frank with one another. I apologize for my inappropriate behavior. It will not happen again. Can you forgive me?"

"Perhaps we should end our sham engagement now."

"If that's what you wish." He took her elbow and untied the leather strap. His eyes told her the truth, but the way he held her arm said more, and it scared her. "Please know this is no longer a game for me. I am quite serious and I believe you are, too." He moved nearer and she closed her eyes, his breath warm on her cheek before he kissed her. In his lips she felt a need and hope echoed in her own heart. She added her silent questions to his, unsure of the answers. No, this was no longer a game. It was something much deeper.

Look for Georgie Lee's debut novel
ENGAGEMENT OF CONVENIENCE
Coming October 2013
From Harlequin Historical

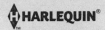

HARLEQUIN®

HISTORICAL

Where love is timeless

COMING OCTOBER 2013

A Date with Dishonor
Mary Brendan

When a mysterious lady advertises her charms in the newspaper, there's no way Viscount Blackthorne will allow his rash friend to attend the twilight rendezvous. Taking his place, Blackthorne is surprised by the reluctant beauty who appears—she's far from the scheming courtesan he was expecting.

Elise Dewey must protect her foolish sister by posing as "Lady Lonesome" in her stead. She's shockingly stirred by the imposing stranger who waits for her in Vauxhall Gardens—but their liaison has been observed…. And unless Elise accepts the Viscount's bold proposal of marriage, they will all be plunged into scandal!

Available wherever books and ebooks are sold.

HH29757

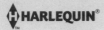

HISTORICAL

Where love is timeless

Look for

Defiant in the Viking's Bed

by Joanna Fulford in October 2013

Captured by his enemy and chained like a dog, Leif Egilsson has one thought in his mind: *revenge.* He'll no longer be beguiled by the treacherous beauty of Lady Astrid. Her innocence, which he so craved, will finally be his.

On his escape, this fierce, proud Viking is bent on making her pay the price of her betrayal—in his bed! Only, Astrid has the heart of a warrior, and she will not be tamed as easily as he believes….

VICTORIOUS VIKINGS
No man could defeat them. Three women would defy them!

Available wherever books and ebooks are sold.

Love the Harlequin book you just read?

Your opinion matters.

Review this book on your favorite book site, review site, blog or your own social media properties and share your opinion with other readers!

Be sure to connect with us at:
Harlequin.com/Newsletters
Facebook.com/HarlequinBooks
Twitter.com/HarlequinBooks

HARLEQUIN®

A *Romance* FOR EVERY MOOD™

**Stay up-to-date on all your
romance-reading news with the
Harlequin Shopping Guide,
featuring bestselling authors, exciting new
miniseries, books to watch and more!**

The newest issue will be delivered right to you
with our compliments! There are 4 each year.

Signing up is easy.

EMAIL

ShoppingGuide@Harlequin.ca

WRITE TO US

HARLEQUIN BOOKS
Attention: Customer Service Department
P.O. Box 9057, Buffalo, NY 14269-9057

OR PHONE

1-800-873-8635 in the United States
1-888-343-9777 in Canada

Please allow 4-6 weeks for delivery of the first issue by mail.